Cover designed by Sharon K Connell using Canva (edited)
Book cover images courtesy of Canva (edited)
Chapter and scene divider illustrations from Canva (edited)

Editing Services: Above the Pages

Hymn and Christmas Carol mentioned in story, *"It is Well with My Soul" and "Hark the Herald Angels Sing"* are in the public domain, as well as "Jesus, Joy of Man's Desiring"
All Scripture is taken from the 1611 King James Authorized Bible

Printed in the United States of America

ISBN-13 978-1-957246-06-2

This book is dedicated to my Lord and Savior, Jesus Christ, who gave me the idea for the story and whose guidance has led me through the writing.

Also dedicated to the Denali National Park and Preserve Kennel Rangers and all the staff for their service in keeping one of Alaska's treasures for everyone to enjoy. This includes the four-legged Denali Rangers, who I've come to admire and respect for their service and loyalty to everyone while working in the park.

And last, but not least, to the indigenous peoples of the Arctic and subarctic regions of North America and Russia, called Inuit. A unique group with homelands including Greenland, Arctic Canada, and parts of Alaska and Siberia.

Acknowledgements

I owe many, many thanks for all the information and advice given during my research. But especially to the following:

The Denali Park Rangers at the Denali National Park and Preserve
The members of Facebook Group, Healy, AK 99743
Justin at the Discover Denali Visitor Center
And my friend and fellow author, AnnaLee Conti, who lived in Alaska
My husband, Arnie Hauswald, retired SGM, US Army, for his service to our country, for his patience with late dinners, and for all the support he gives each day as I strive to make my story the best it can be.
The ACFW Scribes critique group for their help in so many areas of the story.

Fear thou not; for I am with thee: be not dismayed; for I am thy God: I will strengthen thee; yea, I will help thee; yea, I will uphold thee with the right hand of my righteousness. Isaiah 41:10

Back To Denali

Sharon K Connell

Chapter One

Why did her boss insist she do a piece on the sled dogs of Denali?

Rachel O'Rourke grumbled as she pulled a suitcase from the back of her closet and swung it onto her bed. She popped it open and threw items in, then went to her dresser for the toiletry bag. As she passed the oval freestanding mirror against the wall, her reflection bore a frown. She brushed a lock of long, straight, chestnut hair over her shoulder, and spun away. Good enough for a day of traveling.

After graduating from the University of Alaska with a degree in journalism a couple of years ago, she'd been thrilled to land her dream job as a reporter for *The Fairbanks Star* when it started up. She was skilled at her job too. With stories of importance to the public, she'd proven herself. But this?

"Just because she'd engaged in more than one dogsled race in the past." Wa-a-ay in the past—as a teen, having grown up in the area. She wished she'd never learned anything about dogsled racing. Her brother was seriously injured on one of those races. One he shouldn't have entered in the first place with his lack of experience. How could she face being around that culture or environment again?

She slapped a few more articles of clothing into her suitcase as tears ran down her cheeks. *You should have refused the assignment.* "Yeah, sure!" How would that look? *Star Newspaper Reporter Refuses Assignment Due To Out-of-Control Emotions.* If she wanted to get anywhere in her career and work for a major newspaper someday, she needed to do her best on every story she was given. No matter what it entailed. She had to toughen up.

Her cellphone vibrated on the nightstand. "Oh, drat!" Should have turned that off. Though not in the mood to talk to anyone, she snatched the phone and checked the screen. Her boss, *Jess Gibson.* She glanced at the clock next to the phone. 6:00 p.m. Last-minute instructions, no doubt.

"Good evening, Mr. Gibson. Is there anything you've forgotten to tell me about my mission?"

"Rachel. How many times do I have to ask you to call me Jess instead of Mr. Gibson? You make me sound so old." He chuckled.

She distanced the cell from her head and let out a stream of pent-up air through her nose. "I apologize if it makes you feel uncomfortable, but you are my boss, and it's the way I was raised."

"Hmm. It has nothing to do with my having asked you out to dinner a few times now, does it? Even if you have turned me down each time?"

She could imagine his grimace. The same one he'd worn every time she'd made an excuse not to go out with him.

The hair on Rachel's neck prickled as an uncomfortable sensation engulfed her. His persistent pursuit of a date was getting on her nerves. He'd never been insistent or made any comment that led her to believe he expected anything except her company. He'd always kept their conversation about dinner casual. Simply friendly. Then why did it bother her so much?

She shook her head. Her work ethic was against having a relationship with someone at her place of employment. Not that he wasn't a decent-looking man, or too old for her, or... He *was* handsome in a bad-boy way, with his black hair stuck up in front. It reminded her of a cockatoo. She giggled to herself. Well, not really like the bird but... His tall, lean frame, chiseled features, and those deep blue eyes with curled black lashes made all the females at the paper jealous.

"Rachel? You still there?"

"No, Mr. Gibson. I mean, yes, I'm still here. I simply prefer to keep my life at the newspaper strictly professional. That's why I think it's better if we don't... that is... it's why I've not accepted your invitations. It's how I was taught things should be at work."

A sigh came to her ears. "No, there's nothing I forgot to tell you. It's just that you left the office so fast today after our meeting about your assignment. I'm checking to make sure everything is okay. Are you looking forward to being home for a few days—seeing your family?"

A twinge of pain pricked at her heart. If only her brother would be there. She bit her lip. She'd tell her boss why the assignment wasn't for her.

Liam Chadwick shook the snow from his parka and stomped his feet, happy to have a few days off work and wind down from his harrowing experience this week on Denali. *Another careless novice dogsled driver today.* When would these inexperienced mushers learn how foolhardy chances could result in the loss of life—theirs or others? Liam exhaled in frustration. If it hadn't been for the keen hearing, sense of smell, and bravery of his dogsled team... oh, well.

As he carried his gear into the cedar cabin, warmth and a sense of home washed over him. The sensation he had every time he returned to the chalet-style house his father built soon after he, his sister, and their parents had moved from their farm in Minnesota to Healy, Alaska. Almost a decade earlier now… "to experience the *last frontier*," as his dad put it.

His brother, three years older than Liam, stayed behind because of college and a job he didn't want to leave.

After hanging the gear on the rustic, wall-to-wall, natural wood hall tree his dad had built in the mudroom, he sat on the bench and took off his boots. He caught a glimpse of his father's old mukluks, still stuffed under the seat at the end by the rear door. Liam's mind slid back to the day his parents left Healy for Florida.

"Son, we don't need a three-bedroom house anymore, now that we're retired. It's your home now," his father told him. Then he dropped his set of keys into Liam's hand and gave him a slap on his shoulder.

His mother had embraced him and kissed him on the cheek. *"Since your sister has decided not to live in Alaska after she graduates from college, we hope you'll raise many grandchildren for us here."* She winked at him.

Man, how he missed them. They were happy in the Sunshine State at an upscale retirement village in Destin, but they promised they'd visit next spring. He might be able to talk them into coming for Christmas.

As Liam stowed his boots next to his father's, the back door opened.

He rose to greet his best friend and roommate, Anik. "Hey, buddy. Nice of you to finally drop in again. You're home sooner than I expected." The men gave each other a quick hug.

"Yeah. A little earlier. I'll fill you in during dinner. Let me take you to Rusty's for a steak tonight. You haven't rented out my room because I've been gone for so long, have you?"

"Nah. I wouldn't do that to you. Where else could I find a boarder who doesn't involve himself with my love life, or the lack thereof, and doesn't always tell me what I should or shouldn't do, like my siblings?" Liam laughed. "Need help with your stuff?"

Anik held up his hands. "It can wait. I'm starved."

Liam shook his head. This modern-day descendant of an Inuit tribe was always starved. Ever since he met Anik, the guy had been hungry. Where'd he put all that food? He still didn't have a pouch, and he never worked out. Must be their metabolism from living such a hard life off the land since back before who knows when. "Okay, give me a minute to change."

"And it's not that I haven't been tempted to advise you on certain occasions, pal," Anik called after him. "Like relationships." A rumble of a guffaw followed.

Ignoring the jest, Liam ran up the stairs to his second-floor bedroom, flung his dirty clothes into the shower stall to take care of later, and ran a washcloth over his face, arms, and torso. From his spruce dresser, he pulled a fresh navy blue t-shirt and dark gray fleece sweater, which he zipped halfway to his neck while rushing down the stairs, three steps at a time.

"That was fast." Anik grinned as he brought in three of his duffel bags and dropped them on the floor. "Ready?"

"Sure am. I can't wait to sink my teeth into a good steak tonight. You can tell me all about your trip to Finland. Meet anyone interesting over there?" Liam wiggled his brows up and down.

"Ha! Wouldn't you like to know? I'm not telling you until I'm sure I have a firm claim on her. Once the girls see those gray eyes and wavy hair of yours, they have no more use for this Inuk."

Liam gave his stocky friend a weak punch in the arm. "Oh yeah? It'd be more likely that any girls I'd take out would get a load of that genuine grin and happy eyes on you, and they'd be swept off their feet."

The men made their way out the door.

En route to the restaurant, Liam's mind traveled back to his job and the events of the week. The musher he'd helped rescue at the beginning of his shift had been fortunate. Hope he learned a lesson. He could have wound up like the young man who almost lost his life two years earlier in that same wooded area.

Rachel glared at the now quiet cellphone. How could Mr. Gibson be so unfeeling? She dropped the phone on her bed as if it burned her hands. She continued her scowl and shouted, "Of all the insensitive, callous, ignoramuses. You, *Mr. Gibson*, take the cake."

Here she thought he liked her. Pouring out her heart to him about why she didn't have the desire to work on an article that involved dogsled racing, sled dogs, Denali, or anything associated with them had fallen on deaf ears.

"You need to develop thick skin," Mr. Gibson's words still rang in her ears. *"You can't let personal feelings control you, Rachel. Reporters must overcome their own emotional state to get the story."* "Thick skin?" He'd said it as if she shouldn't feel anything over the event that disabled her brother. As if it shouldn't mean anything to her. She shouldn't let it bother her at all.

The echo of her boss's voice filled her mind. *"If you intend to be a top-notch reporter..."* She already was. Her earned awards proved it.

"*Ooo.*" No other choice. Just finish packing and get to bed. It was normally a two-hour drive to Healy if the weather held. She needed to head out when it was light enough... say nine-thirty in the morning at this time of year. With the snow this week and a stop at the roadhouse in Nenana to stretch her legs, she could anticipate adding around an hour to the normal drive. She'd also appreciate relieving the tension from gripping the wheel in the predictable icy patches, even if the roads were well-plowed all the way to Healy. That'd make it a four-hour drive. She'd get there sometime in the afternoon. Probably before three, depending on how long it took her to eat at the restaurant. Should arrive before dark.

"I'd better not forget to pack some matches... a first aid kit... and water... for emergencies." One never knew what would happen on those winter roads.

Rachel finished packing her bags and flopped down in the armchair beside the living room window. She glanced at the digital clock on the end table. Eight-forty-five. *If I go to bed by eleven, I'd be up at seven.* A good breakfast and out the door at nine-thirty. Better listen to the news and weather before getting ready for bed. But first, she needed to call Mom and Dad. Her hope of getting out of doing this story had died.

"Accept the inevitable, Rachel." The only plus thing about this assignment would be time to spend with her parents and younger sister. *I wonder if Anik is back from his overseas trip yet.* It'd be nice to see him again after... too long. How they'd remained friends without actually seeing each other was a mystery to her. He was so easygoing. Never tried to intrude in her life. He was someone to write to and get letters and postcards from... from almost everywhere. The man never stayed in one place very long.

How would you know that? She only heard from him several times a year, if that. He was the only part of the mushing life that didn't still cause her emotional pain. Anik had been there for her when Kalen wound up in the hospital. And ever since, albeit through correspondence that had become less frequent. She assumed he'd been very careful with what he said to her regarding his racing. Anik and Kalen had been so close.

Now that she thought about it, it didn't hurt as much to hear of Anik's mushing adventures, even though Kalen had become disabled. Perhaps she was ready to move on and didn't have to fear her emotions with this assignment after all. She might even enjoy learning more about Denali's Canine Rangers.

Chapter Two

Steaks sizzled on the open grill at Rusty's Steak House. The juicy, caramelized aroma made Liam relish the thought of savoring one. He scanned the room with roughhewn beams and snowshoes adorning the walls. The normally packed watering hole was nearly empty. Not surprised. Tourists and part-time residents had headed back south. It suited Liam fine. He enjoyed the quiet atmosphere.

Lips curled in a sly smirk, his friend reclined in the chair as they waited for their meals to arrive. Liam fidgeted. "What's on your mind, Anik? The last time you had that sneaky look on your face was when you set me up on a blind date with the cute blonde. She turned out to be so clingy I had to cut our second date to a simple pizza dinner. Too much for me to handle. She reminded me of a needy, lost puppy."

"I'm sorry I got you into that. I met her when visiting my cousin. Never expected the girl to latch onto you like Velcro." Anik winced.

"Yeah. I've felt bad about avoiding her the way I did, but I didn't need that kind of female in my life. Ha! With the hours I work, I don't need any female interest at all."

Their server arrived with the steaks, and Liam asked the blessing on the food. He dug in. "*Mmmm.*" He took a mouthful of milk from the glass in front of him. Since he'd landed in Alaska, it wasn't often he had the luxury of drinking milk, with dairy farms being far away and few between. Liam smiled. His friend had insisted he order milk with the meal, regardless of the fact a glass of milk would be much more expensive than a cup of coffee or tea.

"Thank you." Liam raised the glass to Anik. "Even after living here for the past ten years, it's rough not being able to get a glass of milk whenever I want it."

Anik laughed. "I can imagine—growing up on a Minnesota dairy farm as you did. Never cared for the stuff myself."

Liam speared Anik with his gaze. "So... are you going to tell me what scheme you've cooked up in that brain of yours? You're plotting something. Guilt is written all over your face. Give it up."

Anik swallowed his last bite of steak, then sat back with a sigh.

Liam grinned. The man really enjoyed his steaks... as well as added suspense.

His friend chuckled and sat up straight. "I think you need more in your life by now than just working in the park with the dog teams. As satisfying as that may be, what do you do when I'm gone? All your friends are rangers, and they're as busy as you. Most of your schedules don't allow for much interaction apart from work. You get home after your shift, for however many days that is, and what then? You watch TV? I'm not around that much, although I'm grateful you keep the room available for me. Still, I'd hate to see you become a hermit."

After throwing his napkin onto his empty plate, Liam leaned back and studied Anik's face. *So much for this guy not interfering in my life or telling me what I should or shouldn't do.* Where had this come from? Best buds for almost five years, and this was the first time he'd ever brought it up? "Let's get out of here. I'm stuffed. Not interested in dessert."

"I'm full too. Let me take care of the bill." Anik waved his hand in the air.

As his friend flagged down the waitress, Liam feared the discussion of his love life would continue at the cabin.

Anik stretched his legs out as he laid his head on the back of the black leather armchair beside the rekindled fireplace. So comfortable. "Your parents built a beautiful cabin here."

"That they did, but they're happy in the retirement village in Florida. There's much more for them to do there. They'll visit here this spring. No doubt to check out how I'm doing. My sister Ainsley promised to visit then, during her spring break from the University of Alaska in Fairbanks."

Liam placed a mug of steaming coffee on the oak end table next to Anik. "Okay, enough with the small talk. What do you mean by your comment at the restaurant? You said I need more in my life than working in Denali with the dogs, and you don't want me to become a hermit?" Liam plunked himself onto the deep brown leather couch across the room from Anik. As he set his cup of brew on the low table in front of him, he leaned back and drilled his friend with a stare.

A snicker escaped Anik. "Got quite a rise out of you, didn't I? Tell me. Have you been seeing *anyone* since I left on my trip to Finland?" He took a sip from his mug of hot liquid. It warmed his insides as it traveled down his throat.

"When did you become a mother hen?" Liam's brows pinched. "No, I haven't seen anyone while you were gone. I've been busy."

Anik's eyes narrowed. He grinned, nodded, and glanced around the living room. Liam had been busy reading and housekeeping from the looks of it. A bookcase on either side of the fireplace showed books lined up like soldiers instead of leaning this way and that, the way they were a couple of months ago. Not a speck of dust on the shelves and not a dish in the kitchen sink. Everything in the room gleamed as if it had been polished… a multitude of times. "I see you've been busy. You'll make some woman a very good housekeeper."

A pillow from the couch sailed across the room and smacked Anik in the face. He laughed until his sides hurt. When he opened his eyes, Liam was in stitches too.

Once the mirth settled, Anik threw the pillow back to Liam. "Seriously, though, pal, that long face you wore when I walked in here tonight spoke volumes. Isn't there someone you're interested in around here?"

His pal had changed during the time he'd been in Finland. Withdrawn. Over dinner at Rusty's, Liam had told him of the rescue he'd made, which reminded him of the young man he'd helped save a couple of years ago. Maybe Liam dwelled too much on the dangers of life in Alaska. If that were the case, it was time to make sure he found other interests to keep his mind off Alaska's hard life.

With a grimace, Anik waited for Liam to answer. *How can I help him get out of his slump?*

With his lips pressed tight, Liam thought about the young beauty who had strolled into the Human Resources department while he was walking by. Did he dare tell Anik about her? As she walked out again, someone had called her Deirdre. Liam drew in a long breath. It was hard not to notice the flame-haired knockout when she smiled at him before she left the building.

She could've been on a fashion magazine cover instead of applying for a job here in nowhereland. Not that *he* thought they were a nowhereland in Denali. He'd decided this was a paradise as soon as his family moved here. Never was fond of crowds or the fast pace of a city. Even Minneapolis was too big and noisy for him.

"There are several pretty women at my job, but our hours are not conducive to spending much time together away from work because of the sporadic days off, as you pointed out." That wasn't exactly true. If he were interested in a coworker, he could've made an attempt. "I've not been interested in any of them that way."

"None of the females you work with have caught your eye?" Anik grinned.

"They're just friends." Wouldn't be good to start a relationship with someone at work. It might get complicated if it didn't work out." He eyed Anik. "I still want to know why you're so interested in my love life all of a sudden. I don't see you with a fair young maiden hanging on your arm."

Anik finished his coffee and strolled to the kitchen sink with his cup. "Oh, I see several ladies. Nothing serious, you understand, but I have many numbers in my little black book. Just like a sailor in every port. Besides, I'm not the one I'm worried about. I told you I thought it would do you good to get out. You seemed a bit depressed before I left for Finland, and you're even worse now. And I've only been back one day. What about someone outside of the park staff?"

As he returned from the kitchen to the living room, the man still had that scheming twinkle in his eye. Liam made sure a yawn escaped his mouth before Anik could start one of his third degrees. "Any further conversation will have to wait until morning. I'm beat. Good night."

Anik watched as Liam climbed the open stairway leading to the bedrooms. As his friend disappeared around the turn in the stairs, Anik let his eyes take in the rough stone fireplace and then the five floor-to-ceiling, narrow windows. *Yes, sir.* This cabin was a real dream. It was great that the Chadwicks left it to Liam when the couple decided to retire in a warmer climate. A ranger's job was hard enough without having to live in the semi-rough conditions most of them did, sharing a place with fellow employees. At least Liam could come home to a fantastic house and be comfortable in between shifts.

Hmm. This would be an asset in winning over a lady. *Available—rugged bachelor, complete with a beautiful home.* Liam would whack him with another pillow—or worse—if his friend read his thoughts.

Anik washed the two mugs and placed them in the drainer, then returned to the living room. He hadn't had a chance to tell Liam he'd entered the Willow 300 Sled Dog Race for January. Then there was the Iditarod to enter after the New Year. *Can't pass that one up.* Those two races would keep him here for a while before he'd be off to another race somewhere in the world. All while jotting down notes for a future memoir about working with his team and gathering information on other famous mushers. He loved this life.

Speaking of love, he'd better make sure his dogs were settled in for the night. "Best bunch of pups ever," he muttered as he rose from the comfortable couch.

He chuckled to himself. *Don't let Boss hear you refer to them as pups.* He'd give this Inuk an evil eye for sure. But he was an amazing canine anyway. And his other lead dog, Tracker, would give him that cockeyed glare. It was as if the dogs were fluent in English as well as the native tongue. Where had these canines learned to glower like that? *Love those dogs.*

His cellphone rang. Anik dug it out of his jeans. *Mr. O'Rourke?* "Hello, sir. How are you? Did you hear I was back from Finland?"

"Actually, no. I thought you were still over there, hence the late call. I wanted to catch you before you headed out for the day and find out when you planned to come home. It's definitely a blessing to have you back. I had hoped you'd be here soon."

"You had? Is there something I can do for you? We haven't talked in a long time. Sorry about that, but things get busy on the racing circuit."

"I know they do, son. There's nothing wrong, per se. Rachel will be home from Fairbanks, and I wondered if you'd keep an eye on her. She received an assignment to do an article on The Dogs of Denali."

"Why does she need looking after? Sounds like a great assignment to me. I'm sure you and Mrs. O'Rourke are thrilled for her to be home for a while."

"Oh, we are. Believe me, we are. But you saw how she struggled after Kalen became paralyzed while he was mushing with his team. That's why she's not been back for the last two years. I was glad you were around then to give her moral support, being Kalen's best friend."

"Yeah." Anik remembered how broken up she was at the hospital. "I was glad I was there for her, too, but she sometimes acted as if she didn't know me." Then again, after he left for the service at eighteen, they hadn't really corresponded much except for an occasional token letter. She was only what, twelve then? He'd kept in constant touch with Kalen though.

"Anik, my fear is she'll be depressed after she sees her brother in his wheelchair. She may recall she egged him on to join that race with the locals. Of course, she never imagined he'd actually do it and go out on his own before..."

"Whoa. Kalen's home from college? Haven't spoken to him while I was out of the country. Isn't he pursuing his law degree?"

"He is but decided he needed to be here to talk to Rachel when I told him she was coming home for a few days to do a story on the Denali kennels. Kalen thinks she may have a serious problem with the memories while she talks to the rangers. He hopes to convince her, once and for all, that the incident that paralyzed him from the waist down wasn't her fault. She denies the guilt, but Kalen knows Rachel better than even her mother or I do. He says it's still there. I'm sure he could use your support since you're home."

After he dropped back into a chair, Anik shook his head sadly. "Of course I'll be there... for both of them. When does she get here?"

"She's driving in tomorrow from Fairbanks and should arrive at least in time for dinner. How about having a meal with us? Say around four."

"Sounds good. Do you mind if I bring a friend with me? Or will that make too many people?" Teeth clamped together, he winced at the suggestion. This would provide a perfect opportunity for Liam to get to really know these remarkable people. *Hmm*. And Rachel was one fine-looking young lady, as he recalled. She also had a sister, though Anik hadn't been as close to her. She might be there too.

Mr. O'Rourke laughed. "You don't remember my wife? Lady who cooks as if she's feeding a lumber camp? This will cut down on the leftovers I'll have to eat for the next week." Mr. O'Rourke continued his solid, hearty laugh. "Of course you can bring a friend. Female maybe?"

Now it was Anik's turn to chuckle. "No, sir. The guy whose house I've been living in for the last few years when in Healy. He's a ranger. Do you remember him?"

Chapter Three

Why did he let Anik talk him into having dinner with this family? The O'Rourkes were great people, but he didn't know them. Not really. Liam pressed his lips together.

He recognized Kalen O'Rourke immediately when the young man rolled his wheelchair into the living room. The scene from two years ago flashed in Liam's mind. A chill ran up his spine.

Liam recalled he'd been no rookie with the Denali Rangers the day the report came in about an injured musher. He'd volunteered with the search and rescue team many times while off duty. That day, he stopped to talk to one of his friends with the SAR team and overheard the call. With nothing to do that evening, he once again volunteered to help.

What they found still haunted him.

Kalen had stopped his team and run off into the woods to relieve himself when he came upon a small grizzly bear who hadn't yet entered hibernation. The animal, concealed behind thick brush, was either startled or felt threatened and attacked.

Only God's intervention and the protective nature of Kalen's sled team prevented him from being killed that day. The frantic dogs had managed to drag the sled toward their master even with the snow hook engaged and obviously frightened off the bear. But not before the animal's jaws clamped down on Kalen's back. The grizzly had been so close and fast that the young man had no time to get out his bear spray and use it in defense.

The rest of his group hadn't stopped until they realized Kalen's dog team wasn't behind them anymore. His friends backtracked and found him lying in the blood-stained snow, Kalen's dogs frenzied, still trying to reach their master. Someone from the teams called the ranger station, while another musher had applied pressure to the wound to give what first aid they could to Kalen.

By the time Liam and the SAR team arrived on the scene, Kalen had lost consciousness. One man relayed the information Kalen gave him when his group found their friend. Fortunately, SAR was able to keep Kalen alive and get him to a hospital. But it was close. Though paralyzed from the waist down, he lived.

The rest of that day was fuzzy in Liam's mind all the way to his drive home. He'd been so tired after they'd delivered Kalen to the ER staff.

"Hey, Dad," Kalen interrupted Liam's thoughts. "Shouldn't Rachel be here by now? Has she phoned to say she'd be delayed? The aroma of that ham is making me drool."

"Haven't heard from her yet, son. She's not that late."

As she left the café in Nenana, Rachel pulled her cell from her handbag. "Better contact Mom and Dad. I'm sure they expected me long ago." She slipped into the driver's seat of her snow-covered blue Subaru Outback. Should have called before she went in to eat, but she'd been ravenous with the trip here taking so long with snow, ice, and accidents on the highway. Oh, well. At least she was halfway home.

The phone rang as she contemplated what she had said. *Home.* Healy wasn't truly home anymore. She'd get her story done and head back to Fairbanks. "Hi, Mom."

"Hon, thanks for calling. We thought you'd have been here already, but we didn't want to call if you were driving. Did something happen?"

Overprotective family. *Yes, return to Fairbanks ASAP.* "Nothing's happened, Mom. Other than a lot of snow blown onto the roads on top of the ice. I had to slow down, like you always caution me to do. And then traffic was held up by an accident involving a few cars driven by people who didn't slow down. But don't worry. I wasn't involved."

A gasp came from her mother.

Great! She'd made her mom anxious. Definitely should have called earlier. "I'm sorry I didn't phone as soon as I got to Nenana, but I was tired from gripping the steering wheel. And my stomach grumbled. The aromas from the restaurant captured my attention and lured me into the building. Forgive me."

"It's okay, dear. As long as we know you're all right. You say you're in Nenana? What time did you leave this morning? We plan to eat dinner around five. Surely you'll make it before then."

"I'm sure I will. I didn't get a start until ten, and what normally is only an hour drive to Nenana turned into three with the accident backup. I sat in the restaurant for a couple of hours to calm myself and let my fingers relax from the grip of the wheel. But I'm about to leave now. It'll only be a little more than another hour until I get to the house. The traffic has died down."

"Okay, Hon. You be careful. I love you."

"Love you too, Mom." Rachel dropped the phone into the cup holder next to her. She pulled out of the parking lot and maneuvered onto the road. The Alaska Mountain Range formed a backdrop to Nenana, with Denali standing out. *I'm so glad Mt. McKinley was renamed to honor the Native American tradition.* They were here before we were. She'd never get tired of seeing that mountain, no matter the heartache it brought to mind because of the hospital scene with her brother overshadowing it. It was still her picture-perfect sight.

As she drove, the snowfall resumed, and the wind picked up.

Anik took a steaming cup of coffee from the hand of Rachel's mother. "Thank you, Mrs. O'Rourke. So Rachel ran into a delay on the road?" After what her father told him on the phone yesterday, he couldn't help but wonder if she was simply dragging her feet in getting home.

"Yes, she said a multi-car accident delayed her. I'm glad she wasn't involved in it."

How would he help Rachel? Anik sighed into his mug. If her brother had tried and failed over the last two years to make her see his disability wasn't her fault, what could this Inuk do?

Sure, she had egged Kalen on after his friends dared him to join them in a dogsled race in the park, but it was his decision to go. And *he* made the decision to wander off into the timber, not Rachel.

I could've just as easily blamed myself. He remembered the day so well. The O'Rourkes called to tell him Kalen was in the hospital.

Kalen's plan had been to join Anik for the Iditarod the next spring, after Anik suggested it. They'd been working out together and having a grand time over Thanksgiving. But Kalen was still very much a novice.

Anik had grown so close to this family over the years. Well, at least the senior O'Rourkes and Kalen, a year younger than Rachel. She was hardly ever around, yet they'd become close too, right before she left for college. Then they'd written each other.

The year after Rachel left, Kalen had gone off to Alaska Pacific University to study law in their new partnership with Seattle University School of Law. His posts were scarce with the load he'd taken. From what he wrote, he and his sister hadn't been keeping in touch much either.

Anik got the sense Rachel needed him to be her big brother. He gladly filled the role for her. Her letters became more frequent after the bear attack on Kalen.

When Rachel started working for *The Fairbanks Star*, their correspondence slowly became fewer and farther apart. But she did write, and he could still sense the need for support from her elected big brother.

Her brother wheeled back into the room.

"Have you heard from Rachel lately, Kalen?" Anik hoped the two siblings had started writing more often. It would be a good sign.

"Not often. Guess she keeps pretty busy with that job of hers." Kalen shrugged.

Then there was Deirdre, their little sister, a year younger than Kalen. Anik sighed again in silence. The girl had shut herself off from almost everyone. His guess was that she couldn't handle the idea of her brother being paralyzed. Probably missed her older sister too, who might have been a support to her.

Deirdre may have been legally an adult when her brother became paralyzed, but an immature one. As the baby of three siblings, all about one year apart, more or less, she was a tad spoiled.

The front door opened, and the object of Anik's thoughts breezed into the house. "Mom, Dad... I'm home. Sure smells good in here."

She hung up her coat and threw her gloves into the plastic tray on the entry table. Her waterfall of bright red hair whooshed out from under a bright blue knit cap. She turned toward everyone in the living room. Her green eyes rounded.

"Deirdre dear, we have company for dinner." Her mother rose from the couch next to her husband. "Anik got back from Finland... and has brought a friend with him. Come, say hello to Liam."

Deirdre's eyes grew even rounder when she gazed at him.

Anik chuckled to himself. *Oh, boy.* From what he'd been told, Deirdre had always kept several young men dangling on her stringer. Whether that was true or not, it was *not* the kind of involvement Liam needed.

Chapter Four

It couldn't be! Liam's jaw slackened. The redhead from the Human Resources department. He slowly stood and offered his hand. Anik must have his two cents in this somehow.

She sashayed toward Liam. "Hello. Always nice to see a new face joining us for dinner." As she took his hand, she beamed the same way she had outside the HR office before she left the building, her green eyes twinkling.

Quite the flirt. After he dropped his hand from hers, he turned to Anik, eyes narrowed. How had he found out about her? He must've though. Why else would he have invited *his friend* to join him tonight? Especially after the comments he'd made since he got home yesterday. But how'd he know she'd been at the office? Liam's brows lowered. Much less how she'd captured his attention? This was too—

Liam reseated himself, refocused, and turned back to Anik. "Hey, buddy, why don't you regale us with the experiences you had on your trip to Finland?" When they returned to the cabin tonight, he'd better have an explanation for the scheme he obviously cooked up for his *friend*.

Anik grinned. A little too widely, in Liam's opinion. The man was guilty as all get-out.

Highlights of mushing in Finland, the differences between that country and Alaska, and the wonderful people Anik met there were expounded upon. "It was an adventure, to say the least.

"The 2023 IFSS European Championships and European Masters Dryland competitions were held in Jämijärvi, Finland. The Finnish Sled Dog Sport Federation organized the event, with *Länsi-Suomen Valjakkourheilijat*, or the Western Finnish Sledding Athletes, doing most of the work. The opening ceremony was on Wednesday, October sixteenth, and the closing ceremony was on Sunday, October twentieth.

"IFSS stands for the International Federation of Sled Dog Sports. They also host World Championships and World Masters Dryland competitions. Their championships and World Masters Dryland will be held in Ólvega, Spain, from November nineteenth through the twenty-sixth. But I'm taking a pass on that one."

Anik paused for a moment. "Oh, Liam. Did I tell you I'll run the Willow Three Hundred Sled Dog Race in January?"

"Ah. So that's why you cut your trip short. Unlike your rundown of *all* the events." Liam laughed. "Where'd you learn to pronounce those Finnish names?"

Anik laughed with him. "I'm a fast learner. The race is sort of... but not the entire reason I came back early. A friend of mine from Canada is coming in to pair up with me for the Three Hundred. Would it be okay with you if he shared my room at the cabin? Also, he plans to run the Iditarod in the spring. Of course, he'll find his own accommodations as soon as he can. I had planned to put him up in the Denali motel until he finds his own place. Then I decided it might be fun for both of us to have Gordon around for a little while. What do you say?"

Uh-huh. He was calling in reinforcements now. Liam laughed, this time to himself. He'd become paranoid about this matchmaking of Anik's, and the man had only been home for a day. "Sure, tell Gordon he's welcome. We've plenty of space."

Liam scanned the room. Deirdre and her mother must have gone into the kitchen to attend to dinner. Her red hair must come from the mother's side of the family. He'd noticed red highlights in Mrs. O'Rourke's hair. *Wonder what the sister looks like.*

Deirdre stepped back into the living room. "Dinner is ready, gentlemen. Follow me." She pivoted. "Rachel's late for yet another dinner," she murmured.

The comment hadn't been sarcastic—not quite, but it did lack the warmth of sisterly affection. What was the deal there? Liam pressed his lips into a straight line as he followed everyone out of the room.

An aroma of ham, roasted wild game, and fresh vegetables filled the air as they entered the dining room.

Mr. O'Rourke sat at the head of the table, his wife at the other end. Kalen wheeled himself into position at his father's right hand. Anik took the chair across from him. "Aren't you missing classes with this trip home, Kalen?"

"I am, but I can make up most of the missed work when I return to APU. Before I left, I cleared my absence with my academic advisor. A friend who takes the same classes calls and gives me the information on what to study while I'm here."

"That's great. Wouldn't want you to fail. Who knows? I may need you for a lawyer someday." Anik chuckled, as did everyone else at the table.

At her mother's left, Deirdre sat and patted the top of the high-backed wooden chair next to her. "Here's a place for you, Liam, right between my brother and me."

Liam gave her a half-smile, then pulled the chair out next to Anik. "Thank you, but I'm already on this side, so I'll take this one." He sat. She scowled. *Uh-oh, Irish temper.* Was that a snicker coming from Anik? *We'll address that later, too, my friend.*

Mr. O'Rourke held out his hands to his son and Anik, then bowed his head. Anik snatched Liam's hand. This was a little weird. His family never held each other's hands to say grace. And he'd never held Anik's except in a handshake. But okay. New experience.

Mrs. O'Rourke extended her hand across the corner of the table toward Liam. He took it and rested them on top of the linen tablecloth. She stared at Deirdre, who finally laid hers in her mother's and reached across the empty seat toward Kalen.

Everyone else bowed their heads, and Mr. O'Rourke blessed the food.

A knock came on the front door as they released their hands. Mrs. O'Rourke jumped up to answer it.

Outside the door, Rachel stomped off the rest of the snow from her boots and entered the foyer. Her mother closed the door behind her. Rachel placed her knitted stocking cap into her mother's outstretched hand. "Sorry I'm late, Mom. The drive was slower than I would have thought."

"Not a problem, although in another fifteen minutes, I'd've sent the men out to look for you. Why did you knock?" Her brows wrinkled.

Did anyone else on God's green earth have a mother who worried as much as hers? After a brief chuckle to herself, she allowed her mother to remove the wet parka from her shoulders. "Because this isn't my home anymore, Mom."

"Hon, this will always be your home, even if you no longer live in it." Her mother's brows smoothed out, and she wrinkled her nose instead. She raised a hand and waved it back and forth as if she were erasing the irony of that statement. "You know what I mean."

Rachel hugged her mom. "Yes, I do. Thanks."

"Now... come on in and find a seat at the table. We've guests for you to greet."

With one raised eyebrow at her mother's teasing smile, Rachel followed her. She glanced around the living room as they passed. Nothing had changed since she had left. Everything was comfortably familiar. Her heart warmed.

When she stepped into the dining room, she hurried to her father, who stood. Everyone else followed suit, except her sister and brother in his wheelchair. Rachel's eyes caught hold of Kalen's. Tears overflowed as she rushed into his welcoming arms. "Oh, Kalen. I had no idea you were home. Why aren't you in school? Are you all right?"

"Calm yourself, big sister. Mom told me you had an assignment here, so I came to spend a few days with you. I needed time off from the books and classroom anyway."

She lowered her brows at him.

"Don't worry. I cleared it with everyone and can do most of the work online for the next week."

She gave him a hug and kissed his cheek. "It's so good to see you. I'm sorry I haven't been keeping up with our correspondence. I've been pretty busy."

"That's fine. I carry a heavy load myself." Kalen swung his arm toward the man on the other side of the table from him. "Does this character seem familiar to you?"

"*Anik!* Someone else I've been neglecting to write to lately." She ran around her father's end of the table and hugged Anik. "Will you forgive me for not answering your last letter?"

"What's to forgive? You have a demanding job now." He squeezed back. "But I'm sure glad you're here. I've things to talk over with you."

"That sounds ominous."

He laughed. "I understand you're here to do an article about the Denali Canine Rangers. I'd like to tag along... if you don't mind. I'll tell you why later. First, I want you to me—"

The clatter of a fork hitting a plate made Rachel turn her attention to her sister. Deirdre grumbled, "Oh, sure. Say hi to everyone but your sister."

Rachel caught every word. She retraced her steps around her father and down the side of the table to Deirdre. "I wouldn't leave my little sister out for anything, Dee." Rachel bent over and hugged her from behind, then grabbed her hands and pulled her to her feet. "Wow, you look fantastic, sis. I love your hair at this length. So long and beautiful."

A tight-lipped smile emerged on Deirdre's face, who hugged her sister in return, but Deirdre quickly ended the embrace when she pulled back and returned to her seat.

Rachel rounded her mother's end of the table and took the empty chair between her mom and the man next to Anik.

Anik leaned forward and cleared his throat. "As I was about to say, I want you to meet my friend, Liam."

Rachel's eyes locked onto Liam's. Her heart fluttered. Where had she seen those dove-gray eyes before?

After dinner, the men meandered into the living room while Rachel's mind continued to work on where she had seen the gray eyes of Anik's friend. No matter how hard she tried, her memory refused to place them. She collected the dirty plates from around the table and joined her mom and sister in the kitchen.

"Mom, have you seen Liam before tonight? I feel as though I've met him before."

Her mother opened her mouth to answer, but in a smug tone, Deirdre said, "I certainly have."

"Oh? Where?" Something about her sister's attitude bothered Rachel. What was wrong with her? The tone was reminiscent of how Deirdre had needled her when the quarterback had taken her little sister to the prom while they were in high school. *Especially when it was only her and me in the room.* Deirdre had flaunted her conquest.

Rachel tilted her head and raised her brows. She waited for her sister to answer. *As if dating the ego-fed quarterback mattered to me.* Why was it always a competition with Dee?

"The other day, I applied for a job at Denali National Park. When I walked into the building, Liam was talking with another guy at a nearby desk. He noticed me right away, so I smiled at him. When I came out of the human resources office, he was still there. He must've waited to catch a glimpse of me again, so I gave him another smile. He sure seemed happy to see me tonight."

"No-o-ow, Deirdre." Her mother tsked. "How many times have your father and I told you the danger of thinking too highly of yourself? He was simply behaving as a gentleman toward you. And I'm sure there were many good explanations why he remained in that building."

There were times when Rachel wanted to hug her mother to death. This was one.

Usually, Rachel would have shrugged off her sister's jabs, but for some unexplainable reason, her sister's words about Liam bothered her tonight. Rachel sighed. She was just overtired from the drive.

"Well, he seemed very interested in me, Mom. Honestly, Rachel." She turned to glare at her sister. "If you'd do something with that mop of long hair and put on a little makeup, you'd have men clamoring to go out with you too. *Some* women need to work harder at it." Deirdre tossed the dishcloth into the sink and left the room.

Rachel's mouth dropped open. Why had her sister spoken to her in such a rude manner? Did Deirdre resent her that much? Why? There was no doubt—never had been—which of them was prettier. Dee's fire-red hair glowed, as did her ivory skin. Her crystal green eyes and perfect features probably had every boy in town lined up to date her. But, until now, her sister had never said anything so hurtful.

Rachel's mother embraced her. She pulled back with her arms still on her daughter's shoulders. "Don't listen to her, Hon. Honestly, I can't imagine how my two daughters became so completely different. I don't know what to do with Deirdre. And you do *not* need makeup. You are perfect as you are with those warm brown eyes and the gorgeous chestnut hair God gave you."

She smiled at her mother.

"And your best feature is that beautiful smile. It's contagious. Now you go into the living room, and ask the men if they're ready for dessert."

"Okay, Mom. Thank you. Be right back." Rachel reeled in her thoughts and walked to the living room.

Deirdre had ensconced herself on the couch with not more than an inch between her and Liam. A prick in Rachel's heart startled her. *This is silly.* Why shouldn't my sister enjoy the attention of such a handsome man? But the disappointment niggled at her all the same.

Liam's eyes locked onto Rachel's. He stood.

If he's smart, he'll put distance between my sister and himself. That wasn't a nice remark, Rachel. *Pull yourself together.* "Excuse me. Mom said to ask if you gentlemen are ready for dessert."

Chapter Five

Something stirred inside Liam as Rachel walked into the room. He stood. She wasn't the glittery beauty her sister presented, but there was an unpretentious, breathtaking quality about this woman. The ivory skin and facial features of the two were identical, except for their nose and eye colors. Rachel had a cute turned-up nose, as did her mother. Deirdre's Roman nose came from her father, as did Rachel's dark hair. Silky, dark hair.

Rachel's contagious smile had extended to her eyes when she'd seen her brother at the dinner table. *Wish she'd smile at me that way.* Her lips were a perfect shade of pink... *perfect*. Warmth filled his body as Liam stared at them in a dream-like state.

A snicker from Anik, who sat in the chair next to him, snapped Liam's attention back to Rachel's eyes, now focused on him.

Why was he standing? *Think fast, man.* "Well, I, for one, am always ready for dessert. Thank you."

"Yeah." Anik also rose from his seat and placed his hand on Liam's shoulder. "This man's sweet tooth usually rules his head..." The man muted his voice and mumbled the next words in Liam's ear, "...and his heart. I hope."

As more heat shot up Liam's neck to his hairline, he glared a warning at his friend, but Anik already shook with suppressed laughter. *I'll get even with you for this, buddy. You betcha.* "Whose sweet tooth rules?"

For Pete's sake. What would he get even with Anik for? For having brought him to a dinner at a pastor's house where he'd met the two most beautiful females he'd ever set eyes on? Outside of his sister, of course.

Thoughts of his little sister cooled his annoyance. They'd been as close as twins, yet four years apart. He'd always considered Ainsley attractive, to the point where he told his father years ago, *"Dad, if you don't keep a tight leash on Lee, I'll lock her in a closet until she's thirty-five years old."* It was on her sixteenth birthday when a couple of the guys who showed up had made him nervous. He loved his little sister.

Loved. Rachel? Ridiculous. *Don't even go there.*

In the dining room, Liam avoided eye contact with Rachel. He was aware of Deirdre's closeness as she followed him to the same chair he'd sat in for dinner. She sank into the chair Rachel had occupied through the evening's meal. He sighed.

With brows lowered, Rachel stood next to her sister. Then she moved to the other side of the table and sat next to her brother, putting herself across from Liam.

His brows lifted. Perhaps she felt the emotion too? But that couldn't be. Anik's interference in his love life must be the reason for this nonsense.

Liam smiled at Rachel. When she gave him one in return, her entire face lit up. He'd never seen such radiance on anyone. Not even Anik, who appeared to live in a constant state of happiness. How did anyone stay that happy all the time? Liam resumed his enjoyment of the gorgeous view across the table.

Her father broke Liam and Rachel's eye-link when he asked, "So where's the dessert?"

Mrs. O'Rourke focused on Deirdre, then Rachel, and back at Deirdre again. "I was going to ask the same thing. Girls?" She continued to pour coffee into china cups from the large carafe she'd brought to the table.

The girls popped up from their chairs and hastened to the kitchen.

First time he'd ever caused such a distraction. Liam tried to resist the urge to laugh, unlike Kalen, who had no trouble letting a guffaw fly.

The brother eyed Liam. "Guess a new, eligible, good-looking guy in the house has made my sisters forget their duties. A word of advice." He leaned into the table and speared Liam with a brow-raised stare. "If you choose at all...choose wisely. I hear they both have a very protective brother." He peered at his dad. "And father." With a straight face, he fixed his eyes back on Liam. "You *do know* we're Irish."

The last comment made Liam laugh aloud. "Yes, I figured with the name O'Rourke. But not to worry. I'm not in the market for a girlfriend at the moment..." he turned to Mr. O'Rourke, "as lovely as your daughters are. My job keeps me too busy for much of a social life. Especially one that involves paying attention to ladies."

Anik huffed and rolled his eyes. "I've been trying to tell this guy he needs more than working each day with dogs and volunteering on his off time with the search and rescue team." He poked Liam in the chest with a stubby index finger. "You've heard the phrase, 'all work and no play makes...' whatever. I don't remember the rest of it. Something about being dull."

Kalen chuckled. "You mean the proverb, 'All work and no play makes Jack a dull boy.' Hey, if you're working with those great dogs and spending your own time with S and R, you've got to be a decent guy, as if I didn't already know. I wouldn't be here today if not for all of you. You have my permission to choose whichever sister you want.

I'm anxious to become an uncle." He ducked his head and peeked at Liam with an impish grin from under his red lashes. "Please?"

Liam's neck grew warm again. He threw his hands in the air. "I give up. Guys, let me run my own love life, okay?"

"I agree," voiced Kalen's dad. "However, I will say that your working with the Denali Alaskan Huskies would be of interest to Rachel, since that's why she's here."

Rachel stepped into the dining room carrying what looked like a large dish of berry cobbler and placed it in front of her mother. Deirdre followed her with a tray full of whipped cream, plates, and utensils. She set it down in the middle of the table and moved the dishes next to the cobbler.

Rachel grinned at her father. "Dad, what was that you said regarding Alaskan Huskies?"

"I told Liam they were the reason you made the trip from Fairbanks to Healy." Mr. O'Rourke turned to Liam. "Rachel is a reporter with *The Fairbanks Star*. She was sent here to do an article on the Denali Canine Rangers." His line of sight swung back to Rachel. "Liam is a ranger who works with the dogs, dear."

Ever since she walked into the house, there had been something so familiar about Rachel. *Wish I could pinpoint why.*

Rachel's eyes opened wide, again fixed on him.

Liam's brows rose, and a strange tickle ran circles in his chest. The only time he'd ever had that sensation was in high school when the head cheerleader winked at him. *What?* His mind was back in high school now? *Pull yourself together, man.* Should he offer to help her with the article? Maybe that way, he could figure out why she seemed so familiar… and why he couldn't stop acting like a teenage jock.

Rachel kept staring at Liam. *He's a ranger? Works with the dogs. Dogs… ranger.* It struck a bell with her, but why? Had she met him before she left Healy for college? He looked to be around her age. Drat! She was so bad at figuring out ages. "I—"

"I'd—" Liam clamped his lips together. "Sorry."

She continued. "I'll be grateful for any help you give... as I come up with questions." Heat rose in her face. She drew in a deep breath.

He chuckled. "I was about to offer a tour, so you can meet and take pictures of some of the pups. People love to see and hold them."

A thousand butterflies suddenly took flight in her stomach. Why did he have that effect on her? It wasn't as if she'd never met a handsome man before. The excitement of doing this article must have caused it. "That'd be wonderful, Liam. Thank you."

"I'm not scheduled to work again until next Monday. I'll play tourist and have one of my coworkers show us around. That way, you'll get more than my slant on things."

"Sounds wonderful." The idea made her giddy. This was absurd.

Deirdre reclaimed her seat next to Liam. "Would there be room on this *tour* for another? I haven't been to see the Denali puppies in a long time."

Rachel looked on as her sister fluttered her eyelashes at the man. How was she going to get any work done while Dee flirted with Liam the entire time?

"Deirdre." Dad gave her a warning frown. "Rachel has an article to write. Liam is offering to get her the information she needs. This is not a pleasure trip to the mountains. You can see the puppies any time you want during their visiting hours. Not this time."

Little Daddy's Girl was not getting her way. Rachel forced herself to keep from smiling.

Deirdre's lips formed a tight, straight line, while a vein pulsated in her temple.

A guilty sensation overwhelmed Rachel. Maybe Dee really did like this guy.

As the dessert plates, piled high with portions of the cobbler, were handed out to everyone, Rachel pondered Liam and his job at Denali. The warmth she had in her heart for this stranger surprised her. She'd have to be very careful not to do or say anything that made him… or her sister… think she was interested in him. She'd keep things professional. Strictly business. *Do my job.*

Liam sighed a breath of relief at Mr. O'Rourke's words. If their father hadn't said anything, he'd have been obligated to invite Deirdre along. He'd have to put up with her flirtations for the entire outing. They were beginning to annoy him. Was she doing it to irritate her sister? She appeared to be close to the same age as Rachel, but she sure didn't act it. More like a young smitten teen. This had to be the problem between the sisters.

"Shall we go to Denali first thing in the morning?" He gazed into Rachel's warm brown eyes again. His heart skipped. *Whoa!* Who's acting like a smitten teen now? He was too busy to get involved with this woman. Besides, she was going back to Fairbanks after her assignment was over.

"That'll be perfect." Rachel's lips lifted at the corners, causing Liam's heart to skip again.

He pulled out his phone and concentrated on pulling up the calendar. "Okay, what time do you want me to pick you up?"

"How about nine? I can follow you. That way, I won't tie you up any longer than I have to." She left the room but returned with a planner and pen in hand, scribbled something, and then snapped the book shut. "Nine a.m. it is."

Rachel seated herself at the table. The sounds of forks on china resumed as everyone ate their dessert.

A take-charge kind of woman. Liam glanced at Anik, whose brows were raised almost to his hairline. *You interfering Inuit. You are enjoying this too much and getting on my nerves.* Had he known Anik would come back from Finland with an agenda to get his best friend into a romantic relationship, he'd have rented out the spare room to someone else while the meddler was gone. Liam's lips slid to one side. No, he wouldn't.

Anik gave him an all-knowing smirk as if to say, "See? I knew what you needed," and stuffed the last bit of cobbler into his mouth.

Hmm. He'd do a little matchmaking of his own. How could he transfer Deirdre's interest to Anik? It'd serve him right. But who knew what good might come out of it? One side of Liam's mouth lifted. Anik could do Rachel's sister some good. He was mature and sensible. Liam grimaced. *Except when it comes to interfering with my life.*

"Anik, since Deirdre has an interest in sled dogs, why don't you take her to see your team?" He grinned at his friend, whose mouth dropped open.

Ignoring Anik's expression, Liam turned to Deirdre. "Anik Amarok is a well-known name on the mushing circuit. I've lost count of how many races he's won. He and his team travel all over the world. At least where there's a dogsled race." He tilted his head and raised his brows at Anik. "Tell her." *Touché.*

"Yes, we're quite aware of Anik's accomplishments, but—"

"Come now, Anik." Liam turned back to him. "You're always talking about your four-legged buddies."

"Oka-a-ay." Anik narrowed his eyes at Liam. "It's only fair to Deirdre, if she's interested in Alaskan Huskies, to show her the best team anywhere, even though she's seen them many times."

It was Liam's turn for the dropped jaw. "Now wait just a minute there, pal. Best team?"

"Don't interrupt, my friend." Anik turned to Deirdre. "May I introduce you to my *award-winning* team again tomorrow? I promise you'll be impressed."

Deirdre's contemplation bounced from Liam to Anik to her sister and then back to Anik. "Sure. I'd love to. When?"

"Nine okay with you?"

A self-satisfied sensation went through Liam. "My team at the park can match yours any day, pal."

Liam snuck a peek at Rachel. A bewildered countenance took over her face. Her mouth opened in what appeared to be shock as she peered at Anik. *Uh, oh.* Had he made a big mistake? Did a romantic relationship exist between Anik and Rachel that he wasn't aware of?

Deirdre nodded. "It's a date."

Liam thought back to things Anik had said earlier that evening. He'd gotten saved at sixteen in the Healy Bible Church. That would've been fourteen years ago. Rachel must have been a child then. Anik left Healy and joined the Air Force at eighteen. He wasn't around much as she grew up after that. He got out of the service and started mushing and traveling.

When Anik came back to Healy and rented the cabin room a few years ago, Rachel wasn't here. Still, she apologized to Anik for not answering his last letter.

As Liam peeked at Kalen, the scene in the ER flashed where they'd rushed the young man after his bear attack. Anik had been there with the O'Rourkes. Liam's fuzziness regarding the events cleared, and he shifted his gaze to Rachel. It had been Rachel that Anik held in his arms when she fell apart at the hospital. Liam's eyes widened. No wonder she seemed familiar.

Was Deirdre being with Anik a problem between the sisters? If so, he'd just thrown gas on a smoldering fire. Or perhaps he'd thrown his friend into the arms of a female, green-eyed, redheaded she-wolf.

Chapter Six

Before he'd left the O'Rourkes' last night, Liam talked Rachel into letting him pick her up. After her harrowing adventure on the roads from Fairbanks to Healy, she needed to relax and concentrate on her assignment. When he'd reminded her he was off until the following week and had no pressing commitments, she relented.

At nine o'clock sharp, Anik pulled into the O'Rourkes' drive behind Liam to collect Deirdre, whom Anik had said was the youngest of the siblings. She ran down the porch steps, waved at Liam, and jumped into Anik's Jeep Commander. He steered out of the yard before Rachel slid into Liam's truck.

"Good morning, Rachel. Hope you're ready for a fun day."

After she buckled up, she responded. "Busy day. This trip is a work assignment."

Hmm, not in the best of moods today. Probably something her sister had said to her again.

He drove to the kennels at Denali National Park. "Tell me what you do at your job in Fairbanks."

"I'm a reporter. Not much more to say."

Was she angry with him for setting up Deirdre with Anik? Nothing he could do about that now, though he regretted having done it to get even with his friend.

"Here we are. Get ready for some fur-face time. We'll visit the puppies first. These pups are all about getting attention."

"Bring it on. I love dogs, and especially puppies. They have no hidden agendas. They're up-front and open with how they feel."

Finally, an enthusiastic response. But where had that idea come from? Was she talking about dogs or someone in particular?

He hopped out of the Chevy 3500 driver's seat and opened the passenger door for her. She slid to the snow-packed pavement and caught the hand Liam offered. Even though she wore leather, fur-lined gloves, a charge zinged up his arm at her touch. This was getting downright ridiculous. He had a reaction to everything this woman did.

Liam led her to the kennels, where the noise level was deafening. "It's breakfast time, in case you're wondering." He laughed.

She smiled and followed him to the area where they kept the Canine Rangers. More than two dozen puppy eyes observed their steps as they approached the kennel manager.

"Morning, Liam." Annaleise, a full-figured, female ranger with short brown hair and hazel eyes, presented a perfect Colgate grin. "Just can't stay away from your fuzzy buddies, can you? Even on your days off."

The forty-something-year-old woman had worked with the Huskies for seven years and loved taking care of the new pups. She also filled in as an on-site mother to most of the rangers who were far from their families.

"Ha. You've got that right, but today I've brought a guest to see the kennels." He turned to Rachel. "Anna, I'd like to introduce you to Rachel O'Rourke, a reporter from *The Fairbanks Star*. She's here to do an article about the Denali Canine Rangers. I said I'd show her around and answer any questions she might have. Correction. I told her I'd play *tourist* on my day off and let *you* do the honors."

"I love it." Anna extended her hand to Rachel, and they shook. "Ranger Annaleise Kempstead. Everyone here calls me Anna. Great to meet you, Rachel.

"Thank you, Anna. It's nice to meet you too."

"O-o-o-oh, how fun. A special piece on the fuzz-faced, four-legged rangers. That's cool! This guy here is just the man to tell you all about our babies." She leaned toward him. "Sorry, Liam. I'm a little swamped with work. Two of our workers came down with the flu. You'll have to give her the complete tour yourself." She spun back to Rachel. "He was—" Anna looked over her shoulder at Liam. "What, around nineteen when you started here?"

"Actually, eighteen. They hired me to be a kennel ranger right off the bat because of my experience on our dairy farm in Minnesota. And because of the time I spent assisting veterinarians with the Four-H group I was in. Best thing that could have happened to me."

"Yep, Liam can provide you with the lowdown on our ranger fur babies and anything else around here you need for your story. Can't wait to read it. I'm a *Fairbanks Star* subscriber, born and raised in Fairbanks." She winked at Liam. "Now you go show her those littlest guys we have in training." She turned to continue her duties, then swung to face them as she walked backward. "It was good to make your acquaintance, Rachel. Hope you'll visit us again."

"Since my family lives in Healy. I no doubt will make a return visit sometime."

Liam led Rachel to the puppies, where the fluffy balls of hair went crazy at the sight of them. "Judging by the appearance of their bowls, these guys have already been fed, so they shouldn't try to eat your fingers." He laughed again.

He picked up a pup with pale brown markings on its almost all-white body. "This little lady is from Flame's litter. Flame is a Husky on my team and one of my favorites." He leaned in to speak in the fuzzy ear. "But don't tell the rest of the gang, little girl. Remember, I don't *play favorites.* Nevertheless, your mama has stolen my heart." The little dog rewarded him with a head bump to his nose.

Rachel's brows rose. "Is that why Anik is trying so hard to find you a normal relationship?"

He slanted her an amused smirk.

She took the puppy from Liam's arms. The wiggly ball of fluff squirmed until she got into a position where she could wash Rachel's face with sloppy kisses. "Okay, you sweet thing." Rachel giggled and returned the pup to the floor. "She's adorable. Is Flame as pretty as her daughter?"

"Every bit. Wait 'til you see her. But each of our dogs is a beauty. Or handsome, in the case of the males." He scratched behind the ears of a puppy with a few faint brown spots on his otherwise all-white coat. "This one's name is Snowflake."

Rachel bent over, picked up a roly-poly, rust-colored puppy, hugged her, and then put the pup on her feet again. "You're a doll too."

Next, she lifted a black pup to eye level. "Hello there, fella. You sure are a handsome guy."

Liam watched her as she interacted with every ecstatic puppy while they stormed toward her feet, yipping and yapping to gain a response from her. She held each of the canine fluff balls and then cuddled one that was entirely white. "I think I'd call you Snowball."

With a chuckle, Liam leaned over to run his hand over the chubby little body. "That's funny. He's Snowman. The staff gives each pup in a new litter a name connected to a theme. This year, the theme is winter. Hence, Snowflake... Snowman." He pointed to the black puppy. "Coal." Again, he aimed his index finger, this time at the rust-colored puppy Rachel had held. "Poinsettia, but she responds to Po." He swung his arm to include the entire area of pups. "And so on."

Rachel's jaw lowered. She raised the white fuzzy puppy in her arms up in the air as if he were a toddler. "You do look like a snowman." Then she hugged him and put him back with the others. "Coming here was a mistake. I want to take them all home with me."

"We hear that a lot."

"I'll bet."

"You don't have a dog?" Liam tilted his head with the question.

"No. My apartment doesn't allow pets." She sighed.

"Well, maybe someday you'll move to another place where you can have one. The only reason I don't have any of my own is because of working with the Huskies every day. Plus, some of my shifts cover days away from home. Doesn't work if you have a house pet."

She gazed longingly at the pups. "This made me realize what I've been missing. My parents' dogs are wonderful. I've missed them."

"I didn't see any dogs at your parents' cabin."

"They're kept in their own quarters at the rear of the house when we have visitors."

"Oh, okay."

With the puppies back in their pen, still whining for attention, Liam led Rachel out to the adult kennels. He once again leaned in. "I'll show you a few of my favorites from the team I run. But remember, I don't play *favorites*, so don't tell the rest of them." He winked.

She did an eye roll and followed him to an area with many raised wooden doghouses.

"First, there's Canine Ranger Flame. You can see the white flame marking on her forehead from here. Her other markings reminded us of fire with her reddish-brown on white coat."

The moment Flame spotted Liam, the Husky stood on top of her doghouse at the ready. Her tail wagged frantically as she let out a loud bark. Then she jumped off the wooden shelter.

"Hi, girl. Miss me?" Her front paws were up on his chest as soon as he got close enough. "Are the other guys treating my princess well?" She answered with a series of quick yips.

As he rubbed her ears, neck, and down her sides, Liam turned back to Rachel. "I believe she said they've been doing a stupendous job. Every one of the kennel rangers dotes on these dogs, and the feeling seems to be mutual."

"I can't get over her blue eyes. She's gorgeous."

"Yep, that's my lady." Flame approached Rachel, who held out her hand so the Husky could take a sniff.

"Missy Flame has a very sweet temperament. She loves everyone."

The Husky leaned on Rachel's legs, allowing her to stroke her thick coat. "I think I'll steal you from your master."

Liam smiled. This woman was a lot of fun to be with. Easygoing, beautiful, and she loves dogs. *Hey, slow down, man.* He had to get his mind back on the tour.

"Here at Denali, we have a program where we find homes for retired Canine Rangers. You should check into it if you decide to move to another apartment where they allow pets. They each have a different temperament, but they're all extraordinary Huskies. They usually retire after working for eight years. Because of their lifestyle and the excellent health maintained here in the kennel, they have many more years to live after that.

"One requirement of an adoptive family is they must lead an active life. The dogs don't like to just sit around and do nothing. From the conversation last night at your folks' house, I take it you've done your fair share of mushing."

"Yes, I did." Suddenly, Rachel spun away and quieted.

Liam's jaw clenched. She had acted the same way last night when Kalen's mushing was brought up. Tensed up as tight as a twisted rubber band. A sensitive topic for her.

"Over here is Happy, the canine with the happiest face in the kennel." The dog grinned, and his pink tongue hung out, while his eyes formed arches. "Can you see how he got that name?"

Rachel scratched Happy's ears.

They moved on to the next doghouse. "Say hello to Sweets." The medium brown Husky tilted her head to the side, and the corners of her mouth turned up as Happy's had, but with her jowl closed tightly, forming a smile.

Rachel stretched out her hand and scratched the Husky's chin. "She's adorable."

Sounded as though Rachel was relaxing again. Liam led on.

"And this is Hatty. She's modeling the latest in headgear." He roughed up her thick hair, his hands nearly covering her head. She lifted off her haunches and pawed at him with both front feet as if to say, "Leave my hat-like head markings alone." She jumped up and gave him a wet lick on the cheek. "Okay, girl. Sorry I mussed up your cap."

Rachel's lips stretched wider than he thought possible as she stated, "She does appear to be wearing a fur hat. How cute. Another blue-eyed dog."

"Our dogs have a variety of eye colors. Even a couple with two colors, one for each eye, like Anik's lead dog Tracker. But every last one of *these* Huskies is a ranger."

"Are you just calling them that, or is ranger actually their title?"

"The canines' workload for the park is as important as their two-legged counterparts', and they're counted on just as much. They've earned their title of ranger."

Liam explained the history of the Dogs of Denali and how it had changed over the years. Then he described some of what the canines helped the human rangers do in today's world at the national park.

Giving him her full attention, Rachel joined Liam as they walked among the doghouses and met with other canine rangers. She stopped at each one to take a few pictures and made notes of their names. "Wish I had a photographer with me to get the best shot. All this time I lived right here next to Denali and never knew the story about these wonderful Alaskan Huskies."

Time was slipping by too quickly. If only he could slow down the clock. He enjoyed talking with Rachel and wanted more of her company. He wanted to see her again, often... but the drive was more than a hundred miles each way from his cabin to Fairbanks. It was a little too far on a regular basis. *Too bad.*

"Just curious. How long do you think you'll be here before returning to Fairbanks?" He could at least spend time with her while she was staying at her folks' home. Anik was right. He'd missed out on companionship like this.

"I'm not sure. I can email my article to the office when I finish, and I have a fair amount of vacation time I could ask for. It would be nice to devote more time to my parents and brother. But perhaps only a few days this time because I don't want to deduct time from when I come back for Christmas."

She hadn't mentioned her sister. Wish he knew what was going on between them. Then again, it wasn't his business. *Would she consider having dinner with me tomorrow, perchance?*

Chapter Seven

Rachel pulled her bottom lip between her teeth. Could it be that Liam wanted more time to get to know her? He was so different from the majority of the men she'd met in college or at the newspaper. No rushing her, pickup lines, or false compliments. Only an easygoing banter.

While he said goodbye to Flame, Rachel's heart fluttered. He glanced at her. What a sobering and crazy thought—she was jealous of that dog. She giggled to herself. *Rachel!* She had to keep in mind that she'd just met the man, and she'd be gone from Denali and Healy when her article was complete.

Liam rose from his squat and threw his arm out in the direction of a building. "Let's head over to the Doghouse."

"The *Doghouse*?"

He laughed. "Yeah. It's what we call the catch-all project building, where there's a break room. We usually eat our meals there.

You can talk with the other kennel rangers I saw go in, listen to their take on the Huskies, and ask questions to get a variety of perspectives instead of taking my word for everything."

"That'd be wonderful. Not that I don't believe what you say, but it's good to have more than one angle for the story. Thanks."

As they strolled into the lunch area, two rangers hailed Liam and gave an invitation to sit with them. He took Rachel's arm and steered her toward their table. "Exactly what we were hoping for. Guys, I want you to meet Rachel O'Rourke, a reporter from *The Fairbanks Star*. She's here to do a write-up on our sled dogs.

"We've already been to see the pups and met the members of the canine teams. I've given her a brief overview of what they do, but I thought it would be nice for her to get more information from other kennel rangers. If we won't interrupt your lunch, that is."

"Nah, nice to meet you, Rachel." A muscular ranger with short-cropped, blond hair and light blue eyes stood and shook her hand. "I'm Allen Hines, and this tall drink of water," he pointed a thumb behind him, "is Christian Allatori."

The young man with wavy black hair and light brown eyes stood and reached around Allen to extend his hand. "Call me Chris. Welcome. Please join us."

Sure were a lot of handsome guys working at the park. No wonder Dee applied to work here. She stifled another giggle.

For the next hour, Rachel asked questions of the two new-to-her rangers and jotted down information for her story. "This is great stuff. Thank you for taking the time to answer my questions. The readers will be as pleased as I am to learn these dogs are so well looked after."

Liam had been quiet the entire time she talked to the other two rangers. He was definitely a different sort of man than any she knew, except for her family. Not once had he interrupted Allen or Chris to put in his own opinion or correct them. She found him focused on her instead. What was he thinking? *If only I had more time to know him better.*

During the lull that followed, while Rachel made a few notes, Chris asked Liam about a young man he'd helped to transport to the hospital last Friday when Liam had volunteered on the search and rescue team. Chris swallowed the bit of sandwich he'd taken. "Was he in poor condition? Did the guy make it?"

"His condition wasn't too bad." Liam's brows furrowed. "He had slipped off a rock and wound up in a dangerous predicament. He tried to use his cellphone but was in a dead zone of the park. Fortunately, his friends caught up with him. His buddy found a spot where he got a call through for help, and we were able to get him off the ledge and to the ER."

Rachel stiffened. Her eyes locked onto Liam's face, which blurred as her mind transported her back two years to the Fairbanks ER waiting room. Her parents crying—clinging to each other, as they learned of Kalen's horrific injury. She narrowed her eyes. No wonder Liam looked so familiar. He was there. He was one of the rangers who found Kalen. Heat, like that of an angry volcano, filled her chest and threatened to erupt.

Liam's gaze darted to Rachel. Anger flooded her face. What happened?

His mind flashed to when he'd seen Rachel at the hospital two years earlier, after Kalen's surgery. Liam had stopped by to find out his condition. The expression she wore now was the same as it was in the hospital. Fierce anger. He'd chalked it up to the situation with Kalen at the time, but why now?

As if a lightbulb flashed on in his brain, Liam's eyes popped open. *Oh! The question Chris asked about the rescue of the young man in the mountain. Of course.* It would have triggered her memory of Kalen's bear attack and why he was paralyzed. Liam grimaced. He thought she'd be happy over the good news that this young man was doing okay, not angry. He didn't get it.

Rachel shot up from the chair. "Please take me to my parents' house."

She hadn't requested—more like a demand. Liam rose from his seat. "Is something wrong, Rachel? Are you okay?"

"Let's go." She headed for the door.

"Sorry, guys. Not sure what just happened. I'll see you next week."

Question marks filled both Chris and Allen's faces.

"Sure, man. Is she not feeling well?" Chris stretched his neck to peer around Allen as Rachel rushed through the door and disappeared outside.

"Not sure. I'll talk to you later." Liam hurried to catch up with Rachel. What had gotten into her? One second she was sugar and spice and then *blam!* She looked like a fissure ready to spew lava. He had no doubt her sudden change of attitude had to do with Kalen. She was fine until Chris asked about the accident on the mountain. Maybe her ire was directed at his ranger friend. But why?

Liam blew out a frustrated breath. She'd tell him what bothered her on the way to her folks' house.

Rachel hopped into the passenger seat of Liam's truck and yanked the door shut before he even exited the building.

She fumed. It had taken her long enough to put two and two together. Liam was the ranger who had found her brother that day on the mountain. But he hadn't gotten Kalen to the ER in time. She had watched Liam exit the exam rooms, guilt beyond question written on his face. He had to have been responsible for a delay that caused her brother's paralysis. It was all his fault. She hated him.

When Liam jumped into the driver's seat, she wanted to rip into him with her nails as well as words. She bit down on her lips to keep a scream from escaping and clasped her hands. Her blood boiled.

"Rachel? What happened back there just now? I'm sure Chris's question—"

"Just drive." She stared out the windshield and smoldered.

He studied her for a moment, then started the engine.

As they drove in silence, anger raged inside her chest. She couldn't wait to get out of his black truck—which matched her mood.

The drive to her parents' home was excruciatingly long. At least he hadn't tried to talk to her again. She refused to let the welling tears fall from her eyes.

Liam had to have recognized Kalen from that horrific day. He had to have. Hence, he'd known her mom and dad since he talked to them at the hospital when he visited after Kalen's unsuccessful surgery. He knew who she was too.

He'd spoken such sweet words of comfort to her family to cover up his failure to get her brother to the hospital soon enough. She wasn't having any of it. Not then—not now.

At last! Liam pulled up to her parents' cabin. Rachel jumped out of the vehicle, raced to the front door, burst in, and slammed the door shut. She never wanted to see Liam Chadwick again.

As she flew up the steps to her old room, the wall of tears she'd held back overflowed. She dashed in and dove for her bed without taking off her jacket, hat, and gloves.

Minutes later, a soft knock on the door startled her. "Rachel, honey? May I come in?"

Mom. Rachel sat up and reached for a tissue from the box on the nightstand. "Yes," she said, her voice shaky. She mopped her face and blew her nose.

Her mother entered and approached her without asking any questions. "Let me take your jacket for you."

Rachel shrugged out of the parka. Her mother draped it over the small armchair in the corner as Rachel removed her hat and gloves. She tried to keep the tears from flowing, but they forced themselves onto her cheeks. Her mother removed Rachel's wet boots and set them on the scatter rug in front of the armchair.

Sobs erupted and wouldn't stop. Her loving mother wrapped her distraught daughter in her arms and held her until the sobs ended.

After sitting a few minutes in the truck, bewildered and having no idea what to do next, Liam ambled up to the house and rapped on the door. Mr. O'Rourke answered. "Come in, Liam."

He stepped into the foyer. What should he say to Rachel's father?

"Have a seat in the living room. My wife made a pot of coffee. As I recall from last night, you take yours black. I'll be right back."

Liam eased onto the couch, his mind overrun with questions that had no answers. He lowered his head to his hands with his elbows braced on his thighs. None of this made any sense. What had happened to cause Rachel to act that way? Reliving her brother's attack and failed surgery two years ago?

The front door opened, and Deirdre waltzed through, followed by Anik.

He smiled. "Hi, Liam. Did Rachel get all the information she needed?" Anik winked at Liam.

Deirdre had a grin a mile wide. "Where's my sister? I want to tell her *everything* about my morning and what fun we had." She surveyed the living and dining rooms as her father returned with two mugs of steaming brew.

Mr. O'Rourke handed a cup to Liam and placed the other on the table beside his chair. Once seated, Deirdre's father directed his gaze at her. "I'm happy to hear you had a wonderful time with Anik. Your sister is a little under the weather. Leave her alone until she feels better. Okay?"

His younger daughter's lips formed a slight pout. "Yes, Dad." She dragged Anik to the dining room.

Her father took a sip of coffee. He peeked at Deirdre, who pulled out what appeared to be a family photo album and laid it on the table in front of Anik.

Setting his cup down, Mr. O'Rourke peered over his glasses at Liam. "So what happened?"

Liam took in a deep breath, shook his head, shrugged, and spread his hands out. "I have no idea, sir. We listened to two of my kennel ranger coworkers as they told Rachel stories about the dogs, some of the work, and unusual circumstances they'd been in while on duty. Then a lull came into the conversation while Rachel wrote down the information.

"Ranger Chris asked about a young man I helped rescue on the mountain the other day from a predicament he'd gotten himself into. The next thing I knew, Rachel's attention shot up from her writing. She looked as though she wanted to bite off our heads. She demanded I bring her back to your house and ran out the door to the truck."

He dropped his hands onto his thighs, took another deep breath, and blew it out. "When I got to the vehicle and asked her what happened, she said, '*Just drive.*' I thought it best not to ask any more questions until she was ready to talk, but... that didn't happen. She clammed up. I had no idea what to say to her.

"When we arrived here, she jumped out of my truck before I put it in Park, then she ran into the house."

His mouth twisted. "I didn't want to leave without finding out what was wrong, so I decided I'd better come in and ask."

Mr. O'Rourke pinched his lips together and pulled them to one side. He gave a nod. "I'm sure your coworker's question sparked something. My guess is... Rachel finally realized who you were."

"What do you mean by 'who you were'?"

"I mean, she remembered you from the hospital when Kalen had surgery, and you came by to see how he was."

"Okay. I remembered that too. I figured Chris's question might have brought her back to that day. But the young man we rescued wasn't injured, only traumatized from hanging off a ledge."

Mr. O'Rourke's lips relaxed. "You were terrific with our family the day we received the heartbreaking news about Kalen's paralysis. My wife and I could tell you meant every word of Scripture and comfort you gave us. We were grateful. And we're certain you and the search and rescue team did everything possible to take care of and transport him off the mountain and to the ER as quickly as possible. However— "

"Rachel blames you." Deirdre stood and whizzed into the living room. "First for not getting to the site sooner than you did, and then for taking too long to bring Kalen to the ER. She always has. No wonder she doesn't feel well. She figured out who you are. I did too."

Liam's mouth opened. "What?"

The glare Mr. O'Rourke gave his younger daughter could have fried an egg. "What have I told you about eavesdropping on other people's conversations, young lady?"

Her head dropped forward with the smirk still faintly visible. "Sorry, Dad. I thought Liam had a right to know."

"Why did Rachel blame Liam?" Anik stepped up next to her, his brow furrowed. "Nonsense. I never heard her say that. We haven't corresponded much since then, but still. Surely she would've given an inkling of her anger over two years if she blamed someone."

The cup Liam held clattered as he set it on the coffee table. His gaze swept from Anik to Deirdre to Mr. O'Rourke. "She blames me for Kalen's paralysis?" Liam's brows rose. Bewilderment flooded him. "How? Why? I don't understand."

Chapter Eight

Liam awoke in a state of turmoil. Yesterday, he'd headed back to his cabin with no answers for why Rachel blamed him for her brother's paralysis. Her father had rushed Deirdre out of the room, and Anik shrugged and said nothing.

The search and rescue team had responded to the call for help that day as soon as they got it. Liam paced with his cup of early morning coffee. Why did she think he'd caused a delay? He'd only been a volunteer. His only thought had been to deliver Kalen to where he would receive immediate trauma intervention. *How could Rachel believe I was negligent in rescuing her brother?*

He stopped his tour of the kitchen and placed his mug on the counter. Perhaps when he spoke to Anik today, he'd find out more about what happened then to make Rachel so angry.

As he sipped the hot brew, Liam shook his head. He'd never seen Rachel before Kalen's accident. Where had she gotten her information? Surely Anik hadn't said anything to make Rachel come up with such a horrible accusation.

Fatigue from a restless night's sleep hit Liam. He shouted into the air, "Where did Rachel get the idea I'm to blame for Kalen's paralysis, Lord?" Could it be possible Anik had said something to lead her to that belief without realizing it?

Glaring at the staircase, Liam yelled, "Anik! Come down here. We need to talk."

Rachel awoke with a throbbing head and her heart still full of anger. Yesterday afternoon, she'd been too distraught to talk. Not even to her mother, the most understanding person in the world. Nightmares had haunted her fitful sleep as she relived the doctor's pronouncement that Kalen would never walk again.

After a soft knock on the door, her mom entered her bedroom with a breakfast tray. She set it on the dresser. "You remembered Liam, didn't you?"

Of course, Mom read my mind. She always did. "It was *him*, Mom. *He's* the reason Kalen is in a wheelchair. How dare he come here and attempt to endear himself to our family? Offering to help me with the article. What was he thinking?"

Her mother sat on the side of the bed. With a gentle smile, she took Rachel's hands in hers and peered into her eyes. "Honey, we've been through this before when you first blamed yourself. You have no basis to accuse Liam either. You didn't then, and you don't now. Both your father and I appreciated Liam's genuine compassion toward us at the hospital. Kalen also felt it when he spoke to him in the helicopter on the way to the emergency room. If anything, Kalen was grateful Liam kept him from going out of his mind with pain by quoting Scripture to him all the way to the Fairbanks ER."

"I don't remember you telling me any of this back then."

"At the time, you were hurting so much for Kalen you probably lashed out at the first person you saw. I thought you'd gotten over this anger a long time ago. If we had known you were still harboring all these negative feelings, Dad and I would have talked to you about it again."

Rachel pressed her lips together. Tears burned in her eyes. "But he recognized me and said nothing."

"To me, it means he was waiting to see if you remembered him, or maybe he couldn't place you right away any more than you did him. But I don't think Liam was aware you thought the worst of him. Why would he, when he didn't do anything wrong, and he'd volunteered to help search and rescue that day? SAR got Kalen out of the mountains and to Fairbanks in record time. If he recognized you, Liam probably thought you were still sensitive about your brother's loss of the use of his legs and didn't want to bring up something so painful."

Rachel squeezed her eyes shut. The thought she had blamed Liam for Kalen's paralysis all this time added more heaviness to her heart. If her mother was right, she had some apologizing to do. Rachel hung her head. Her mother lifted her chin with an index finger.

"Eat your breakfast, hon. Food in your stomach will perk you up. Then wash and come downstairs."

Her mother headed for the bedroom door but spun. "Before you hear it from Deirdre, she blurted out your accusation to Liam. Yes, she's in the doghouse for it. But... at least you don't have to explain everything to him about why you were so angry yesterday." Mom pursed her lips. "You must have voiced your anger near your sister. Regardless, he's confused. All you have to do now is tell him you were wrong. Can you do that?"

Rachel bit her lip. For two years, she'd blamed him as much as herself for a result he had no control over. Thought he was in charge. Assumed he hadn't done his job right, when in fact he'd volunteered to do something not even his job. He'd acted so confident and offered kind words to all of them. How could she know?

I needed someone to share the burden. She'd chosen Liam to carry all the responsibility.

Mom approached the bed and patted Rachel's back. "Honey, Kalen's injuries from the bear attack were too critical. It's nobody's fault. Sometimes things just happen."

Rachel nodded. She'd blamed herself for Kalen having gotten injured in the first place. He'd forgiven her for egging him on about going with the guys, though she'd been teasing. Her brother told her his paralysis wasn't her fault. He said the blame was his for not being more careful, and... if she *had* been to blame for that day, God had already forgiven her when she cried out to Him.

Kalen had quoted Matthew 5:45 "...he maketh his sun to rise on the evil and on the good, and sendeth rain on the just and on the unjust." Then her brother told her, "Bad things happen to everyone. All you have to do is forgive yourself." Yet she still thought she was responsible. She'd blamed herself and no one else... until she saw Liam. But it wasn't Liam's fault.

Rachel's heart broke all over again. "Mom, all I can do is try to apologize. But I can't do it right now. I need time." More tears flooded her eyes.

Mom kissed the top of Rachel's head and left the room.

After Rachel had mopped up her tears, she nibbled at her food. Should she go back to Fairbanks? She had enough information for her story. And if Mr. Gibson wanted more, he could make the trip down here and fill in the gaps himself.

Anik hadn't answered Liam's shout. The man must have gotten in late last night. *Much later than when I went to bed.* Frustration set in. Liam pursed his lips. Better go outside and walk this off.

When Liam had walked off his exasperation, he came in and climbed the stairs only to find his friend's bedroom door open.

Liam ran down the stairs. He was *not* going to let Anik leave until they had this out. Liam entered the kitchen, where he dropped into a chair across the table from Anik. His friend buttered a slice of toast as if nothing of significance had happened yesterday.

"Were you aware Rachel was so angry at me? I remembered you talking to her at the hospital when Kalen had surgery... and how she fell into your arms. What did you tell her?" The irritation mounted again.

Anik's brows puckered, but he didn't answer.

As Liam waited, his friend's eyes rounded like a deer caught at night in headlights.

"Anik, what did you tell Rachel about me at the hospital a couple of years ago? She thinks I'm to blame for the paralysis. I remember you kept talking to her and nodding toward me. Never thought to ask you about it back then."

"What are you talking about?"

Is he playing me? "The night Kalen and his parents found out Kalen was paralyzed because of the damage the bear had done to him, I was leaving the hospital when the doctor told his family. Rachel stood next to you. You spoke to her. You nodded toward me. Then she fell into your arms. What did you say to her? You heard Deirdre. Rachel blames me. Why?"

Anik moved into the living room with his toast and coffee. He stood before the couch, set the plate and cup on the table, then dropped onto the seat like a load of timber. His jaw hung open as he stared blankly at Liam. "I don't recall what we were talking about two years ago, pal. But if I nodded at you, it must have been because I was trying to get Rachel's mind off her brother at the time."

The stocky man stopped and lifted his gaze as if he would read the words he'd spoken on the ceiling. He snapped his fingers. "Yeah. I do remember. The doctor had already advised the O'Rourkes of Kalen's condition. I remember you coming out of the recovery area. I figured you were there to check on him, being the way you are. When I saw you, I told Rachel you were part of the team that brought him in, and you were a friend of mine. I would never have said anything to make her think you were to blame."

"I doubted you would, but I remembered you talking and nodding toward me. We didn't know each other that well yet back then."

Anik pointed to the chair across from him. "Why don't you sit down and chill out for a few minutes? This thing has gotten blown all out of proportion. Like I said last night at the O'Rourkes', Rachel never said anything to me about blaming you or the search and rescue team for what happened to Kalen. This could all be one of her sister's fabrications. There seems to be a wide green streak running through the girl—Deirdre, I mean. Something must have happened to put a wedge full of briars between her and Rachel. I don't remember such animosity when I was around while they were younger."

Liam slumped into the chair and rested his elbows on his knees. He lowered his head into his hands. "SAR did a fantastic job with Kalen when they transported him to the hospital in Fairbanks. Somehow, he and I connected that day as he regained consciousness on the ground. He reached out to me. The crew thought it would be good for me to keep talking to him."

As Liam slowly shook his head, the sound of Anik's scuffling boots went into the kitchen. Liam's heavy heart broke over what Rachel thought of him. *Lord, I hope what Deirdre said last night isn't true.* Why would she have said it if it weren't though? *If there's something wrong between those girls, please fix it.*

The scuffle of boots sounded again. Liam raised his head to a cup of steaming liquid.

"Here." Anik handed him a mug. "Drink this. My grandmother always said you should go with cocoa and peppermint when stressed out. Fortunately, you had both in the cabinet. My favorite of Aanaa's remedies." He snickered.

Liam accepted the mug. The smooth chocolate and peppermint combination soothed his rattled nerves. Maybe this entire thing was a mistake. Perhaps Rachel did have a stomachache yesterday. At least he could hope, though he didn't want her sick.

He still had three days off before he'd return to work on Monday. He'd call the O'Rourkes and find out if she'd talk to him.

Anik observed the tortured look on Liam's face as his friend drank the hot cocoa. This love story was headed for tragedy. The spark of interest in Rachel could wind up being a deep wound if it were true that she blames him. But why would Rachel blame Liam for Kalen losing the use of his legs? Would Deirdre deliberately say such a thing? Why make her sister out to be so hateful?

"Hey. I have an idea. Rachel is obviously having a problem with the idea of mushing, which came across through our written correspondence."

"Yeah, so?"

"So, I have a plan to get her past the possible fear she's developed since her brother's accident. If you join me in the kitchen, I'll make one of my infamous breakfasts for you. I'll bet you haven't eaten at all since yesterday morning, have you?"

"No. I haven't, except for a couple of antacid tablets and toast before I fell asleep on the couch while I waited for you." Liam followed Anik back to the kitchen and sat at the table.

As Anik pulled out pans from the lower cabinets and food from the refrigerator, Liam hopped up and got plates and utensils out. "My stomach was upset, along with the rest of me."

"Sorry. I stopped to visit with an old friend before I came back. You had already gone to bed when I came in. I'm surprised you didn't hear the dogs when I took care of them before coming inside, or me when I entered."

"I was out for the count when my head hit the pillow. But it didn't last long. I wrestled with the covers for the rest of the night.

They were in a ball this morning. I kept dreaming about Rachel's reactions. Still can't figure it out."

The bacon sizzled in the frying pan. Anik poured oil into another pan, heated it, and added frozen shredded potatoes. He adjusted the heat. "Well, last night I received a call from my friend, who I said would stay with us while we practiced runs in Denali. He'd gotten a call from his dad. His mother was taken to the hospital with a ruptured appendix. He can't make it. Thought I'd ask Rachel if she'll help me practice with the dogs."

"Why?"

"Kalen was out with his friends and lagged behind. You know the rest. No doubt her time with the dogs, talk of mushing, and her recollection of her brother's bear attack from the question your coworker asked brought on the reaction yesterday."

Liam nodded.

"If she helps me, it might help her. And if you're there to assist… well… besides, she owes me a favor."

"What a harebrained idea. Rachel may have already left."

The aroma of bacon filled the kitchen. "But maybe she hasn't, pal."

Anik slid bacon, eggs, crispy shredded potatoes, and toast in front of Liam. "Put something in your stomach. Then we attack." He snickered. "We can't let her leave Healy like this." *Or leave you.*

Chapter Nine

After half an hour, Anik stared at Liam, who toyed with his breakfast. "Something wrong with the food? You've hardly touched a bite."

"No, this is great." Liam shoved a forkful of what had to be ice-cold, sunny-side-up eggs over shredded potatoes into his mouth. He followed it with a noisy bit of crisp bacon. His expression was priceless, like a chipmunk with his cheeks full of nuts to store for the winter.

Anik grabbed the plate and stuck it in the microwave. "Well, if you're still going to eat it, at least let me heat it up. But it won't taste as good as when it was fresh from the pan." He closed the machine, set it on Defrost to warm the food, then turned to Liam.

"Come on, guy. Snap out of it. It's awfully fast, but I know you already have feelings for Rachel. You wouldn't be as bummed out as you are if what happened weren't under your skin like a tick."

Liam's eyes narrowed. His jaw twitched. "Will you please stop with the matchmaking?"

Anik held his hands up, palms out. "Whatever you say. But we *will* go over there this morning. If I have to tie you up and drag you, I will. It'll be for your own good. Get this settled. Find out what's wrong with her. Is that so hard to do?"

The nuker dinged. Anik lifted out the plate and deposited it in front of Liam. "Now eat!"

"You sound like my mother."

Anik laughed. "You need someone to act in the place of your mother. If that has to be me, so be it, unless you'd like me to call her." He picked up Liam's fork and held it out to him.

Liam snatched the utensil, blew out a stream of air between his teeth, and speared a helping of eggs and potatoes.

As Rachel hid in her room, her mind traveled to Liam and the day he left the hospital after Kalen's surgery. She'd blamed him for not immobilizing Kalen properly, delaying the trip to the ER, and so many other things in her state of distress. She shut her eyes and hurt everywhere as she reflected on the injustice of her false accusation.

While working with the dogs for her article yesterday, everything about him impressed her. He was different from any other man she'd met. She even hoped he'd ask her out, and they'd become better acquainted, even though they lived so far apart. Until she realized who he was. Then all those ugly accusations she'd come up with flooded into her brain.

The attitude she had shown him, too much for anyone to bear, made the idea of his wanting to date her vanish.

She accepted he wasn't at fault. *Why didn't Mom and Dad correct me back then?* They actually did. They thought she had gotten over her misplaced anger. *How can Liam ever forgive me?* She owed him an apology, no matter how much embarrassment it would cost her. She wouldn't blame him if he turned his back on her and walked away. Then she'd never see him again.

Her mother's familiar knock came to the door. "Hon, are you up and functioning? I'm getting lunch on the table. And you have a guest."

"I'll be down in a minute." Who could it be? Surely not Liam.

Liam got ready to leave the cabin with Anik. "I'm still uncertain this is a good idea, buddy. If she's mad at me, it'd be best if I wait for her to cool off before I face her. And if she has problems dealing with mushing after what happened to her brother, I doubt she'll want to have anything to do with helping you. This could result in her being twice as mad."

"You're a worrywart, you know that?" Anik opened the front door and stepped out, dragging Liam with him.

All the way to the O'Rourkes' home, Liam tried to dissuade his friend from asking Rachel to assist him with his practice for the upcoming dogsled race. Nothing worked. "Anik, you are one hardheaded Inuk."

He grinned. "Ain't it grand? When I set my mind to do something, that's it. It gets done."

"I hope she doesn't throw something at that hard head of yours... and mine too, for good measure. I'm not in the mood for a flight to the ER in Fairbanks or Anchorage." He needed to stop worrying about what Anik would say to her and figure out what *he'd* say. But how could he do that when he had no real clue what upset her? Maybe he should start by telling her he was sorry for not saying something when he first recognized her. Then what?

Anik pulled his Jeep in at the O'Rourkes' home and got out. Liam pressed his lips together, took a deep breath, and stepped out of the vehicle. Beyond Anik's Jeep sat a four-wheel-drive, cherry-red Chevy Tahoe. *Wonder who that belongs to.* He hadn't noticed anyone driving an SUV like that in town since the tourists left.

He caught up to Anik, who knocked on the front door. Mrs. O'Rourke answered.

"Welcome back, Anik, Liam. We're blessed with visitors today." She turned to lead them into the living room.

A lanky man, who looked like he was a member of a rock group, rose from the couch. He'd been sitting next to Rachel, with Deirdre on his other side. Hadn't seen him around here either.

Mr. O'Rourke stood. "Anik, Liam, this is Rachel's boss from Fairbanks. Mr. Gibson, these are friends of ours, Anik and Liam. This young man," her father laid his hand on Liam's shoulder, "is the ranger who helped Rachel acquire the information for her article on the canine rangers."

Liam felt his brows lower. This was her supervisor? More like a refugee from the goth subculture of the eighties. But he had to be at least thirty. Did he have mascara on his lashes? Probably not, but they sure were long, dark, and thick.

Mentally jerking himself to attention, Liam checked his thoughts. What was that, jealousy? Won't do to insult or aggravate him. You already have Rachel angry.

So this was the kind of guy Rachel was interested in, even if a little outdated with that hair, shaggy sideburns, and leather jacket. *You're acting like a jealous fool again. Get a grip.*

After Anik shook the man's hand, Liam offered his. "Welcome to Healy, Mr.... Gibson. Do you always drive so far to monitor your reporters?" Now, why had he said that? *Not your business.*

Rachel's eyes widened.

Mr. Gibson clasped Liam's hand and grinned. "I'm not here to keep an eye on my star reporter. It's not the way I run things at my paper. I decided to take a couple of days off and help... with anything she might need." He smiled. "When I gave her this assignment, I assumed she'd be back in the office by now, but she called yesterday morning and told me she still had work to do on the story. So... here I am... to contribute my time."

The man returned to the couch and sat down—a little too close to Rachel, in Liam's opinion.

She popped up. Her eyes locked on Liam's. "There's something I want to ask you... about the kennels. Could we talk in the kitchen where it's quiet?" She turned to her sister. "Maybe you can show Mr. Gibson Dad's dog team."

Deirdre sprang from the couch. The boss's brows furrowed.

No doubt, Rachel sought to put some distance between herself and her superior. *What's up with that guy anyway?* Liam extended his arm toward the hallway. "Ask away, Rachel. As I said earlier, I want to help make your article the best it can be... and accurate."

As Mrs. O'Rourke encouraged Deirdre to wear her warmer coat outside, Rachel led the way through the dining room.

Liam glanced at her boss, who appeared none too happy. Mr. O'Rourke posed a question to the man about his newspaper as she left the room, Liam on her heels.

"Is Gibson coming on to you? You seem nervous. He's not a problem, is he?"

His question went unanswered.

She went through the kitchen's work area and slipped into the small alcove. Rachel closed the double door that led back out to the hallway and into the front foyer. She sat in one of the wooden chairs around the huge oak table in the center of the nook and folded her hands on the polished surface.

"Liam," she breathed in, "I need to apologize to you for the way I acted yesterday. I've been so wrong."

He lowered himself to a seat. "You have nothing to be sorry about. I figured the question Chris asked bothered you... because of Kalen's situation. Your brother's injuries back then were traumatic for everyone. You love him. It's understandable—you lashed out. I made a good target."

She rumpled her brows. "Quit being so nice. This is hard enough as it is."

He wanted to wrap his arms around her and make her feel better. But she needed to talk this out. "Okay. I'm listening."

She took a deep breath and let it out as if she'd counted to twenty. "I chose to blame you instead of myself. Did Dad explain to you how I egged Kalen on to join the practice run with his friends? Of course, I was only joking with my brother all the time, since he had no experience, but I guess Kalen thought I was serious."

Liam shrugged. "I don't really remember that. Too shocked over what Deirdre said about your blaming me."

Rachel's face filled with pain, as though she'd bit her tongue. "Kalen tried to tell me the accident was simply something that happened. He quoted the Bible verse that says the rain falls on the just and the unjust. Still, I couldn't get rid of the guilt. God understood and had already forgiven me when I cried out to Him, but I needed a scapegoat. Then I saw you and decided it had to be your fault."

"But you do understand and believe what God said, correct? And that neither of us is to blame?"

"Yes, but how do I pardon *me*? I thought your kind words to me and my parents were a farce that day. But I was wrong."

She laid her forehead on her arms atop the table for a moment, then lifted her head. "I convinced myself you didn't do something right. Mom told me you had volunteered with the SAR team. It wasn't even your job. You essentially risked your own life to save Kalen." Tears burst from her eyes.

Liam took her hands in his and massaged the backs of them with his thumbs. "Rachel, my life wasn't at risk. Please don't cry. If you need my forgiveness, you have it. I understand the trauma you were under. It's okay."

With tears pouring, she gazed at him. He let go of one hand and brushed away the drops from her cheek and smiled at her. He rose, pulled a paper towel from the holder on the kitchen counter, and held it out to her. Rachel mopped the waterworks from her face.

As Liam returned to his chair, he scooped up her hands again and grinned. "You didn't answer me about your boss. Is he a problem for you?" Liam's pulse sped into overdrive.

The door from the entry hall to the breakfast nook opened. Mr. Gibson stepped through and glared at Liam.

Rachel had been about to tell Liam her boss was not a problem, per se, although in her heart it wasn't entirely true. Mr. Gibson annoyed her on occasion when he insisted she call him by his first name. Then there were the invitations to eat with him. But other than his interruption now, she could handle it.

She dragged her hands out of Liam's and faced her boss. "Mr. Gibson, did you need something? Coffee?" As she stood, heat raced from her collarbone to her cheeks.

"Ah. No. I came to ask you if you'd have dinner with me. Is there somewhere in this town where we can find a decent steak?"

Liam rose from his seat. "Sorry, *sir*, but I've already asked Rachel out tonight." He gave the man more of a smirk than a smile.

The guy narrowed his eyes. "Sir? That's what my dad is called, not me."

Though the rest of her overheated, chills attacked her spine. Like a winter rabbit sensing a predator nearby, while faced with a trapper in front of her, Rachel's jaw dropped open. *Huh? Wait.* Liam had given her an excuse. "That's right, Mr. Gibson. And I accepted before you walked in." *Liar.* Both of them were.

She grinned to herself at the smug expression that still rested on Liam's face.

Mr. Gibson returned Liam's smirk with one of his own. "Well, perhaps we can make it a threesome."

Please think of something, Liam. I don't want to spend an evening with my boss.

"That would be great, but—"

"But..." Anik strode into the room. "They're joining me at my aunt's home for dinner." He helped himself to a cup of the dark liquid from the carafe on the counter. "And I'm afraid the table is already full, otherwise I'd extend an invite."

Her boss abruptly left the room, Anik behind him.

Rachel blinked. How did Anik do that? He had to have a sixth sense or extremely good hearing to have heard them.

Liam escorted her out of the breakfast nook and through the hallway after the two men. Before they reached the foyer, Liam leaned over and spoke into Rachel's ear, "You did a wonderful job with that pickup."

With a tap on Anik's shoulder, Liam asked loud enough for Gibson to hear, "What time did you say we have to leave?"

She whispered back to Liam, "Anik's the one who did a great job. But thanks."

"Right now, if we plan to arrive on time," Anik announced in a volume to match his friend's. Then he chuckled, turned, and winked at Liam and Rachel.

Mrs. O'Rourke's visage showed surprise. "What's this about leaving? I thought you'd all stay for lunch."

Rachel smiled at her mom. "Anik's aunt invited Liam to dinner, and Liam invited me... with Anik's permission, of course. We'll grab some snacks to eat on the way there." Although she hadn't the slightest clue where, since neither Liam nor Anik had mentioned a destination. Fortunately, Mom and Dad didn't ask.

Deirdre conveniently commandeered the conversation by asking Mr. Gibson to join the family for their meal.

Liam tossed Anik his parka. Rachel snatched her jacket from the coat tree in the hall, while Liam slipped his on. She watched her boss's every movement in her peripheral vision. As his eyes stayed glued to her, he agreed to eat with the O'Rourkes'.

Mr. Gibson began to pace the living room like an angry mountain lion.

Will I still have a job after yet another rejection?

Chapter Ten

Before Rachel, Liam, and Anik left her parents' cabin, she glanced again into the living room. Her boss stopped pacing, lowered himself into a chair, and glared at Liam. She'd have to thank both Anik and his friend for their quick thinking about dinner. But how did they know she didn't want to go out with Mr. Gibson? Men's intuition? She was sure Anik had it? Didn't matter. She was grateful to both of them. The two men seemed to be tuned in to each other's wavelengths.

Anik used to do that spontaneous *knowing* when they were younger and hung out at her house. She'd taken for granted it was an Inuit cultural thing back then, but now?

Once outside, Liam opened the passenger door and assisted her into Anik's Jeep. Liam got in the back, and they traveled in comfortable silence, with Rachel delighting in the scenery she had loved since a child.

Soon, they pulled off the road. Anik shifted into park in front of an idyllic, two-story rustic cabin on the west side of town, elegant and sophisticated in its natural surroundings of woods. She snapped her slackened mouth closed.

"Welcome to my home." Liam helped her out of the vehicle. "Come on in and have a cup of coffee while we figure out where to go for dinner tonight. I'm assuming Anik's aunt is not expecting us." He grinned as they watched Anik, who rounded the front deck and entered the garage man-door on the far left corner of the building.

"Hope you didn't mind our hijacking your evening. But you looked a bit—I don't know—let's say uncomfortable with your boss's suggestion for a night out."

"You're very astute, Liam. And I was grateful for the rescue. Thank you. Mr. Gibson keeps saying it's only two coworkers sharing a meal, but he's been trying to persuade me to go out with him. He's not pushy or threatening. I mean, I haven't felt like he's holding my job over my head or anything." She grimaced.

Liam directed her toward the cabin. "Watch your step on the icy patches." He took Rachel's elbow and led her onto the steps of the front deck. "I'll take you in the *formal entrance*, as a regular first-time guest. Anik and I always enter through the garage, the mudroom, and then into the kitchen, but it's because our feet are usually pretty dirty."

A raised cedar walkway with a fence ran the entire length of Liam's house. They passed by five narrow, floor-to-ceiling windows centered on the front. "This is a beautiful cabin, Liam."

"Thanks. My father had it built when they sold their dairy farm in Minnesota and moved here to appreciate the 'last frontier,' as Dad put it. He always wanted to live in Alaska."

"Oh. You live here with your parents?"

"No. They retired from being retired," he snickered, "and moved to Florida."

Her brows pulled together as she considered that statement. "If they retired from the farm... what did they retire from here?"

"When we were in Minnesota, my father also had a tax prep and consulting business, which he continued here. Then one day, he up and said, 'Son, Mom and I have decided to retire completely and move to Destin, Florida.' They took off for the Gulf Coast.

"My older brother, Lucas, had moved there after college, and after a trip to visit him, both my parents fell in love with the Gulf."

They turned the far corner of the deck, surrounded by trees and bushes. A few feet farther brought them to the entrance.

"Dad gave me the keys to the cabin with both their blessings. He knew I had no intention of going to college or leaving Alaska. My sister Ainsley, four years my junior, left home for the U of A in Fairbanks, and didn't plan to return here, except to see me."

"Wow!"

Liam unlocked the door and ushered her into the arctic entry. At the end of the walk-in, closet-sized space was a bench with hooks on the wall behind it. They removed their jackets, hats, and scarves.

They kicked off their boots and placed them on a tray under the seat. Liam handed her a pair of fur-lined moccasins from another tray that ran along the wall and back to the door. "These were my mom's. She left them for any..." he cleared his throat, "female guests. Said she didn't need them in Florida." He cocked his head and eyed her feet. "They should fit."

She took the footwear from his hands and slipped them on. "Perfect size. Thank you. I like arctic entries. Makes a big temperature difference in the rest of the house, especially when it gets down as cold as it does."

"You've got that right."

Liam opened the door to the living room. Anik crouched as he stoked the fireplace at the end of the room on the other side of the long windows she'd noticed outside. "What a lovely room."

"Thanks. Dad did an outstanding job with the help of some local craftsmen here in Healy. Have a seat while I get the coffee on. Regular or decaf?"

"Whichever you two want is okay with me. It all tastes the same."

He gave her a thumbs-up and left the room.

Anik put the fireplace tools away and sat on a chair in front of one of the matching bookshelves framing the hearth.

Rachel lowered herself to the couch across from the set of long windows. "So, this is where you live now, Anik?"

"I do. That makes Liam my landlord." He laughed. "I rent a bedroom upstairs. I'm sure he'll show you around. It is a nice cabin. Quite a fine place for a young married couple." He winked at her, causing heat to rise in her neck.

What did Anik imply by that comment?

Liam walked into the room from the hallway. "Anik... remember, I can always cancel our non-written lease arrangement." He sounded irritated. Then he shifted his icy gaze from his friend and softened his tone, smiling at her. "Pay no attention to his pipe dreams. But I'd be happy to show you around if you like."

"Yes. I would." She cast a glance at Anik, who wore a super-grin with his lips clamped shut and brows raised. *These two men have a peculiar friendship.* "Anik has always been a tease." Even when he'd written to her over the years.

"Just ignore him." Liam headed toward a hallway.

She followed him down the hall past the polished wooden staircase, which led to the second floor and another enclosed set of stairs. "A basement too?"

"Mom and Dad thought of everything."

Beyond the stairwells, the space opened to a spacious dining area. "Did your parents leave you all this too?" The rustic-styled furniture appeared brand new.

"They gave it all to me. Mom said it was time for a change in styles and they were basically going to be beach bums." He chuckled.

"*Beach bums*? She really said that?"

"Oh yeah. My mother's a real character. If you're here in March, I'd love for you to meet her and my sister, who will also be visiting during UAF's spring break."

"You said she attends the University of Alaska in Fairbanks? That's my *alma mater*. What's she studying?"

"First, let's go in here. This is the kitchen, as you can see." He strode to the coffee machine, pulled down two mugs from the overhead cabinet, and filled them with aromatic liquid.

Anik came in and secured his own cup.

"Let's enjoy our coffee before I show you the upstairs." Liam motioned for her to sit at the table. Anik joined them.

Rachel took a sip of coffee and pinned Liam with her gaze. "Now, what's your sister studying?"

He settled his mug in front of him. "Lee—that's what I usually call Ainsley, will graduate next June with a degree in Arctic Research. She's taken an interest in all things Alaskan since we got here. When that girl has something grab her attention, she throws herself into it all the way."

"That's wonderful. It's the way I feel about journalism. My heart's in it."

He gazed at her with his dove-gray eyes. Her stomach flipped.

"I can tell."

As Anik picked up his coffee cup and left the room, Liam tried to drag his gaze away from Rachel, but his *will* refused to cooperate. It enjoyed her warm, soft brown eyes... too much. *Steady*. Remember, she'd only be here for another couple of days.

Rachel broke the intense stare they'd entered. He must've made her uncomfortable. The way her boss did. "Let's continue the tour and then decide where we'll have dinner, since I did invite you... in a roundabout fashion."

The corners of her pretty pink lips curled into a smile. She finished her coffee. "Again, thank you for that rescue. But you don't need to take me out to eat. Once we left, and he had his lunch, I'm sure Mr. Gibson went back to the motel where he's staying. He's never handled conversations with older people like my parents well."

But what if I want to take you?

"Nonsense, Rachel," Anik called out from the dining room. His head popped around the kitchen doorframe. "When a gentleman says he's asked you to dinner, he'd better come through with it. But my aunt lives too far from here to drop in on her, and she never invited us in the first place, so you two are on your own. I've an appointment with that memoir I'm working on, so get on with the tour, Liam, and pick a mouthwatering eatery."

"I fully intend to make good on my invitation, so mind your own business, buddy." Liam lifted one side of his lips and shook his head. "But you can join us if you'd like."

Anik grinned. "Nope. Like I said, I have some writing to do." He disappeared from view again.

That had better be the last of his friend's matchmaking. Liam's head swung back and forth. He peeked at Rachel, who took her cup to the sink and ran water into it. He wouldn't mind spending a lot of time with her.

Liam led Rachel upstairs. They turned on the landing and climbed the rest of the way to the hall. "Remember, these are now bachelor quarters, so don't expect much—not even clean rooms." He snickered.

She grinned. "I have a brother, *remember*? I know what male-occupied rooms are like, but thanks for the warning."

He waved to the left. "My room."

She took a quick peek inside. He was happy he'd picked up his clothes before they'd left that morning.

"The entrance to the master bath and walk-in closet is to the right."

When she shifted her gaze ahead to the double doors that led outside, she let out a tiny gasp. "You have a balcony. Like in *Romeo and Juliet.*"

"I do. It's enjoyable during the warm time of the year. I sit out there and read."

She spun and headed back into the hall. Her face turned a bit pinker than it was downstairs. What could she have been thinking?

This would be a perfect time to develop mind-reading skills. "The door on our left is the upstairs bath."

"This is a gorgeous place."

"The door straight ahead is Anik's room. It's a little bigger than the one to the left that Mom made into the guest room. Anik's room used to be Lee's room. When she visits this spring, she'll be staying with a girlfriend in town, and Mom and Dad will have the guest room."

Liam pursed his lips. "They already told me they are not taking over the master bedroom. One does not argue with my parents when they put their foot down. Old habits, you know." He was becoming a motormouth. *Calm your nerves, man.*

"I understand. I try to avoid arguing about things with mine too, although my mother is a worrywart, and sometimes it gets to me."

"That's only because she loves you." Warmth flowed through his chest and rose to his face. *Stop doing that.*

They descended the stairs to the first floor and then continued to the lower level. "Over there is the utility room and half-bath in the corner of the family room." He pointed to the door next to the utility room. "That's the game room. Spent a lot of time in there when I was younger. The rest is pretty much storage."

They headed back upstairs. "Would you like to see around the outside? Or we can do that when we leave for dinner." What was he doing? He was treating her like a prospective buyer—or maybe—

She takes my breath away.

How many times did he have to remind himself she was leaving? He gulped in air and let out a long stream.

"I'd love to see the grounds. I know I said it before, but this is such a lovely cabin."

Not half as lovely as you. Admit it, man. You're infatuated with her.

He heard Anik's snickers from the dining area, as if the man had read his mind. *I'll get even with that dude.*

While Liam and Rachel discussed possible places to eat, Anik came downstairs and joined them in the kitchen. He poured himself another cup of coffee. "So, did you two decide where you're going?"

"I was telling Rachel there's a new restaurant in town that hasn't closed their doors for the season. What did you think of The Brown Bear in Ferry when you ate there before you left on your trip, Anik?"

"It was impressive. Great atmosphere. And the tourists have made comments saying it's like living the real life in Alaska. I'd offer to cook tonight, but I think you two need more discussion of Rachel's article, without my interruptions." His lips stretched into a self-satisfied grin. *Liam will do something horrible to me to get even.* But perhaps he'd find he liked being on her hook. *He'll forgive me.*

"Eat your cooking?" Liam's brows did some serious crunching. "I'll pass."

Anik's mouth dropped open. "Hey, you liked my breakfast, and I can pop TV dinners in the microwave with the best of them." He chuckled. "So...you're going to The Brown Bear?"

"Sounds good to me if Rachel agrees. Oh, is your boss staying in Healy?"

"No, he said he couldn't find anything available here, so he got a motel room in Anderson. We don't have to worry about running into him. He told me once he hates to drive any farther than he has to, especially in the snow. Tires him out."

Inside, Anik was grinning from ear to ear. *Let's hope he stays there.* He'd like to see these two spend an evening together and see if the fiery sparks would fly.

Anderson was only about half an hour north of Ferry, but... they should be okay. Wouldn't they?

Chapter Eleven

Liam led the way out of his cabin and gave Rachel a quick tour of the surrounding land. He got a kick out of the surprise people had on their faces when they gazed off in the northwest beyond his backyard to the snow-covered peaks of Denali. Her expression was priceless, eyes rounded, lips parted. Like a little girl in a candy shop. "You obviously love the outdoors. I can see it in your eyes."

"I do. This has to be one of the best views of Denali in the area... outside of the national park."

"I neglected to take you onto the deck at the back of the dining room." He pointed to the sliding glass door at the rear of the cabin. "You can see it from the kitchen window too."

"Most people only dream of a view like this from their homes." She pointed toward Denali. "I've always relished being outside. Kalen and I were hardly ever inside. Dad used to take us to the Iditarod each year. Both of us wanted to run in the race when we were old enough. I ran in a couple of smaller races with my team, but then I went to college." She took in a deep breath.

"Since Kalen had decided to take his courses online at first after high school, he continued getting ready to compete. Since he'd spent so much time with them, I let him have my dogs." Sadness filled her eyes.

"I'm sorry, Rachel. I didn't mean to bring back sad memories."

"It's okay. There were good ones too. My dogs loved Kalen and vice versa."

She slipped on a slick spot in the packed snow and lost her balance. Liam reached out and caught her before she hit the ground. Their gazes locked. As he held her, his focus dropped to her parted lips.

"Ah-h-h, thanks for the save." She twisted in his arms.

He lifted her upright and gulped in a lungful of air. "Sure. All part of my duties as a ranger. Always glad to help." He smiled and willed his heart to stop pounding. "Maybe we'd better get going to the restaurant."

They trekked back to the vehicles. Liam helped her into his truck and got in behind the steering wheel. "Ready?"

She smiled in return. "Ready. I've not told you yet how much I like your ride. This black and tan leather." She smoothed her hand over the console, then the seat. "It's very rich."

"Thank you. I like it."

On the way out of Healy, talk turned to her career at *The Fairbanks Star*.

"So, you've worked at the paper for two years now. Has Mr. Gibson always come on to you?"

"No. It's only been a while since he started asking me out to dinner about once every month or so. He's not aggressive, if that's what you're thinking. And as I mentioned, he's given me no reason to fear for my job. But I never date a fellow employee. He's handsome... but not my type."

Liam covered his mouth with his hand in an effort not to grin. That was music to his ears. Did he dare ask? "Does he wear eye makeup?"

Her soft laugh settled over him like a sunny day.

"One day, Mr. Gibson told me that people are always asking him about his long, thick lashes. Curled, too, as you've noticed."

"Hard not to."

"He said it's a family trait on his dad's side. They all have ample black hair and lashes women would die for." She laughed again. "I think that's why he adopted his bad-boy appearance. He doesn't look the part of a newspaper owner by any means."

"Hardly. So that makes him in charge over there."

Liam caught how she scrunched up her face, but then released her muscles.

"Yes, he's the *big* boss, but he doesn't act like it. It's a small business, and he likes to be easygoing with his employees." She spread her arms as if to display the scenery they passed by. "This is a beautiful area. Gorgeous sights are all around. You're fortunate not to live right in town."

Okay, she didn't want to talk about work or Gibson. "Dad was particular about where he decided to build the cabin. I'm blessed that he wanted me to have it." *Better not mention his parents also expect me to fill it with their grandchildren.* Heat rose in Liam's neck.

The Brown Bear Restaurant came into view with a life-sized upright statue of its namesake near the road where they turned in. The two-story structure, the width of a hotel, resembled a huge log cabin stretched across the parking lot. Bear cub figures in a variety of positions climbed the outside of the building to the second-floor balcony and even appeared to wrestle on the roof. A giggle bubbled up inside Rachel. "That is so cool."

Liam parked his truck, and they walked to the entrance. A lifelike carved grizzly stood on its hind legs to greet them, its front paws spread on either side of its head, and its mouth mimicking a Cheshire Cat. Rachel patted its stomach. "Thanks for the welcome, big guy."

Inside, a hostess showed them to a table beside a window overlooking the mountains. Rachel couldn't take her eyes off the image before her. The sun hadn't set yet, and the glow from the west produced a miraculous effect on the snow, turning the scene to pale coral. "Oh, Liam." She pointed. "The mountain range is stunning tonight."

"It is indeed. It's one of the reasons I love living here."

A waitress in a stylish black uniform, with her brunette hair pulled back into a low bun, came to the table and handed them each a menu. After she perused the items, Rachel blinked at Liam. "Everything sounds so delicious I can't make up my mind."

Liam chuckled. "They do make it mouthwateringly difficult, don't they? Let's start with the Chef's Lobster Ravioli appetizer."

Rachel read the description. *Bits of lobster enveloped in pillowy dough and topped with mozzarella cheese, swimming in a basil cream sauce.* "Oh, my."

"Do you need a few more minutes while I get the appetizer?" The girl showed her pearly whites.

Rachel nodded once. "Please."

"What would you like to drink?"

"A Coke with no ice."

"And for you, sir?"

"A glass of milk."

"Excellent. I'll bring your beverages right away." She left their table.

Rachel's eyes snapped to Liam's. "Milk? Didn't see that coming."

"Dairy farm boy, remember?" He laughed. "What kind of meat do you have a taste for? Order anything that strikes your fancy. I plan to."

She inhaled the aromas wafting through the room, then went over the choices again. "The braised pork chops."

"That does sound good."

"Must be a popular choice for tonight. I can taste it in the air."

While they waited for the appetizers to arrive, they scanned the side dishes. The server brought their drinks, the lobster ravioli, and two plates. "Have you decided on your main courses?"

Rachel handed her the menu. "Yes. I'll have the braised pork chops, garlic mashed potatoes, and sautéed spinach."

The girl turned to Liam.

He peered up. "Make that two."

She thanked them and once more left them alone.

After a bite of the appetizer, Rachel gazed around the room. "What a fantastic rustic setting. So appropriate for Alaska and yet more elegant than most places to eat in this area."

"The Brown Bear will be a big hit in the years to come." He checked out the décor as she had. "People need a nice place to go for dinner. I'll bet their business will attract many from as far as an hour away. Even from Fairbanks or Anchorage for special events. I saw doors marked Private Dining Room. And Anik said they don't plan to close at the end of the tourist season either. Like he said, good food and atmosphere. He also mentioned they're attentive to their customers."

"You're beginning to sound like a travel guide, Mr. Chadwick. I might do an article on The Brown Bear for *The Fairbanks Star*."

He laughed, but his laughter didn't last long.

Rachel's brows lowered at the sour expression. She sensed a presence on her left. Foreboding replaced the easygoing sensation from Liam and his casual banter as a hand rested on the back of her chair. She glanced up into the deep blue eyes of Jess Gibson.

He glowered at Liam.

Her jaw slackened. *Oh, no!*

"What happened to *dinner* with your Eskimo friend's aunt?" Jess pinned Liam with a glare, then shifted his gaze onto Rachel. "Did he get you to go out with him on false pretenses? Come on, Rachel. I'll take you back to your parents' house." Jess took hold of Rachel's upper arm.

Liam stood. "Our change of plans isn't really any of your concern, Mr. Gibson. And in case you are not aware, *Eskimo* is a term we do not use around here. Our indigenous people consider it derogatory. I would think a newsman from Fairbanks would know that. Take your hand off of her."

"Or what?"

Jess and Liam locked eyes, but Liam's gaze broke as he focused over Jess's shoulder.

"Or there'll be a not-so-nice scene." The voice had come from behind. He let go of Rachel and spun to find Liam's friend. The expression on the stocky man's face spoke volumes. "You're in this *Eskimo's* way, *sir*."

Jess huffed. *Great! I drive all the way back to Ferry from Anderson to sit in a decent restaurant and eat, and now these two clowns get in my face.* "Hey, sorry I jumped to conclusions. I imagined that one glimpse of this lovely lady," he laid his hand on Rachel's shoulder, "would cause all kinds of finagling to be in her company for an evening. My apology."

The waitress reappeared. "Will there be two more at your table?"

Anik slid into the chair between Liam and Rachel. "*No! Just. One.*" He gave her an order for his meal, then turned to Jess. "*Please...* excuse us, Mr. Gibson. We weren't able to join the party at my aunt's, so we decided to discuss business tonight instead. It wouldn't be of interest to you."

Jess's neck smoldered with anger. Who did these guys think they were, to dismiss him that way? "Perhaps I should take Rachel back to her parents' place if you have *business* to tend to. It would probably be boring to her."

"Oh, no-o-o. On the contrary. Part of this involves Rachel. So. Again... please excuse us."

Jess narrowed his eyes. If looks could kill, he hoped his would not only do in the *native*, but the temperature would fry his ranger friend as well. *You'd better cool your jets, Gibson.* Getting into a fracas with them would only turn Rachel off. "In that case, I'll leave you to your *business*." Jess smirked.

"Rachel, I'll see you tomorrow. I want to talk to you about the article. Would you set aside some time for me? I'll come to your parents' home around one in the afternoon if that's okay with you."

"One will be fine, Mr. Gibson." Only one side of her lips rose.

He'd find out if the story had enough information in it already—probably—and then press Rachel to return to work on Friday for another assignment. That should get her away from these backwoods bumpkins.

Rachel watched as Mr. Gibson walked out the front doors of the restaurant. He didn't act as though he believed the excuse Anik gave one bit. She'd been caught in a fabrication to avoid going to dinner with her boss, even if the lie wasn't her idea. The whole situation was odd. Mr. Gibson almost sounded jealous.

"Glad *he* left," Anik muttered under his breath, then faced and studied her. "Rachel, is your boss hitting on you?"

"As I explained to Liam, Mr. Gibson asks me to go for a meal with him on occasion, but I don't. I've told him my reasons. It doesn't seem right. I'm his employee, and he doesn't go out with other females at the newspaper. He insists it's simply a friendly request, or sometimes he says it's to talk about work."

"Be careful, Rachel. When he asked Liam what happened to our dinner plans at my aunt's, Gibson didn't have the demeanor of a concerned friend. He had possession written all over his face… and his hand on your arm."

"Possession of whom?" Her brows pulled together. Her focus bounced between Anik and Liam.

Anik grinned and shifted his attention to Liam without moving his head. "Well, it wasn't either of us. We're not the ones he tried to ask out at your folks' home."

Rachel's stomach soured. Deep down, this was what she'd been afraid of all along, though she'd never considered it harassment. Still, it didn't seem harmless anymore either. What would she do now? Her position at *The Fairbanks Star* was important to her.

"Rachel?" Liam's hand covered her wrist as she rested it on the table.

"*What!*" That came out harsher than she'd meant it to. Her boss's actions weren't Liam's fault, and Liam hadn't acted any differently toward her than Anik had all these years. *Well, not much more.* She closed her eyes. Had Mr. Gibson sensed the attraction she'd felt for Liam?

"Do you fear you'll lose your position at the *Star* if you continue to turn down your boss's requests to go out with him?" Liam removed his hand from hers. "Could be that's why I picked up on the vibes at your parents' house… that you didn't want to have dinner with him but didn't know what to say."

Her eyes burned as she forced back pending tears. "I don't think I have anything to worry about regarding my job or Mr. Gibson. He's always taken my no for an answer… before. And it sounded like he accepted the reason you gave him about discussing work when you asked him—in a roundabout way—to leave."

She grimaced at Anik.

"Did you want him to stay?" He tilted his head to one side and bunched his brows.

"No, but that's not the point." Still, if Anik was right about Mr. Gibson and he planned to give her a hard time about refusing his advances in the future—

Her head ached. "I should go back to my parents' cabin and allow you two to discuss whatever business you mentioned. It doesn't involve me."

"But it does."

Anik gave her an impish gleam, the way she remembered he did when they were younger, and he wanted to get her to do something she didn't want to do. The scallywag.

"And besides, here comes our food." He popped a ravioli into his mouth and leaned back in his chair.

The waitress placed steaming plates in front of the three of them.

Rachel glanced at Liam, who pressed his lips together and focused on his friend.

She clamped her lips together too. Then said, "Okay, what are you two *gentlemen* up to that involves me?"

Chapter Twelve

Hands up, palms out, Anik tried to give her his best innocent smile.

"Come on, Anik. Out with it." Rachel tilted her head. "You're up to something. You haven't changed one iota in all these years. What are you trying to rope me into now?"

She had him. The girl could always tell when he had a scheme up his sleeve. But it was worth a try—for her own good. She needed to move past the guilt she carried over her brother's accident. And if he had his way, she'd wind up in a solid relationship with a terrific guy before she went back to Fairbanks.

"Why don't we eat dinner before the food gets cold? It'd be a shame to waste one of The Brown Bear's outstanding meals."

They bowed their heads, and Liam gave thanks.

In a flash, Anik dug into his elk steak. "Mmmm. Now this is what I'm talking about. This place will become famous."

"I second that." Liam cut off another chunk of his pork chop. "This is as tasty as Mom's. How's yours, Rachel?"

"It's fabulous. Yes, for sure, I'm going to do a write-up on The Brown Bear for the newspaper." She smiled. "You know, I might even find I prefer reviewing eating establishments to the writing I've done for the past two years. Think of all the great restaurants I'd visit." She chortled through another bite of her chop and then a mouthful of roasted-garlic mashed potatoes.

Anik's eyes widened. "You can't leave your family and travel around the world. They'd miss you too much." And how would he get her and Liam together if she became a jet-setter?

"Don't worry, Anik. As exciting as it sounds, Alaska is in my blood. I wouldn't be happy anywhere else."

Whew! Anik stuffed another piece of meat into his mouth.

After they finished their desserts of chocolate mousse with almond sauce, Rachel took a sip of coffee. She placed the cup in its saucer and folded her arms across her midriff. "Okay, Anik. Dinner's done, so let's have it. What have the two of you cooked up that involves me?"

And there it was again. Anik chuckled to himself. That direct, no-nonsense, get-to-the-point girl he knew and loved like a sister. "Right. Here it is. I couldn't focus on writing and got hungry." Plus, he had a nagging hunch about *good old Mr. Gibson.* "So, I thought I'd join you two here at The Brown Bear for a meal." Tilting his head forward, Anik peered at Rachel and then at Liam. "Hope you didn't mind the intrusion."

"Your timing was appreciated, considering our intruder." Liam glanced at Rachel.

She continued to stare at Anik.

"Anik."

That one word, spoken in her forceful tone, told him he'd better get to the crux of the matter, or she'd up and leave—even if she had to call someone to pick her up. "Yeah. Well. On the way over here, although it's not the first time I've thought about this," he saw the puzzled look on Liam's face, "I started thinking about the race I have coming up. Also, about the fact I won't have anyone to help me with the team during practice." He peeked at Liam, who gave an eye roll. *No, Liam. I haven't given up on this idea.*

Liam smiled and pursed his lips. "Anik, it's unnecessary—"

"Just hang on for a minute, pal, while I explain my proposal to Rachel. We've already talked about this. You don't have time to give me a hand with my preparation, and I understand."

Anik pasted on his signature poor-puppy expression for Rachel. It had always worked when they were younger. "So... I really want help with the dogs, if nothing else. I figured working with my team could even benefit you with your article. You know. Show what other dogsledders are like compared to the Denali Canine Rangers?" He shot Liam a look. *Come on, Liam. Give me an assist here.*

Liam's brows lowered for a second. He nodded. "That's not a bad idea, buddy." He smiled at Rachel. "Your readers should find interest in the differences between a dogsled team gearing up for a race and how our park sled dogs get ready and perform their duties."

Rachel's gaze darted from Anik to Liam and back again. Anik envisioned gears spinning in her brain.

In a near whisper, she said. "That would mean I'd have to stay in Healy longer than planned."

A glint brightened her eyes as she turned to Anik.

Thoughts about not going back right away to Fairbanks—to her possessive boss—seemed to agree with her. Anik gave himself a mental high-five. But would she guess his hidden-to-her matchmaking agenda?

Rachel's eyes narrowed. The thought of not going back to the office and having to deal with Mr. Gibson and his latest attempt to date her, let alone his attitude when he grabbed her arm, appealed to her. But knowing Anik the way she did, she'd bet he had something else up his sleeve with this request for assistance.

However, now that she'd gotten back in touch with her love for the wonderful sled dogs, working with Anik's team would be fun.

"Can you give me a few hours before I make a decision?" Rachel finished her coffee. "I'll have to have time tonight to consider how to present this idea to my boss… if I decide to assist you. I guess he'll be okay with it, considering the additional interest in the story. But I need to word it the right way to convince him it will result in a better article and not simply add fluff to the piece."

Anik's smile reached from ear to ear. "Of course. No problem." He grinned at Liam and then back at her. "Say, do your folks still do that Friday night get-together with the bonfire in the backyard? I haven't been to one of those sing-alongs in ages."

"Yes, they do. Tomorrow night at seven." She turned to Liam. "It's a big event, held the last Friday of the month in Healy. This will be the last one until spring in my parents' huge yard. Everyone brings a dish to share, and we have a late-night dinner, toast marshmallows, and afterward, the sing-along. At evening's end, Dad usually gives a devotional. It's become a tradition, so there's no reason things should have changed. Are you interested in coming? Obviously, Anik plans to. But dress warmly. Temps are supposed to drop tonight. Dad'll put out the patio heaters."

"Sure, thanks. Sounds like fun. I've heard rumors of something like this happening, but I'd never been invited. And while we're on the subject of tomorrow, shall we continue the tour of the kennels at Denali earlier in the day? Or have you collected all the information you need for your article?"

"I have more questions about the work, the dogs, and the rangers in general, both two and four-legged." She smiled. "So, a continuation of our visit at the park would be helpful, especially if I can talk to more of your fellow rangers. Some of the females in particular."

Anik cleared his throat. "Hey, you two. Remember me?" He waved his hands in front of their faces. "Liam, could I tag along on this outing? It's been a long time since I visited the Denali Canine Rangers. They're one of the reasons I got into mushing in the first place."

"Sure, you can. You can supply some differences for Rachel between our furry rangers and regular dogsled teams." Liam faced Rachel. "If it's okay with you."

"Sounds like a plan. And I promise, Anik, I'll have a decision for you by the end of the evening." She almost had her mind made up now, but there was her boss to convince.

Her eyes wandered to Liam, who was telling Anik about some of his canine buddies at the park. It would be a joy to spend another day in the company of a special guy like Liam.

Remember, your life is in Fairbanks, not Healy. Her focus needed to remain on writing the best article she could for the paper. Then, and only then, she'd think about romance. *Maybe.*

Liam reached for the check, but Anik beat him to it.

"Hey, you crazy Inuk. Give that to me. You didn't ask Rachel to dinner. I did."

Anik laughed. "But if it hadn't been for my quick subterfuge about my aunt's dinner invitation, where would you have been?"

"All the more reason I should pay for tonight's meal." Liam tried to snatch the bill from Anik, but his friend twisted away.

"You can get the next one. This is my treat. Now take your lady home."

Liam glanced at Rachel from the corner of his eye. *If only.* Her brows had risen, but she didn't say a word. What would it be like to spend every evening with this wonderful, intelligent, beautiful woman?

"Okay, Anik. You win. Meet you back at the cabin." Then he'd fill in the stubborn Inuk on Rachel's change of attitude about her brother's accident. *And give him an earful for that crack about whose lady she was.*

After Anik placed his credit card in the black folder with the bill and a cash tip, Liam and Rachel left the table. At the door, Liam gave his friend a two-finger salute. He escorted Rachel into the parking lot. He was beginning to like the idea of being matched with her. Only one problem. When she completed her assignment, she'd be gone from Healy. Possibly with his heart. *Ever think of that, you meddling matchmaker?*

And she'd shown no sign of romantic interest in him thus far.

Chapter Thirteen

Liam led Anik and Rachel through the kennels, stopping at each canine. Anik spoke to every one of them as if they were kindred spirits. Liam shook his head. He should have foreseen this. His friend was a modern-day dog whisperer with ingrained heritage from his ancestors—especially his grandmother, who had instilled in him a strong connection to the animal world. He always referred to his own team as his brothers. At this rate, they'd be here forever.

As Anik held a conversation with Flame—words interchanged with various tones of yips—Liam leaned over and whispered to Rachel. "I think we'd better leave Anik and move on to the human doghouse so you can get some interviews, or we'll be here until midnight." He laughed.

After a giggle, she joined him. "He certainly has a way with dogs."

"He does. It's inherited from his grandmother. He calls her his *aanaa* in the Inuktitut or Inuit language. She believed in a connection between the Inuit people and God's creatures. From what I've seen of Anik with his Husky crew, I can't deny it." He took her elbow to keep her from slipping on the icy patches and led her back toward the breakroom. He was sure she already knew all that, having known Anik for so long. Yet she listened intently and hadn't interrupted him once. Quite a lady.

"Anik's familiar with our layout here at the station, and everyone knows him. He'll find the Doghouse on his own."

His friend glanced up as Liam and Rachel strode off. "I'll catch up with you two in a while."

Liam waved without turning around. He yelled out, "When you get cold enough, come to the break building for some coffee." Liam chuckled. "Yeah. He won't feel the chill until he's had a talk with each and every one of our Canine Rangers."

Rachel stole a glance at Anik. "You know, that's another aspect to include in my article. I'll have to ask Anik if he'd mind discussing his Inuit beliefs and traditions."

"He won't. He does his best to teach people how to view animals as more than simple wildlife."

"But Anik is a saved man—a Christian." Her brows rumpled. "My father led him to the Lord when he was young."

Liam smiled. "True. He makes no secret of his faith. But his ancestry runs deep. Still, the Bible talks about animals in a way that explains in no uncertain terms how God expects us to take care of them. Proverbs twelve, ten says, 'A righteous man regardeth the life of his beast...' Obviously, we're to treat them well."

They entered the Doghouse and spotted two rangers taking their lunch break.

"Come on, Rachel. I'll introduce you to Verity and Ericka."

She followed him to the picnic bench toward the rear of the room, where the taller of the two, Verity, in a black pixie cut, lowered herself to a place at the table. Next to her, petite Ericka, with sandy hair pulled back in a low ponytail at her neck, was situated with food in front of her.

As Liam and Rachel neared, Ericka looked up with bright, sparkling blue eyes.

"Verity… Ericka… this is Rachel O'Rourke. She's working on an article for her newspaper featuring our canine rangers, but she'd like to get information about the two-legged variety as well." He grinned. "Would you mind?"

Verity reached out and shook Rachel's hand. "Not at all. Although I doubt we can tell you more than Liam, Allen, or Christian have told you. They mentioned your interview with them. But go ahead." Her hazel eyes held a welcome. "Right, Ericka?"

Ericka swallowed. "Shoot. We'll be glad to help. Always ready to answer questions about the work here or our furry buddies. One of our favorite parts of this job."

While the rangers finished their sandwiches and chips, Rachel posed additional queries she hadn't asked Allen or Christian. An hour later, she tucked her mini-recorder and iPad into her tote bag and pulled out a Sony camera. "Mind if I take a few shots of you?"

The girls stuck their heads together, and their lips turned up at the corners. "Anything for the press."

As the rangers rose to clear their trash, Ericka asked Liam, "Did you hear about the suspected poachers in the Dry Creek region? Remains of a bull moose were found."

Liam's brows lowered. "Those guys will be in a world of financial hurt when they're caught, not to mention they'll lose their privilege to hunt."

"Serves them right." She huffed.

"Does that happen often?" Rachel inquired. "Poachers, I mean."

"Not anymore. It used to be a serious problem years ago. But there are some fools who still insist on taking a chance. Some people never learn."

Rachel nodded. "So we read in the papers and hear on the news all the time—that people never learn." She faced Liam. "What's next on the tour?"

Liam called out to his coworkers, "See you around, girls."

He and Rachel headed for the entrance.

"Let's find Anik and see if he's ready to continue. Then I'll take you into the park so you can get some pictures for your article."

Her smile warmed Liam's insides.

"As long as we don't run across poachers." She bumped her shoulder into his.

Arriving back at her parents' cabin, Rachel's heart was light. What a spectacular morning. She slid out of the passenger side of Liam's vehicle before he released his seatbelt. She turned and leaned into the cab. "The ride through the park was wonderful. I took so many interesting shots." When he opened the driver's door, she leaned farther in and grabbed his arm. "You don't have to see me to the door. The potluck dinner starts at seven, followed by the sing-along. You'll probably want to rest up this afternoon. See you later."

He pulled the door shut with a thump. "I'll be here." He winked at her. "And you know Anik. He wouldn't miss a meal he didn't have to cook."

Liam's soft chuckle lingered in her ears as she closed the passenger door and headed for the cabin.

She'd regret ending her time here in Healy and the Denali National Park. She and Liam had formed such a sweet relationship already. He was everything in a man she wished to fall in love with. Rachel sighed. *But I'll be leaving in a few more days.* And that was only if her boss allowed her to stay for the extra information Anik could provide about mushing while she helped him practice for the Iditarod.

Mr. Gibson's bright red Chevy Tahoe was sitting in the backyard.

Rachel slipped into the house and tossed her tote with purse, iPad, and notes on the desk in the corner of the kitchen. A tray of brownies with M&M's peeking out of them sat on the table. *Wow!* Mom really went all out with her baking today. She picked up a decadent square, laid it on a paper towel next to the sink, broke off a piece, and popped it into her mouth. *Mmmm.* They tasted like the ones at the local bakery.

When Rachel strolled into the living room, she found her family in conversation with her employer. She swallowed the evidence of her appropriated treat.

"Here she is. Right on time." Mr. Gibson showered her with a brilliant beam.

As Kalen rolled his wheelchair out of the room toward the kitchen, her parents rose.

"Hon," her mother patted her on the shoulder, "We're about to make some sandwiches for lunch. When the two of you finish talking, come into the kitchen and eat."

Mom followed her dad and brother.

Taking a seat in the armchair across the coffee table from her boss, Rachel asked, "So you're returning to Fairbanks?"

"Yes. I hoped you'd have enough for your feature by now and would join me. We could stop on the way for dinner and discuss what you've written. I have a new assignment waiting for you when we get back."

"Mr. Gibson, I'm not finished collecting everything I want for this story yet. A local musher has offered to explain the differences between the Denali Canine Rangers and their work in the national park and the lives of regular sled dogs. I'll help him for a few days while he prepares for an upcoming race. It's an opportunity I don't want to pass up. The information will add interest to the article. Our readers will love it."

Her supervisor pinned her with a narrow-eyed stare.

"This *musher* wouldn't be that *Eskimo* you were with last night, would it?"

She rose from her seat. "May I remind you the word Eskimo is one we do not use here? Anik is of the Inuit people, indigenous to Alaska, and a famous dogsled racer, having won competitions all over the world. He's the perfect person to show me what I need for—"

Mr. Gibson held up his hands in front of him. "Okay. Okay. I apologize for using the slur yet again, but is this information really necessary for the article? I was hoping to get the story into the coming edition. I have a couple of other ideas for future issues. You're my top reporter."

Rachel retook her seat. "Then let me do my best. It's not ready for this publication of the Star, but you won't be disappointed if I stay and give it the attention it deserves."

A huffed sigh pushed through his lips. "All right, Rachel. You win. But I want you back in Fairbanks by the end of next weekend at the latest. That'll allow enough time to get the feature into the first Sunday edition in November."

"You'll have it." If only she worked for another paper instead. Suddenly, Fairbanks held no pull on her to return. She should check for openings in Anchorage while she was here.

Rachel led Mr. Gibson into the kitchen. Her mother had moved the tray of brownies to the counter, and a platter of cold cuts and cheeses with bread, buns, rolls, condiments, and napkins took its place.

"Ah, just in time. Help yourself." Her mom added a large pitcher of lemonade.

"This is wonderful, Mrs. O'Rourke. Thank you for inviting me." Rachel's boss sat in the open chair beside Kalen.

Rachel rounded the table and chose a seat by her father and across from her brother. "Where's Deirdre?"

As he squirted mustard onto a bun, her father answered, "She ran out to meet with someone about an hour ago. Didn't say who." He frowned.

Her mother gestured to the counter. "Wasn't it thoughtful of Mr. Gibson to bring all these brownies for our potluck and sing-along tonight?"

Rachel's head popped up from building her sandwich. *Oh, no. Please tell me he's not staying.* He said he was leaving.

A couple of hours later, Mr. Gibson said his farewells to the O'Rourke family with a reminder to Rachel that he expected her to return to Fairbanks by a week from Monday, if not before.

As they waved and watched the man head out to the road, a renewal of her thoughts from earlier grabbed hold of her. She'd check out Anchorage and see if there were openings at one of the newspapers published in that vicinity. She'd even settle for a smaller publication in a nearby town where she could drive from Healy, if there were any. Her dread of returning to Fairbanks was growing. Or was it something else that made her not want to leave? Liam's face flashed into her mind.

"Well, Mr. Gibson, though unconventional, is a nice man, hon. I'm glad we got to meet him." Her mother wrapped her arms around Rachel's waist and steered her into the cabin.

Should she confide in Mom about the irritating way he insisted on asking her out? No. Mom would tell Dad, and then they'd both worry about her when she went back to her job. Better leave that can of worms alone.

Inside, they hung up their parkas. Rachel joined her mother in the kitchen, where they worked on food for that night's potluck. How she missed this—side by side with her mom, talking about the week's activities in Healy and the surrounding towns. A homesick sensation hit Rachel.

"Honey. I really miss having you here. I know, I know. You're all grown up and have a life of your own now. But your absence leaves an emptiness in the house... and my heart."

"My exact thoughts, Mom." Rachel gave her mother a quick hug. "At least we have extra week together."

Then she'd have to go back to Fairbanks… and *Mr. Gibson*. He'd become a problem—him—as her boss. She loved being a reporter. But what else would she do if she couldn't find another job writing and had to return to the paper?

Chapter Fourteen

At ten minutes to seven, Liam and Anik arrived at the potluck sing-along in Liam's pickup. Liam checked his hair in the rearview mirror. Seeing Rachel and spending the evening in her company had his insides turned upside down. He'd never felt like this about any woman before, and no matter how hard he tried to tell himself he had to stop because she'd be leaving, it wasn't making a bit of difference.

"Every hair is in place, as always, pal," Anik teased. "Now let's go. I'll grab the back ribs. You get the dessert."

Liam gave Anik a sideways glower. He hopped out of the driver's seat, opened the door to the crew cab, and lifted the box with the cake they'd ordered from The Brown Bear. "Good thing the restaurant has takeout. Hope everyone is hungry for ribs and chocolate."

"Hey... if they're not, I am." A hearty guffaw escaped Anik as he strode toward the O'Rourkes' front door.

As Anik rang the doorbell, Liam caught up to him. Deirdre answered the door with a flirtatious flutter of her lashes directed at Liam. *Oh boy. Here we go again.* He sure didn't want to hurt Rachel's sister, but he had to nip this in the bud. "Hi, Deirdre. Where's Rachel?"

She frowned at him.

After Liam and Anik entered the cabin, Liam led Anik to the kitchen to deliver the food they'd brought.

Rachel spun away from the counter as they came into the room, her fingers covered in raw ground meat. "Welcome, guys. What do you have there?"

Liam's brows felt as though they had touched his hairline. "Do I want to know what that is on your hands? Should I search for the body, or call the state troopers?" He narrowed his eyes suspiciously as his lips quivered with suppressed laughter.

"Funny. Real funny. I'm helping Mom make the hamburgers Dad will grill over the open fire. So, what kind of goodies did you two bring?"

Anik slid the huge tray onto the kitchen table. "Picked up some barbecue baby back ribs from The Brown Bear for tonight's feast. Liam is holding one of their scrumptious dark chocolate cakes. And we haven't even sampled any of it."

Liam put the box down next to the meat. "It was difficult having this grub in the house before we left and not taste test it, but we disciplined ourselves." Besides, his thoughts had not been on food at all today. He grinned at Rachel. If only she didn't live in Fairbanks. It was only a one to two-hour drive away, and they could always stay in touch by phone and online, but he wanted more. There had to be some way to keep her here.

"*Mmmm,*" Rachel moaned as she peeked into the cake box. She glanced at Liam. "How did you know my weakness is chocolate?"

"Isn't it everyone's?" Anik chuckled.

"Not so, buddy. My sister, Ainsley, believe it or not, hates chocolate. She's a strawberry girl."

"Remind me to have a talk with that sibling of yours." Anik snickered, then faced Rachel's mother, who was trying to contain her laughter while she kept cutting raw vegetables. "Mrs. O'Rourke, is there anything I can do to help?"

"Actually, my husband would love some assistance with the bonfire. He's out in the back."

"On it!" Anik disappeared out the door.

Rachel turned and resumed mixing the seasonings into the hamburger and making patties.

"Guess I'll go out and see how I can lend a hand." Liam left the kitchen.

Christmas lights had been strung all around the yard. He caught sight of Anik jogging toward a prepared log-cabin-shaped structure. *Sensational.* That was going to be one big blaze. *It'll last all evening.*

Stumps of various sizes sat around the fire pit that the minister was about to set aflame. Liam glanced over his shoulder. He had forgotten to ask Rachel if her boss agreed to allow her to stay longer and work with Anik to add interest to her article. She sure was a dedicated writer. When she returned to Fairbanks, would Mr. Gibson become more of a problem for her? The idea smoldered in Liam's chest.

After everyone had their fill, Rachel helped her mother put away the cold food and set out munchies on the kitchen island for snacks. Then, she stepped out onto the back porch and gazed at the bonfire. Orange and yellow-white fingers reached skyward. As the branches collapsed into the center, sparks flew like fireworks. A sweet, slightly smoky aroma mixed with one reminding her of Christmas filled the crisp air.

The rest of the party had donned their parkas, hats, scarves, and mittens and meandered into the backyard, where the sing-along would be held. Rachel leaned on the railing. How she missed these Friday get-togethers. Sure, she had friends in Fairbanks, but they never did this.

She spotted Liam and Anik pushing the burning wood into the fire. Soon it would be a mound of embers.

Liam turned and obviously saw her on the porch. When he waved her over, she skipped down the stairs. Even though she couldn't see his facial features, her mind's eye brought his image clearly into her memory. He was a handsome man... but more than that. He was thoughtful, kind, and considerate. Her heart fluttered. *Don't go there. He lives here, and you live in Fairbanks.*

"We saved you a seat between Anik and me. That way, if the temp drops, you'll be sandwiched and keep warm."

She gave Liam a wide-eyed stare.

"Don't blame me. It was Anik's idea."

"Speaking of Anik." She searched among the group but didn't see him. "Where'd he go?"

"Who me?"

Rachel jumped at the deep voice behind her. "Don't do that. You'll never change." She read the questioning expression on Liam's face. "Anik always used to sneak up on me when we were kids. At least *I* was a kid."

His energetic laugh bounced through the air. "Sorry, Rachel. I couldn't resist."

Settling onto a stump on the other side of Liam, Deirdre joined their group. Kalen rolled his wheelchair into an open spot next to his younger sister.

Anik took the empty seat by Rachel. "So, have you decided whether you'll assist me with my practice?" His eyes pleaded with her.

"Yes, I told Mr. Gibson you'd give me additional information for my article. He reluctantly agreed to let me stay." She smiled. "I'm excited about working with you."

"Hey." Deirdre bent forward and peeped around Liam at Anik. "I'd love to help with your dogsled team."

"Thank you, Deirdre, but I only need one person to give me a hand. Besides, didn't you say you were hired by the national park and start on Monday? Rachel's going to be busy all day, every day. Maybe next time."

Before Deirdre could respond, Rachel's father called for everyone's attention. "Let's get this sing-along underway." He began singing *The Old Rugged Cross*. People joined in, several breaking off into parts.

Yes, she really missed this.

"Rachel," Liam whispered in her ear. "What's wrong with your sister? She looks angrier than a bear with a sore tooth. I thought at first you and Anik might be a couple, but he straightened me out. Is she jealous of your time with him? If so, why does she flirt with me?"

"No. No jealousy. We think of Anik as a brother." She leaned toward Liam. "I'm not sure what's wrong. She's been this way since I got home. I need to talk to her."

By the time Liam and Anik helped Mr. O'Rourke put out the fire, the other guests had left. Liam followed Anik into the cabin to say good night to everyone. Liam found Rachel alone in the kitchen. "Rachel, would you have dinner with me after church on Sunday? I have to return to my job on Monday, and you'll be helping Anik all week. We won't see much of each other before you leave for Fairbanks, but I want to get to know you better."

Deirdre glided through the doorway and fixed herself a cup of cocoa, taking what seemed like longer than necessary to complete the task. Rachel's brows rose.

Uncomfortable silence prevailed until Deirdre spun around and faced them. "Oh, don't let me interrupt whatever you had going on." She stormed from the room.

Liam's eyes widened. "What was that all about?"

"I have no idea." Rachel gaped in the direction her sister had gone. "I plan to find out tonight though. Something is eating her. She never used to be like that. I didn't come home much while away at college, and I haven't for almost two years while working at the paper."

Rachel shook her head, then turned to Liam. "To answer your question, I'd love to have dinner with you Sunday afternoon."

Anik's comment from the day he came back from Finland popped into his mind. *"I think you need more in your life by now than just working in the park with the dog teams."* He was so right.

Liam's heart warmed. Not sure how this was going to turn out, but he'd do his best to become a part of this fascinating woman's life. He'd start by attending her church.

From the front picture window, Rachel watched Liam's truck disappear into the night. An empty sensation filled her heart. How was it she had such strong feelings for the man after so short a time? She could no longer deny them. He obviously was interested in her. It was going to hurt when she had to say goodbye. They'd keep in touch, but it wouldn't be the same. Would the feelings she had now diminish after a while? Would his?

Rachel recalled the two female rangers she'd interviewed at the park. They were both single and pretty. And it was obvious they considered Liam a wonderful guy. Yet, he didn't seem to be attracted to either of them.

Was he as dedicated to his job as Anik had indicated? The crazy Inuk, who admitted he'd set them up. He also said this was the first time he'd ever seen Liam *lovestruck*. She chuckled to herself. She'd simply laughed it off then, but now?

Her sister broke into her thoughts. Deirdre had never acted as rudely as she had lately. Time to confront her about it. Why was Deirdre mad at her all the time? Rachel couldn't put her finger on anything she'd done to hurt or make her sister so angry. "No time like the present, late as it is." Deirdre always stayed up way past midnight on the weekends.

Rachel climbed the stairs to the second floor, where her sister's room was at the end of the hall. She knocked softly on the door. No answer. Surely Dee hadn't turned in for the night already. Rachel rapped again. Still no response. She opened the door a crack. The light was off. A shaft of moonlight shone through a break in the drapes on the window and illuminated a form in the bed. All was silent.

Chapter Fifteen

Liam found it hard to concentrate on the sermon, his focus broken by thoughts of his upcoming dinner with Rachel. He'd listen to her father's message online later.

After church, he drove her to The Brown Bear. He wasn't sure, and maybe he was fooling himself, but he'd sensed a strong chemistry between them. Long-distance relationships had worked with couples from much farther away than Fairbanks and Healy. Why not for them? They'd not known each other long, but what difference did that make?

Liam pulled into the parking lot. "Hope you're okay with coming here again."

"More than okay. Delightful décor. Extraordinary food. A smiling grizzly to greet you. What's not to like?" Happiness showed on her face as they approached the entrance, and she patted the grizzly statue's stomach. Shivers raced up his spine. He *had* to convince her this relationship was doable. If he guessed right, she was as much attracted to him as he to her.

They entered the restaurant, and the hostess seated them next to a window, beyond which an expanse of birch trees stretched as far as the eye could see.

"Beautiful." Her words had barely reached his ears.

He followed her line of sight. "Birch has always been my favorite species. They grow in Minnesota too."

She shifted her gaze to him. "Do you still miss Minnesota?"

He shrugged. "It was my life for sixteen years. Along with my parents' dairy farm, until one of our competitors convinced Dad to sell. That's when he decided we'd head to Alaska. I already mentioned my father's investments, which he'd made over the years, and his side business, which he continued here. He was able to retire early. It worked out well."

A waitress appeared at their table with menus and water. "I'll give you a few minutes." She shot off to serve another customer.

While they perused the offerings, Rachel said, "I remember you telling me about your father's success. Wasn't moving hard on you?" The concern in her eyes melted his heart.

"It was a challenge for my sister and me, but nothing we couldn't overcome." He laid the menu down. "Lucas, three years my senior, went off to college right away. He's an investment broker now, married with two kids, and lives in Destin, near our parents. Ainsley has always been flexible. She shifted easily from high school in Minnesota to Alaska. As I said the other day, she'll graduate this spring from UAF. Then, she'll go on to earn her masters in biological science."

"Wow! Quite the undertaking. And you chose not to go to college?"

"I take online courses in biological science too. My job at Denali goes hand in hand with my studies. It'll take me a little longer to graduate than Lee, but I'm doing work I enjoy, and my degree will come in handy in the national park system."

"That's wonderful. I believe few people truly love their jobs."

The server returned. "Do you need more time?"

Rachel handed her the menu. "I've chosen grilled salmon, wild rice and mushrooms, fire-roasted vegetables, and a Caesar salad."

"And to drink?"

"I'll have an Italian raspberry cream soda."

"And for you, sir?"

"Braised boneless beef short ribs, mashed potatoes, the fire-roasted vegetables, and king crab and corn bisque. And a glass of milk."

"Yes, sir." She left the table.

"Now that you've heard about me, how about you, Rachel? You said you graduated with a degree in journalism and landed the job you wanted."

She slanted her lips in a lopsided grin. "Yes, I love being a reporter. Finding interesting stories."

"You love the *job*." He tilted his head. "But not *where* you work?"

"Oh, don't get me wrong. People at the *Star* are wonderful. They've all been supportive of me ever since I started. But..."

"But... your boss."

She peered at him with wrinkled brows.

"Rachel, you said he hasn't harassed you."

"No. I mean, I couldn't call it harassment. Although he annoys me with invitations to lunch and dinner, he never gives an ultimatum. I'm not even sure why I find it annoying. He did it again before he left for Fairbanks. I don't intend to go out with the man, but he's persistent, if nothing else."

Her frown deepened. "It's like having a neighbor who always asks you over to his house, but you don't want to get into a relationship with that person, no matter how nice he is." She huffed. "And yet he doesn't take the hint."

The waitress slid Rachel's salad and Liam's soup in front of them. She gave a brief nod and left.

Rachel leaned forward and breathed in with her eyes closed. "That smells divine. I wish I had ordered it."

"Trade?" He didn't want greens, but if it would make her happy, so be it.

"No. But thank you. I'll remember to order it the next time I come here."

"Then you do plan to return to Healy?" *Say yes.*

"Eventually. To visit my family."

A sinking sensation hit Liam's stomach. Not quite the words he'd hoped for.

After Liam gave the blessing for the food, silence ruled for a few minutes while they ate their salad and soup. As soon as they finished, the server delivered their meals.

"Liam, thanks for bringing me back to this wonderful restaurant. I really will push to do some reviews on restaurants in the paper. It should be a winner with our readers. I've jotted down several notes on The Brown Bear."

"You're welcome. I'm glad you're pleased with it." He cut into his short ribs and took a bite. After he swallowed, he glanced up to find her eyes closed again. "Is everything okay?"

A flash of delight stretched across her face. "I'd forgotten how delicious fresh-caught salmon can be. Everything's perfect."

She was perfect. A *perfect Irish angel.* His pulse quickened. "Rachel, I know we haven't known each other for more than a week, but it seems longer."

Her eyes popped open. "You feel that too? Of course, I met you a couple of years ago at the hospital when my brother had surgery, but I guess that doesn't count."

He puckered his lips. "Right." *Especially when you were so mad at me.*

"The feeling that we've known each other longer is probably because we've spent so much time together."

He stopped cutting his meat and searched her face. Light from the chandelier hanging overhead made her soft, warm brown eyes sparkle. "We've a special connection. At least I'm hoping that's the case." He reached his hand across the table and touched her fingers resting next to the plate.

A rosy glow filled her cheeks.

As Liam's hand covered hers, warmth traveled through her. Liam was a great guy. And so good-looking. Would it be possible to maintain a relationship where we wouldn't see each other for months on end?

"Rachel, I want to keep in touch with you when you return to Fairbanks. Not an occasional email, but often. We're both very busy, but I think we can work something out... if you're willing. What do you say?"

He slipped his fingers under hers. His hand was strong, secure. Her heart skipped a beat. She'd never felt this way before. How could she not try?

"I'd like that, Liam."

The smile that lit his face spread to his eyes. He was sincere.

"I suppose we'd better finish our meal, or it'll get cold." He withdrew his hand. "Then let's celebrate with one of The Brown Bear's decadent desserts."

"Mmmm. Bring it on." Rachel's attention returned to her food.

Several minutes later, the waitress picked up their empty dinner plates and came back with a card listing the choice of dessert items. As they concentrated on the luscious treats, a comfortable quiet between them reigned aside from the murmurs from other diners, an occasional laugh, and the soft clinks of china and crystal.

Liam lowered the menu. "I'm getting the one called a chocolate caramel entremets." He picked up the menu again and read, "With layers of chocolate cake, chocolate mousse, caramel ganache, and raspberry puree." He peeked at her over the card. "Have you decided yet?"

She watched as he licked the corner of his mouth. She bit her bottom lip. "It's a tough decision, but I guess I'll have the same. Chocoholic, remember? My waistline will hate me for it, but..."

With his head tilted, he gave her a sideways glance. "You don't have to worry about weight, from what I've observed." His face turned a ruddy hue while heat rose to hers.

After the server took their dessert orders, she suggested coffee. "Yes. Please." Liam handed both menus to the girl, and she left.

"Liam, you were blushing."

"What? I was not."

"Yes! You were. Your neck rivaled the stop sign at the end of my parents' street." She studied his reaction from under her lashes.

"Okay. You've got me. But I thought I saw a rosy glow on your cheeks."

"Well, the color was charming on you." She smirked. "You are so different from most of the men I know. That must be why I'm comfortable with you. Relaxed."

The desserts arrived at the table, and Rachel's eyes widened. "It's huge."

"Enough to take some home for tomorrow." He laughed. "Or not."

When they finished eating dessert and took their last sip of the rich brew, the server brought to-go boxes for the remains of their entremets. She cleared the dirty plates and utensils. "Will there be anything else?"

"No." He turned to Rachel. "I, for one, don't have a spare space left for anything. How about you?"

"I don't think I'll eat or drink for two days."

The waitress giggled. "We hear that a lot here. Can't have our customers going away hungry." She strolled away.

"Sweet girl." Liam watched her for a moment before turning to Rachel.

Was he interested in her? *While sitting here with me?* She shouldn't have even thought that. He just had a natural response to the girl. She *was* sweet. Was that a spark of jealousy? Rachel lowered her brow.

How would she handle Liam here and her in Fairbanks… away from him for several months at a time? This long-distance thing might not be such a good idea.

Liam ushered Rachel into the pew beside her mother for the evening service, and then he seated himself next to her. He could feel the heat coming from Rachel's sister as she slipped in and sat on his right—a little too close for comfort. He moved over farther, brushing Rachel's arm.

She leaned forward, peered around him, and straightened in the pew. When she scooted closer to her mother, a chain reaction of people in their pew shifted toward the far end of the row. Rachel and Liam chuckled softly, but Deirdre's face stiffened.

Why did Deirdre act that way? He'd done nothing to encourage the girl, outside of having observed her at the HR office at the national park the day she came in. It wasn't as if the rest of the guys hadn't noticed her too.

The sermon Pastor O'Rourke preached was on waiting on God when you had a need. It had been a topic Liam's dad mentioned to his children often when they were growing up.

Perhaps that was why he'd not been interested in any other woman until Rachel.

After the service, as Liam followed Rachel's family out of the pew and toward the exit, he touched her shoulder. "Can I interest you in a cup of coffee?" One last chance to be with her before he had to start his shift at Denali.

"Sounds wonderful. No food though." She laid her hand on her midriff. "I'm still stuffed from dinner."

"You and me both. We'll go to the espresso bar in the lodge nearby. They stay open late."

"Did someone say something about stopping for java?" Liam jumped from the voice behind him. He turned to see his friend grinning.

Anik snickered. "Gotcha."

Liam glared.

Anik gave a tiny nod that he'd taken the hint. "Espresso bar... terrific idea... but I have to get back to the cabin and prepare for our first day of working with the team." He showed his snowy choppers as his index finger pointed to himself and then at Rachel. Anik slapped Liam on the upper arm and winked. "Have a cup for me, pal."

Liam let out a sigh of relief. *God bless that buddy of mine.*

Anik turned to Rachel. "See you around nine tomorrow morning." He rushed past everyone and exited the church.

"What was that all about with you two?" Rachel raised her brows. "Since when does Anik pass up coffee?"

Busted. Liam had a hunch she knew what the understanding had been between Anik and him. Liam chuckled. He'd have to keep in mind how smart she was. "A friendly warning not to cut in on my date."

The right side of her lips rose in a half-smile.

After a delicious cup of peppermint mocha at the lodge, Liam drove Rachel to her parents' cabin. She wouldn't see him for at least the first part of the week. Homesickness engulfed her stomach. The entire day spent with him had convinced her this was a relationship worth working on. Whenever she looked at him, her pulse went crazy. Yet, she had an overwhelming sense of peace. He was a kindhearted man, someone she definitely wanted to spend more time getting to know. But it would take a lot of effort.

He walked her to the front door. "Guess this is good night then. Wish I had more days off."

"But we'll talk tomorrow at some point, right?" She searched his eyes. "You have my number."

He moved closer. "Got it, and I'll use it first chance I get."

Her pulse sped into overdrive. Liam leaned down, and his lips found hers.

Rachel's knees buckled as he circled his arms around her waist. She slid her hand under his parka hood into his hair. The kiss deepened.

She pulled back and gulped in a breath of air.

In her peripheral vision, she saw the drapes on the picture window swing in place. If that was Kalen watching, she was in for a lot of ribbing.

Liam tapped her nose with his finger. "I promise I'll call the minute I get a break tomorrow."

The door to the cabin flew open, and Deirdre stormed down the steps. She hopped into their father's car, gunned the engine, and raced off.

Chapter Sixteen

Rachel awoke with a start, the cabin quiet. The clock displayed one-twenty-three in the morning. She'd stayed up that night, hoping to catch Deirdre when she came back from wherever she rushed off to in their father's car. Rachel rubbed the sleep from her eyes. She'd dozed off in her bed, propped by pillows, reading the Bible.

Mom and Dad were upset with Deirdre for taking off as she did without a word, but they were worried too. Rachel frowned. So was she. Deirdre acted so unlike the sister she'd left behind six years ago. *Deirdre has changed so much since I was home last.*

Surely she'd returned from wherever by now. Would she still be up? Rachel listened to the quiet house. Her parents must have retired.

Rachel tiptoed across her room and out the door into the dark hallway. She approached Deirdre's bedroom and leaned her ear against the wood. Not a sound. She inched open the door. Once again, the outline of her sister's sleeping form appeared in the moonlight. *Drat!*

Hadn't she told everyone her first day of work at Denali was today, or did she begin the following Monday? At any rate, her shift wouldn't begin until the afternoon, so she could sleep late. *And I have to meet Anik by the time the sun is up.* She sighed. May as well go back to sleep. Her talk with Deirdre would have to wait.

Rachel shuffled to her room and undressed. As she slipped between the sheets, she replayed the scene with Liam on the porch. His kiss. The embrace. It gave her goosebumps all over again. Joy morphed into concern. She recalled the movement of the drapes in the window and her sister's abrupt departure into the night. Had she been the one peeking out? She'd seen them. It wasn't Kalen. Could Deirdre be jealous... of me? Could it be?

Their sibling relationship had gone from bad to worse. She'd never meant to hurt her sister. *What can I do to fix this?*

Rachel's alarm went off at seven. The sky was still dark, with a faint glimmer of light. She slipped her feet into fuzzy slippers and trudged across the hardwood floors and large braided rug to the wooden chair that held her clothes for the day. A hot shower would bring her to life.

She eyed Deirdre's room as she passed, tempted to enter and wake her sister for the much-needed talk. Did she dare? No, not now. Dee would not be happy if awakened this early... considering. Better wait until tonight.

After Rachel showered, dried her hair, and dressed, she proceeded to the kitchen without a sound. She grabbed one of the leftover cinnamon rolls from Sunday's breakfast, a hard-boiled egg her mom always had available for snacking, and a cupful of granola cereal.

Rachel sat down at the end of the table and poured milk into her bowl of granola, then peeled the egg. Thoughts about how her sister had stormed away last night consumed her. Summers during college were spent taking extra classes. She recalled the short weekends she'd come home, except for holidays, but every time, Deirdre had made herself scarce.

The wall between them had started after she left for college and had grown thicker ever since. Rachel shook her head. Why had she not noticed it?

And now she'd gotten Deirdre angry with this budding relationship with Liam. *I had no idea Deirdre had feelings for him?*

After Rachel finished eating, rinsed out her dishes, and placed them in the dishwasher, she donned her gear and drove to Liam's cabin to meet Anik. As the sun began to break over the horizon, purplish and coral stripes of clouds stretched from north to south. It would be a perfect day.

By the time she reached Liam's property, the sky had cleared and lightened to pale blue. She parked her car next to his pickup. Wonderful. She'd get to see his cheerful face. But then they'd only have phone conversations for the next few days.

As she exited the vehicle, Liam ran down the front porch stairs and straight to her. "Good morning, gorgeous." He cupped her face in his warm hands and lowered his lips to hers. "I'm so glad you got here before my mad dash for work." He enclosed her in his arms, swung her in a circle, then set her back on her feet.

She laughed.

"I dreamed about the most beautiful girl with long, dark chestnut hair last night." He planted another kiss on her mouth. "What a fantastic night's sleep. But now I have to run. I'll call you the first chance I get."

"Good morning to you too, handsome. I'll be waiting. Stay safe out there."

"I will. You and Anik too." He hopped into the driver's seat and took off down the drive toward the highway.

What a fantastic way to start my day. She couldn't contain the happiness in her heart, nor how her cheeks burned while her lips stretched and turned up at the corners.

Anik was next out the door. "I can see from your face that you had a moment with the ranger who hangs out here." He laughed. "That's great. He told me you two agreed to work on a relationship. I couldn't be happier for both of you. He's an exceptional guy, that one." Anik focused on Rachel. "And *you* are a special lady. The two of you suit each other." He tweaked her nose. "Now, let's get our team ready."

Rachel followed Anik to the kennels in the backyard. "Okay, big brother, lead the way." She would always think of Anik as family. "Thanks for the compliment, but it's kind of out of character for you, isn't it? You used to do nothing but tease me... mercilessly."

He laughed again. "Yeah, well, I was being more of a stinky brother to you then. We're friends now."

"We are. Anik, what's the real reason you wanted me to help you? You've never had anyone assist you except for handling the dogs at the beginning and end of the event. So why now? You're not getting old, are you?" She shoulder-bumped him.

He spun and gave her a pointed stare. "Do I look like I'm getting old?"

She bit her lower lip to keep from laughing. "Not really."

He grabbed her gloved hand, and they ran to the rear of the cabin. When they reached the kennel, his huskies gave them a hearty welcome.

"Hey, Tracker." She held out her hand. "Remember me?" He jumped up and almost hugged her with his cold paws. "What a welcome, boy."

"To answer your question, Rachel, when I asked for your assistance, my thoughts were to get you over your animosity toward dogsled races and Denali Park. I thought if we took a few runs there, you'd snap out of it. But your brother and Liam have already accomplished that by talking to you."

"They did. Kalen's reasoning made me see how illogical I've been about his accident. I think my boss did me a favor by handing me this assignment." She turned to Anik. "So why didn't you cancel, if you don't need me?"

"Well, you do have an article to finish, don't you?" He displayed his toothiest grin.

"That I do." A pang hit her heart. And then it was back to Fairbanks and life without being with Liam.

The frown on Rachel's face pained Anik. "What is it, Rachel? Are you all right?"

She smiled, but the fact that it didn't reach her eyes meant something bothered her. Thoughts of her brother's accident? She said otherwise. She'd never held anything from him in the past. Not since a teen, as he recalled. Then again, she was older and had been away from Healy for a long time. *People change.* But everything else about Rachel remained the same. Maybe it wasn't connected with mushing or the canines.

"I'm fine, Anik. You worry too much." She showed a funny face with her nose crinkled. "Okay, worrywart." She pulled out a recorder. "Let's start with some information about the differences between the dogs you and your fellow mushers have and the Denali Canine Rangers. Then you can dive into your vast knowledge of mushing and the way the animals take to racing."

"Sure. You're fortunate that I've been living with Liam. I can't tell you how many times he's gone into a lengthy seminar about his four-legged coworkers. Still, I'd suggest you verify anything I mention about his furry buddies before you take it as concrete information." He smirked. "Besides, it'll give you more to talk about with him, unless... you have other things to keep you busy."

She punched his arm. "I'll do that. So... what do you know?"

They moved around the kennel Anik had set up in the back of Liam's cabin. The dogs demanded their attention with barks, yips, and mumbles. "They've already eaten and are telling me, in their own way, they're ready for some action."

He reached out and scratched each of their ears as he checked on them. "Easy, brothers and sisters. We'll take care of all of you. I know you want to stretch those legs and get some exercise."

He peered up at Rachel. "The Denali canines—while genetic cousins to my pack here—differ from most used in a dogsled race. Dogs that take part in racing the Iditarod and other races are bred for long-distance running. The Huskies at the national park are bred for freight hauling. Did you notice the Canine Rangers were larger and had heavier coats than my guys? Or any other mushing team, for that matter?" One of Anik's females grumbled a half-growl on cue. "Easy, Trixie. No offense meant by that remark." He peeked at Rachel. "She's very sensitive."

"Did she understand you?"

He laughed. "It was a well-timed grumble for attention."

Rachel joined him in laughter.

He led his team out of the kennel. "The Denali Huskies are tougher too. They have to be with the work they're expected to perform. Like I said, they're bred for it."

"What do you mean?"

"Well, one of Liam's friends at the park said, 'It's the difference between a sports car and a Mack truck.' I guess they pick out the male and female *Mack* dogs that fit the bill to pair and produce a litter."

Rachel nodded. "Why do they have to be so big and heavy?"

"In early fall, when there's insignificant snow, the Huskies pull metal carts that resemble the frame of a ride-on lawnmower from one dormant campground to another. When the snow accumulates on the park road, they switch to ATV four-wheelers in neutral. They do five to nine miles per day with that year's puppies running alongside, so the offspring get a feel for the work." He rested his hands on his hips. "Liam invited me to watch them one time. It was a sight, seeing all those pups keeping up with the team."

He glanced at Rachel, whose grin grew wider. That girl had always loved dogs and couldn't get her fill of puppies. "Around late November or early December, when there's enough snow, the Huskies patrol the range from one to five nights away from the station."

Rachel eased herself into the sled basket with her recorder in hand while Anik made a final check on the team.

"Okay, here we go." He let up a little on the brake and called to his lead dog, Tracker, "Easy, boy." The sled moved forward, and Anik let up more on the brake.

As they moved forward, Anik lent more volume to his voice. "Liam said, by March, when Alaska has its peak snowfall and best conditions for dogsledding, they spend up to three weeks straight patrolling the farthest reaches of the protected public lands. The Denali Park Rangers and their canines scout the entire grounds. And that's about an area larger than the state of New Hampshire. Those Huskies have to be bigger and tougher than a regular mushing team to do the work. They aren't bred for racing."

Her brows lowered. "Isn't it kind of hard on the animals?" Worry lines formed on her face as she pursed her lips.

"Are you kidding? That's when the fun begins for those sled dogs. The Denali Canine Rangers live to perform their duties. Liam said if one of their Huskies doesn't act like it enjoys the job, the kennel staff will put it up for adoption. They won't make their beloved fuzzy buddies do something they don't want to do. Those fur-faces are guaranteed an ideal forever home, whether they remain with the park service for years or don't work out."

"I remember Liam telling me about the adoption program. I'm so glad they'll all be taken care of."

Anik laid his hand on her shoulder. "Yeah. You'd be a good adoptive former-ranger parent."

"I wish."

"Or a *partner* for a particular ranger." He wiggled his brows up and down.

She grimaced. "Don't get ahead of us, buster. Liam and I are only friends."

Right. Anik had seen the expression on Liam's face during breakfast that morning and how he'd run out the door when she'd pulled up. He'd also witnessed the happy interaction between the two of them. *Friends. Ha! We'll see.*

Chapter Seventeen

Rachel worked a full day with Anik and his team of sled dogs. Liam had called her twice during his breaks. She enjoyed every minute spent with both men, but missed having her personal one-on-one time with Liam.

"Thank you for all the material you gave me today for my article, Anik."

"You're welcome. Tomorrow we'll visit not only another Denali Kennel Ranger but a couple of other mushers in the area who've received awards in the Iditarod and other races. They might give you information neither Liam nor I have thought of."

"Sounds wonderful." She waved goodbye and headed back to her parents' cabin. On the way there, she mused over her conversation with Liam earlier. He was so easy to talk to. And he cared. When she told him of Anik's teasing throughout the day, the way he used to when she was a kid, Liam's boisterous laugh through the cell thrilled her. He was a man she could spend every day with.

Again, her heart plummeted with the realization that she was expected to leave Healy at the end of the week... or Sunday at the latest. Then it would be phone calls like today, emails, or live chats via the internet. They'd have to make it work.

"Deirdre." Her sister's possible reaction to seeing her and Liam kissing hit Rachel. She had to discuss this with her. Tonight!

After she parked the car, Rachel hurried into the cabin. The aroma of marinara sauce filled the air. Her mouth watered. *Mmmm. Mom's spaghetti.* She hadn't tasted it for at least two years. Mom's was the best she'd ever eaten. She'd wager Mom had made melt-on-your-tongue, homemade Italian meatballs to go with the meal, garlic bread, and a seven-layer salad with her mother's signature strawberry and pecan vinaigrette dressing too.

She tossed her parka, which landed on a hook on the coat rack. Rachel hurried down the hall to the kitchen. "Hi, Mom. What can I do?"

"Glad you're back, Hon. You can stick the garlic baguettes in the oven. Everything else is done." Her mother dropped the spaghetti noodles into a pot of boiling water.

"I'll set the table. When does Deirdre get home? Did she start her new job today?"

"No, not until next Monday. And she has a date tonight."

"With whom?"

"She didn't say. She rushed into the house and hurried out as fast as she came in, telling me she wouldn't be here for dinner. Your sister was invited to eat with a *"handsome"* man, as she put it. I didn't have time to ask a single question. That girl drives me to distraction at times. Dad caught her last sentence and peeked out the window. He said the car's interior light came on when Deirdre entered the car, but he couldn't see the man very well."

The clock on the mantel showed after eleven. Crunching sounds from outside alerted Rachel to a vehicle pulling into the yard. *Finally.* If Deirdre's date had a job, this was a late hour for him to bring her home. Maybe his schedule was odd like Liam's.

Liam. She'd not heard from him this evening. But he'd said there'd be times when he was in a dead zone at the park and unable to make a call.

Her sister's infatuation with him came to mind. *Don't let jealousy over nothing get a grip on you.* He'd made it clear he had no interest in Deirdre.

What was taking her so long to come inside the house? Rachel snuck a peek through the front window and wished she hadn't. *Really, Dee?* It wouldn't surprise her to see steam rise from the top of the car. She'd been mooning over Liam, and now in a lip-lock with who-knows-who? What was wrong with the girl? Their tête-à-tête was way overdue.

Several minutes later, Deirdre entered the cabin. "Why are you still up?"

"I'm waiting to chat with you about something."

After Deirdre hung up her parka, she slipped off her boots and shook the light snow from her knit hat. She stuck it on a peg. "We've *nothing* to talk about." Deirdre headed up the staircase to the bedrooms.

"Yes, we do." Rachel followed in her sister's footsteps. "First, I want to know why you're always so mad at me. What've I done? Is it because of Liam?"

Halfway up the stairs, Deirdre spun and pinned Rachel with an angry stare. "This has nothing to do with *your* ranger. You think that because he chose you, it means anything to me? I don't need any guy who's charmed by a woman as selfish as you."

Rachel's mouth dropped open, while Deirdre sprinted up the rest of the stairs. *What?* Rachel continued to the second floor on her sister's heels. "You're saying I'm '*selfish*?' What are you talking about? Why'd you call me that, Dee?"

Before her sister could turn the doorknob, Rachel grabbed it and pulled. "Talk to me. If I hurt you by letting Liam kiss me Sunday night..."

Her sister whirled to face her. "I'm not jealous of you and that pretty boy. Yeah, I flirted with him and would've been happy if he'd paid attention to me, but he's not the only man in the world. And, by the way, I've found my own musher to assist. So leave me alone."

She tried to open her bedroom door again. Rachel kept a firm grip on the knob. "We *will* hash this out tonight, little sister. I've been home for a week, and you've done nothing but show me your ire. If this isn't about Liam, what is it? You were angry the day I arrived. What's eating you?"

Deirdre's eyes filled with tears. "Leave me be. I'm tired."

"Not until you tell me what's wrong."

Her sister's eyes narrowed. "You've no clue, do you?"

"No." Rachel's voice softened. "But I need to... so I can make it right. Please, Deirdre. You're the only sister I have. This animosity toward me makes my heart sick. I don't understand what I've done to earn it."

Dee's face lost its hardness. Her head dropped forward.

Rachel let go of the doorknob and placed her hand on her sister's shoulder. "Let's go to the kitchen. We can make hot chocolate and sneak into the cookie jar like we used to when we were kids. Then you can tell me what I did to upset you."

Rachel sensed how reluctant her sister was to go with her. But Deirdre finally relented. As they walked down the stairs side by side,

Rachel half expected Dee to turn around and dash back up to her bedroom.

They entered the darkened kitchen. Rachel flipped on the light switch and found the room spotless. She looked around and smiled. If only she could be as good a housekeeper as her mom someday, she'd be happy. "Would you get the cocoa out of the pantry, sis? Bring the milk too."

Without a word, Deirdre retrieved the items and placed them on the counter next to the stove while Rachel measured water into a saucepan. "This shouldn't take long. See what kind of cookies Mom has stashed in the cookie jar."

"She keeps the ones for guests tucked away in a storage container in the pantry now." A soft giggle escaped her sister. "Mom has no idea Kalen and I know about her *stash*." She stepped into the small storeroom.

"Will she mind if we take a couple?"

When Deirdre returned with the plasticware, she placed it on the table and opened the lid. "Not if we only have two. She'll never find out."

"I'll never find out what?"

Dee spun to face the door behind her. "*Mom*. Ahhh..."

"Yes, dear. I'm *quite* aware that you and Kalen have been filching from my *company* supply of cookies. That's why I made so many." Their mother grinned. "What are you two doing down here in the middle of the night? It's past midnight."

Rachel half-turned while she stirred the cocoa and hot water. She met her mother's green eyes. "We disturbed you? Did we wake Dad too? Dee and I needed to have a *sisters'* chat."

"No. He's still sawing logs. The floorboards squeaked as you two descended the stairs. My curiosity got the better of me." She handed the sugar canister to Rachel, took an oatmeal chocolate chip cookie from the container, and bit into it. "I'll leave you ladies to your talk. If you have plans for tomorrow, I hope you won't stay up too late. Breakfast is at seven." After a kiss for each of them, she turned and sashayed from the room.

As Rachel glanced at her sister, her brows lifted. "I'd say Mom agrees that we need to straighten things out between us." She lowered the temperature on the burner and added milk to the dark liquid. Then she put in the vanilla and removed the cocoa from the burner. "Grab two mugs."

Rachel reached for a ladle and brought the pot to the hot plate on the kitchen table. After she filled the cups with the steaming mixture and sank into a chair, she selected two cookies for each of them, then arranged the treats on a dish from the cabinet.

"So, please tell me what has been eating at you, sis. I'm clueless. I hate that you're unhappy about something, and it appears to be something I've done, or said, or..."

Deirdre half-turned away from her. She pressed her eyes shut. "*You left me.*" Tears seeped from under her lids.

Rachel swallowed a mouthful of cookie and shook her head. "I left you? When? Left you where?"

Deirdre turned to Rachel and pinned her with a glare. "*Here*. You took off, and I was all alone—with nobody to talk to."

"Sorry, Dee. I'm not following you. What do you mean?"

Her sister wiped the waterworks from her eyes with the palms of her hands. "You've no concept of what I went through with no girlfriend to talk to once you weren't here. The other girls in high school ignored me or made nasty jokes behind my back. I wasn't in their clique. They said I was a snob. I wanted to be a part of their group, but I could never approach them. You were gone, and you were the *only* one I ever confided in. Kalen was too busy with his pals, and he was a guy." The tears fell faster.

Rachel's mouth drooped. Her sister must have become an introvert. *How did I not see this?* Rachel jumped up from her seat, snatched a paper towel to wipe Deirdre's cheeks, and wrapped her in a hug. "I'm so sorry, Dee. I never knew. You said nothing to me. Did you tell Mom and Dad?"

As she sobbed, Deirdre squeaked out a shaky, "No. I was too embarrassed to say I didn't have any friends. I felt like a dummy."

Her arms circled Rachel's waist. Her sister's weeping slowed. "I guess I allowed the anger to grow. You never said goodbye to me. You drove off to college while I was helping my Sunday school teacher with something at her house. I spent the night crying and then decided I'd never speak to you again."

"Oh, Dee. I remember leaving and hugging our parents. With the excitement, I never thought about your being absent." Her brother hadn't been there either. He'd not said a word. "Wait! That isn't exactly true. When I got to my dorm room that evening, I realized I didn't get to say goodbye to you or Kalen. I planned to call, but a gaggle of giggling females burst into the room I was to share. They were all introducing themselves at once. Then my roommate and I went to work on settling in. I'd never been away from home, so I was caught up with the new things in my life, familiarizing myself with the campus, my classmates, and everything." She'd put everything and everyone else before her sister.

"Can you forgive me? I didn't think. I guess I *have* been selfish." She hugged Deirdre. They clung to each other for a few minutes before Dee let go of her.

They sat at the table, and Rachel touched her sister's wrist. "You had no friends at church?"

"No. One day a guy in my class came up to me and said the girls there were jealous because I was so pretty. I hadn't an inkling how to handle it, and you weren't here." Deirdre dabbed her face with the paper towel.

"Dee, why didn't you call me? We could have discussed all this."

Her sister hung her head. "Since you left without saying goodbye, I figured you didn't care."

"I did ask to speak to you when I called home, but each time I was told you were out or couldn't come to the phone."

"Yeah, I used to leave as soon as Mom or Dad said your name once they answered the cell."

Rachel wrapped her arms around her sister again. Dee had always seemed immature for her age. Not physically, of course, but emotionally. *Guess I dropped the ball.*

Her sister pulled away. They ate their cookies and finished their cocoa.

Deirdre gazed at her. "I am *not* jealous of you."

The corners of Rachel's lips tugged up. "Okay. You're *not* jealous. I'm glad. Now, who is this guy you're helping with his dog team?"

"Look, sis. It's almost two in the morning, and I'm beat. Can we talk tomorrow?"

Chapter Eighteen

Rachel startled at the knock on her door. Her mother said, "Rise and shine, sleepyhead. Breakfast is in an hour." She listened to the same message as her mother rapped on Deirdre's door. "Six in the morning came too fast." This was going to be a long day after less than four hours of sleep.

A hot shower and dressing in clean, warm clothes for a day of helping Anik with the dogsled team made her at least look human. She brushed her hair, swept it up into a ponytail, and breezed out of the bedroom.

In the kitchen, her father sat at the end of the table, Kalen to his right and Deirdre to her father's left. Her sister looked as if she'd slept a solid eight hours. Not fair. She quirked her smile with a slight shake of the head and slipped into the chair between Dee and their mother's chair.

Mom set a platter of pancakes surrounded by crisp bacon and sausage links in the middle of the table. A bowl of mixed berries flanked the serving dish, and a variety of syrups stood sentry on the other side of the feast.

"Pass the butter, please." Her father held out his hand. Kalen complied.

"It smells wonderful in here, Mom." Rachel speared a sausage. "I haven't had this good of an appetite since I went to college." She gave Dee a sideways glance. "Must've been a guilty conscience."

Dee giggled.

Their father's brows pinched in question. "What's that all about?"

"Private jest between us, Dad." She elbowed her sister, whose lips angled upward on one side.

He nodded and resumed his pancake prep.

After breakfast, the men slid their empty plates and utensils into the sink full of soapy water and refreshed their cups of coffee. "Come into the living room, son. I have a document I want you to look over for me." They exited the room.

"Mom," Rachel took her dirty dishes to the counter, "Dee and I can handle cleanup."

"I appreciate the assistance. Will you both be here at lunchtime, or have you made other plans?"

"I'll probably eat lunch with Anik. He has the entire day planned for us."

Deirdre stacked her plate, mug, and utensils next to the sink. "And I'll be working with another sled dog team. I'll be back for dinner though."

"Good. I'll expect you then, unless you call and say otherwise." She left the room but peeked back in. "And thanks for the kitchen duty reprieve." She disappeared into the hallway.

"Do you want to wash or dry, Dee?"

"I polished these yesterday, so I'll wipe." She held up her shapely, long fingers with perfectly sculpted nails, painted with sparkling maroon nail polish.

Rachel glanced at her own hands. "Wish I didn't have to cut my nails so short. If I don't, I make too many typing mistakes."

Deirdre stood poised with the dishtowel, ready for the first clean, wet plate.

"You said we could continue our discussion this morning. Who is this musher you'll be helping with the team, sis?"

"He's a guy from high school. The only one who wasn't put off by my quiet treatment. We used to sit next to each other in study hall. We weren't supposed to talk, but he'd whisper to me and make comments about other students. Nothing bad, just funny things, and he made me laugh."

A sense of joy filled Rachel's heart until guilt pushed it out. If only she'd paid more attention to her little sister back then. "Does this knight in shining armor have a name?"

"Dan. Dan Harris."

"Dan from church?"

"Yes."

"Did you two date in high school? Do you date now?"

"What's with the third degree, Rachel?"

A second twinge of guilt assaulted her. These were the things she should've been asking her sister over the past six years… or six years ago, before leaving for college. She didn't blame Deirdre for being hostile to a certain extent. "Forgive me again. It's my feeble attempt to make up for lost time. I'm concerned about you, Dee. Please bear with me while I try to put our relationship as sisters back on an even keel."

"Okay." Dee narrowed her eyes. "But no more interrogation." She sighed. "No, we never dated. He asked. I guess I was scared. I don't know what was wrong with me. Then he stopped asking. At least he didn't ignore me. After graduation, he went away to school, and I had nobody again." She frowned. A moment later, her face brightened up. "When Dan returned this year, he started talking to me at church. He's hoping to enter the Iditarod for the first time. I like him."

"One more?" Rachel raised her brows. "Is he an experienced musher?"

"Aren't all the guys?" Dee shrugged. "He was born here. It's a man thing, right?"

Rachel's concern over Deirdre helping Dan with a dogsled team ate at her. Maybe it was because she wasn't very familiar with him. *Or maybe you're being the overprotective big sister you should have been.*

"You said Dan plans to enter the Iditarod for the first time, didn't you?"

"Yeah. Why?"

"I'd find out how much experience he has in sledding... well, don't go off on a run alone with him if he's a novice."

Deirdre tented her hands on her hips. "I'm smarter than that."

Is she? An uneasy sensation snaked its way through Rachel's stomach.

As Anik and Rachel readied his team for a run, their conversation was one-sided. Had she heard a word he said? "What's wrong with you, girl? You haven't spoken more than two sentences all morning. Am I that boring?" Anik chuckled.

Her head whipped up. "I'm sorry. Guess I'm a little absorbed." She stared into the distance.

"Care to explain? It's always good to talk things out with a good friend when something bothers you."

Rachel exhaled loudly, as if she carried a ton of bricks on her back. "I'm worried about Deirdre."

No wonder she couldn't focus. "Over how she acts toward you? I'd call it jealousy."

A smile spread across Rachel's face. "Exactly what I thought, but after a good discussion last night and this morning, I found it wasn't envy that made her act out. It was a different kind of resentment, and it was my fault. I'll tell you about it another time. We've settled our problem."

He nodded. "Then what's got you so discombobulated?"

"So *what*?" Her head popped up, and her nose scrunched.

Anik laughed until he almost doubled over. "Guess it's not a word you reporters use in your articles, huh? It means confused, perturbed, thrown off balance."

"Oh." She checked the tow line that connected the rear dog's harness to the sled. "I'm worried about Dee."

"Yeah, you said that already."

"Well. When you said you only needed one person to assist you with your team, she found someone else to help."

"And you don't trust him?"

"It's... not that I don't trust him *around* her. They went to high school together, and apparently, he was sweet on her. She was too shy to allow him to get close, but she likes him."

Anik shot up from his squatty position where he was scratching Tracker's ears. "Deirdre... your sister... *shy*? Are we talking about the same girl? Red hair. Emerald green eyes. And a tongue capable of whipping a man... or woman... into silence?"

Rachel's laughter echoed against the metal shed where he stored his racing equipment. "Surprising, isn't it? She was until she got out of high school. She's kept her introverted side so well-hidden since then... I had no clue. And now she's teamed up with Dan Harris to prepare for the Iditarod. Something tells me he's had no experience in mushing. Not sure. It's only a hunch. That's what I don't trust... I guess."

Anik concentrated on what he knew about Dan, which wasn't much. "I've met the Harris family at church and spoken with Dan's parents. They'd never mentioned their son running a dogsled when the three of us yakked about various races. You may be right, Rachel. And he plans to enter the Iditarod?"

"That's what Dee said. Now I'm even more worried if you've never heard of him racing."

"Before we jump to conclusions, the race is still some time away. If he's only starting to prepare, I doubt he'll take off across Denali until he gains experience in what he's doing. Why don't you ask Liam when he calls if he's met Dan? If Liam isn't acquainted with him, he could find out if other rangers are."

Rachel's face relaxed, and she smiled. "Good idea. I may be worried about nothing."

Or is she? Anik finished checking the harnesses.

Liam finally caught a break and entered the Doghouse. He grabbed a cup of coffee, pulled out his cell, and tapped Rachel's name on his favorites list. "Hi, beautiful. I wasn't able to call before now. By the time we finished our duties last night, I figured you'd be asleep, and it's been crazy here today so far. How's your day going?"

She told him about her talk with Deirdre and that they'd settled things between them. Then she brought up Dan Harris and how excited Dee was to help him with his dogsled team in prep for the Iditarod. But something in her voice said there was a problem. "I sense a *but* coming. Why?"

Rachel sighed. "While I'm happy for her to spend time with the guy she had a secret crush on in high school, I can't shake an ominous sensation when my mind strays to them. I've no idea if he knows what he's doing, and Dee never came with me or Kalen when we ran dogs in the past. Have you met Dan?"

"No, I'm sorry. I haven't. However, if he's run a team, someone here could have. Let me ask around. A benefit of working and living in a small community is that everyone is connected to someone who is connected to someone else who's connected to you. Or something." He laughed. "Hold on. I did meet him. At your church, when I went with you last Sunday. Seems like a nice guy. It's good to hear you and Deirdre straightened everything out, though."

They spent several minutes talking about Anik's team and Liam's events of the day at the Denali kennels.

"Rachel?"

"Yes?"

"I hope you haven't any plans for Friday night. I want to take you to dinner after my shift ends and spend the evening with you."

Had he imagined it, or did her warmth seep through the phone? He could almost see her smile.

"Sounds wonderful, Liam. This has turned into a long week, and it's only Tuesday." She giggled.

"You're right on both counts. Now, don't get stressed about Deirdre and Dan. I doubt he plans to do anything he's not skilled at. From what I've learned of this area, if you are born and raised here, you're at least somewhat familiar with dogsledding."

Chapter Nineteen

The next day, while Anik checked his team's harnesses, Rachel's cellphone rang and Liam's face appeared. Her heart soared. She hadn't expected a call this early. He must have gotten a morning break. Her stomach flipped as she answered. "I was thinking about you, handsome. How are my fur buddies?"

"Ha! Is that what you mean by thinking about *me*? I'll have to have a serious discussion with Happy. He was your favorite all along, wasn't he?" Liam's hearty laugh carried through the speaker. "To set your mind at rest, the Canine Rangers are all well and always raring to go."

She laughed. "He's such a sweet dog, but *you* were the one in my thoughts. We spent so much one-on-one time together before you returned to work that I got used to having you around."

"I know what you're saying. I'm starved for some attention from my Irish lass. Only two more days until I'm yours again."

"Hmm."

"What's with the negative sound of contemplation? You don't believe me?"

"Oh, I believe you. That doesn't mean I'm not wondering *whose* you are in the meantime with all those pretty female rangers around you." She had to clamp her hand over her mouth to keep in a laugh.

"Awww. You don't trust me? Ha! I've worked with each of those women for at least a year now, much longer for some. It's strange, but I've never had the notion to date any of them. I've been so busy here at the kennels, putting in overtime and volunteering with the rescue teams that I've not been interested in dating... until you came along. Even in high school, when I went out with a girl, I wasn't drawn to her like I was right from the start with you."

"Really?" A tingle ran circles in Rachel's stomach. "The day at my parents' house, when I arrived and saw your gray eyes... something happened. Well... let's say you made an impression on me."

"Ah, yes. I recall the opinion you had of me."

"Was that a snicker, Mr. Chadwick? I don't mean the *misunderstanding*. I'm talking about... when I looked at you... there was something. Aside from the anger that surged once I realized who you were."

Her chest fluttered as usual. He was literally a heartthrob. He had to be the one God intended for her. *Had* to be.

"I'm relieved that we got the problem straightened out." His tone of voice softened. "I never want to cause you any pain again."

"I know you don't."

"Good. Well... I have to go. But, I—"

"It's okay. Anik's waving at me... so I guess we're ready for our practice run this morning. Will you call later?"

"Actually, no. I phoned early because our team of rangers is setting off for Denali to check on things in the park. There's no service where we're going. We probably won't get back until late Friday afternoon sometime."

"You'll be with other rangers?"

"Don't worry, we do this all the time. I was so independent growing up, my folks were used to my taking off for long periods—as long as I showed up for dinner." He laughed. "Which made it easier for them when I joined the Rangers. They knew I could handle myself. I like that you care."

"I do care, Liam. Even if I realize you're experienced in the wilderness, I'm still glad you won't be by yourself. I look forward to hearing about what all you do on these runs."

"Basically, we check on any winter recreationists who explore on snowshoes, skis, or dog teams, and the rest I'll fill you in on later."

"You might see us if Anik decides we'll head that way today." *If only.* "Anyway, I can't wait to find out what else you do at work." She willed her warmth and smile to pass through the cell. "Consider yourself hugged."

"Mmmm. Nice. I'll miss talking to you, beautiful."

"Me too, 'til you can get a call through. Wish us well on our run. Anik said we're doing great so far."

"The man lives for mushing," Liam said with a slight chuckle.

As she turned toward Anik, she was sure Liam's mind could picture his friend standing ready with the dog team, an infectious smile from one cheek to the other.

"I'll pray for both of you," Liam added. "Stay safe."

"And we'll pray for all of you." She threw a kiss through the line.

"Hang on for a minute and close your eyes while you imagine my face." A couple of moments later, a muffled noise came to her ear. Liam said, "Did you feel my lips on yours?"

"I did. Thank you. You felt a little silly doing that, didn't you? Bet you turned around to check if any of the other rangers were watching before you smooched the cell."

He issued a loud laugh.

Her heart warmed.

"Talk to you Friday, sweet lady."

The line went dead. She rushed over to Anik and the dog team. *Drat!* He didn't say whether or not he'd found other rangers who knew Dan.

After their day in Denali Park, Anik settled his dogs and turned to Rachel. "I'm sorry we didn't come across Liam out there today. That was my real reason for heading into the park for our practice. I thought we'd see the rangers."

"You surprised me. I told him we probably wouldn't head that way." She chortled. "But thanks. It just wasn't meant to be."

What *was* meant to be was Liam and Rachel together. Anik would stake his life on it. Must be the native intuition his old *aanaa* passed down to him. He loved this particular gift from his grandmother, but he preferred to call it reading the signs. He chuckled to himself. Instinct or not, he was sure he'd guessed right with those two. "Well, Friday isn't too far off now. So, cheer up, girl."

"Who said I was down?"

"Can't fool me. You've missed talking to him all day."

As he walked Rachel to her car, she elbowed him in the ribs.

"*Ooph*. Cut that out. My belly can't take this kind of abuse when it's empty."

She giggled. "Why don't you come over to my parents' house for dinner? Mom and Dad would love to have you."

"Thanks. What's she making tonight? Never mind. Whatever it is, it'll be tasty. I'll change and be over in a flash." He tapped her on the top of the head, the way he used to when she was a kid, and they parted.

Anik jogged to the cabin. *Like old times, her and me.* He had to think of a way to talk Rachel into not going back to Fairbanks. She didn't belong that far from home, and he didn't like the way her boss ogled her. Liam was a much better choice.

As she pulled the car around the garage to head back to the O'Rourkes' residence, Anik waved from the back door. He shot into the basement's arctic room, ran up the flight to the first floor, and took the stairs three at a time to his bedroom on the second. He clutched a fresh pair of jeans and a shirt, then headed for the bathroom.

After he'd cleaned up, he surveyed his sleeping quarters. "If those two do wind up together, I'll have to secure another place to live." But first, he'd have to do more to encourage the relationship, which would not be easy if she left at the end of the week. There wasn't much more information to give her on mushing and the dogs. So no more stalling her boss. He pushed his lips out in frustration.

The drive to the O'Rourkes' home produced no new ideas of how to delay Rachel's departure for Fairbanks. He drove into the family's yard and parked, hopped out of the vehicle, and ran up the front porch stairs. After only one knock, the front door opened.

"I thought I heard your Jeep." Rachel swung the door wide for him to step inside.

"Did you tell your mom you invited a hungry polar bear for supper? Hope she made enough. I'm starving after our day of mushing."

"Anik, my boy." Mr. O'Rourke stood from his recliner and held out his hand. "Glad you came this evening."

Rachel hurried down the hall to the kitchen.

"Yes, sir. Your daughter took pity on me. It looked like a can of beans for my meal until she suggested I join you."

"Still haven't learned how to cook, huh?" Mr. O'Rourke ducked his head and gazed at Anik over the top of his glasses.

"Ah, not unless it's breakfast. Been a little too focused on other things to learn."

"What you need is a wife, Anik."

His neck warmed. "Too busy for that, too, sir."

Rachel returned and announced dinner was on the table. They sat down in the dining room, and Mr. O'Rourke bowed his head. "Our dear heavenly Father, please bless the food You've provided for us and the hands that prepared it."

After everyone said, "Amen," plates full of steaming potatoes, vegetables, and a platter of meatloaf circulated.

Rachel passed the meat to her father along with a question. "Dad... the Harris family from church..."

"Yes?"

"Does Dan have any experience mushing?"

"Not sure the subject has ever come up. Why?"

"He's the young man Deirdre is assisting to prepare for the Iditarod."

"Huh. Is it that time of year again already?"

Anik took a helping of the meatloaf and pursed his lips. Rachel was still fretting about the boy and her sister.

Deirdre and Dan strolled in through the back door.

"Hi, everyone." The redhead shrugged out of her parka. "You all know Dan. Sorry I'm late for dinner, but I'm happy to see my portion won't go to waste since Anik is here." She giggled.

"Not to worry, girl." He gave her a thumbs-up.

"Dan asked me out to The Brown Bear tonight anyway. Need to change first."

She ran out of the room, calling out behind her. "Be right back." Her footfalls announced her trip up the stairs.

"Welcome, Dan." Mrs. O'Rourke smiled at him. "Have a seat, or you can wait for Deirdre in the living room."

Dan drew out a chair across from Rachel and sat down. "This will be fine, Mrs. O'Rourke."

"Would you care for something to drink?"

"No, thank you. I'm okay. We had some cocoa at my place before we came here."

The stern expression on Rachel's face told Anik she was about to give the boy a third degree. She'd take her concern for her sister out on Dan. He'd better intervene and save the poor guy from Rachel's wrath. If Deirdre walked in on the cross-examination, she'd pitch a fit.

Rachel faced Dan. "Do you—"

"Dan," Anik cut in. "How'd your team do today?"

Rachel's eyes widened. She pressed her lips together in a tight line.

Anik chuckled to himself. *Better for her to be angry with me.*

Dan's face brightened. "We learned about commands to give the dogs while we hooked them into a team. You know... like when you pull them out straight from the sled. And about the rigging. It was fairly easy. Wish I had learned earlier. I've missed out on a lot of fun."

As he continued to talk about his plans for the race, Anik observed Rachel's face ease. Dan had mentioned nothing about trying any difficult runs. Plenty of rookie mushers had entered the Iditarod, but they each had to have a report card from qualifying races completed by race officials. That meant Dan couldn't enter this coming March. He'd practice for quite some time yet. It should help Rachel relax.

Anik released a silent sigh. *In all honesty, me too.*

Dan would get all the training he needed before he signed up for the big race. And Rachel could finally stop agonizing about Deirdre.

Chapter Twenty

Friday had finally arrived. Rachel stared at the time on her phone—after six. They planned to have dinner together. When would she hear from Liam? It had been a sensational day with Anik and his dogsled team, but she'd waited on pins and needles all afternoon for Liam's call.

The familiar ringtone sounded. Rachel grabbed the cell. "Hi, handsome. I was about to head to my parents' house to prepare for our date." She gasped in a breath. No need to tell him how concerned she'd been.

"I'm so sorry, Rachel."

"Why? What's happened?" Her jaw muscle clenched.

"We'll have to have a *very* late dinner... if you still want to go out. The guys and I returned to the station only moments ago. What a day. But if you don't mind the hour, I'm ready to spend an evening with the prettiest girl in Alaska. What do you say? I should be able to pick you up by… let's see. I'll tie up some loose ends here, drive home, clean up, and get to your parents' cabin. Is nine too late to eat?"

She laughed. *Whew! That's a relief.* "No. Not at all. I'll have a snack at Mom and Dad's. I already missed dinner, but I'd told my mother not to count on me. She probably thinks we headed straight to a restaurant instead of me coming back to change."

"Okay, I'll pick you up at their place as soon as I get cleaned up. If Anik asks, tell him, no, he's not invited. I want you all to myself."

She preferred privacy tonight too. Rachel's heart sang with excitement.

They ended the call, and she glanced at her phone to check the time. Another two and a half hours to wait until she'd see him again. She'd never been this anxious before. Rachel sauntered toward Anik, who had settled his team in for the night.

"So, Liam finally made it back, huh?" Anik grinned. "I wondered where he was. Knew he wouldn't have stood you up."

She grimaced at his teasing.

"Where's he taking you to supper, and when will he be there? I can be ready and meet you two." His smile grew.

"Oh, no." She shook her head. "Liam knew you'd say that. He said, 'No, he's not invited.'" She giggled. "At least not this time." She bumped him with her shoulder.

With a horselaugh, Anik almost doubled over. He straightened. "That's what I thought."

Rachel helped him put away the rest of the equipment and then hugged him. "Thanks for a fun day and all the information I got for my article. This should make Mr. Gibson pleased."

"If it doesn't, he'll answer to me." Anik guffawed again and walked her to her car.

As she rolled the Subaru Outback out of the driveway, he waved, turned, and slipped from view.

Before long, she drove into her parents' front yard and hurried to the cabin, famished.

Kalen sat in his wheelchair, his lips clamped tight, his brows knit together, while her mother paced the living room floor. Stress lines creased her forehead.

"Mom, what's wrong?"

Before her mother or Kalen could answer, her dad strode into the room, his cell attached to his ear. "Thank you, Trooper Dunlap. I appreciate it." He dropped the phone onto the coffee table and pulled his wife into an embrace. "They'll send out the notices right away. Don't worry. They'll find her. They couldn't have gone far."

"Who hasn't gone far?" Rachel's stomach churned. She pinned Kalen for an answer. "It's Dee, isn't it?" He nodded.

Tears coursed down their mother's cheeks. "Deirdre didn't come home by three as she told me she would. That's what she promised before she left this morning for the park to meet with her new boss and pick up her uniform. She told us she was going to assist Dan with something afterward, but also that they didn't plan to do much today. She expected to be here early enough to help me with dinner. And she's not answering her phone."

Mom wrapped her arms around Rachel as if she were a life preserver. "I'm so worried. It's not like her."

She let go of Rachel and resumed pacing.

"Dad, have you called Dan's parents?" Rachel lowered herself to the couch. "Maybe Dan took Deirdre there to eat and her phone is simply dead."

"Yes, I did." Her father guided his wife to the couch and made her sit between Rachel and Kalen. "It's the first place I tried when your mother started to fret. Turns out, not only are they *not* at the Harris's, but Dan doesn't live at their house anymore. His mother gave me his roommate's number. His roommate, Ken, said he hadn't seen Dan since early this morning. He told Ken last night that he wanted to do a run in Denali Park today."

Mom wrung her hands. "Where's Liam? I thought you were having dinner with him tonight. Did something happen to him too?"

Rachel rubbed her mother's shoulder. "Nothing happened to him. He'll be here in a little while. Then we were going out to eat.

But not now." How could she convince her mother to remain composed when her own pulse beat at the rate of an Irish jig? "Try to calm down, Mom."

"I can't, honey. When I realized Deirdre was so late, a niggle began to nag at me. It was the same premonition I had when you were seven and didn't tell me you decided to visit a friend of yours after school. I was beside myself until your father found you walking home from the other side of town right before dark."

Oh, yeah. She remembered the day well. She'd walked toward home through Healy, her skin tingling with anxiety because she hadn't meant to stay late. She'd never seen Daddy that angry and happy all at once. "I never tried that stunt again. Perhaps it's something along those lines with Dee." *We can hope and pray.*

Dad had disappeared into the hall again. Several silent minutes passed before he returned with a cup of hot tea for Mom. "Here, honey. Drink this. It's that camo... whatever you always say calms you."

A slight giggle came from her mother. "Chamomile, dear." The humor didn't show on her face.

The melodic ring of the doorbell sounded from the entrance. Rachel almost jumped out of her skin. *Dee?* She ran for the front door. That was dumb, Rachel. Why would your sister use the doorbell? Possibly one of the state troopers with good news... or not? *No. Lord, please protect my sister.*

She hadn't spent as much time in prayer as she should. Not since she moved to Fairbanks. Would the Lord even hear her anymore?

The door flung open to the O'Rourkes' house. Instead of the smiling woman Liam had anticipated spending the evening with after a long week's work, Rachel appeared to be on the verge of tears. "Hey, what's wrong?"

She stepped back to allow him into the foyer without a word.

Liam glanced toward the living room, where her mother had the same anguished expression. Mr. O'Rourke's face showed fatigue, as if he'd not slept in a week.

"What's going on?" Liam drew Rachel to him and hugged her.

"I'm sorry. I forgot all about you." The dam that stayed her waterworks crumbled. He held her at arm's length to read her face. When she didn't say anything more, he pulled her back into his arms. "Shhh. Everything will be okay. Tell me what's happened."

Rachel buried her head in his parka-covered shoulder. After a second, she stopped crying and straightened.

He took off his coat. She hung it on a hook as she explained why they were all upset.

Liam strode into the living room beside her. "So, everyone who might know anything has already been called or notified."

After Rachel grabbed a tissue, she wiped her eyes and blew her nose, then sat between Liam and her mother. "Yes. There's no one else to contact, and the state troopers don't want any of us to go off on our own to search for her. They said it's their job, since Healy, like the rest of Alaska, has no county sheriff. The state troopers are the only law enforcement officers with jurisdiction in rural areas. But you already knew that, being a ranger."

"Right. It's *their* job." He squeezed the hand he held. "They'll do their level best to find out where she is, but I can check too. They didn't say *I* couldn't leave. I'll go back to the park to get some support. I can contact the law enforcement ranger on duty and talk to those at their station. Maybe they can tell us where Dan might have gone. In such a small community, someone might have an idea." Liam rose to don his parka.

"I want to go with you." Rachel jumped up from the couch. "If I stay here, I'll go crazy. I've had this foreboding about Dee working with Dan from the minute she told me about it. I can't sit here and do nothing."

Liam glanced at her father, who nodded.

Kalen turned his eyes from his mother to Liam, then to his sister. "Go with him, sis."

Liam dipped his head to both men in understanding. Rachel couldn't help her mother in the emotional condition each of them was in. "Okay. Let's go."

"You're not going without eating." Her mother hurried from the couch to the kitchen. "Don't make me worry about you too. I will if you don't take along something to eat." Her voice trailed off down the hallway.

She returned with a bag and thrust it into Rachel's hands. "I threw together a couple of ham sandwiches, chips, and drinks. Please be careful. Promise me." Her mom latched onto Rachel's shoulder, but her eyes pleaded with Liam.

"We'll be safe, Mrs. O'Rourke. And we'll call as soon as we have information."

"Or if you don't," Mr. O'Rourke said and rumpled his brows as he laid his hand on Liam's back. "Thank you, son."

Rachel chewed the inside of her lip as Liam drove to the Visitor Resource Protection Building at the park. "I sure hope someone can give us a lead on where to find them."

"I'll check with everyone who's there, but I suspect most have left for today." Liam reached his hand to her shoulder.

The ride seemed to stretch in Rachel's mind, but he finally pulled into the parking lot. She reached for the door, but his hand caught her wrist. "We should pray before we get out. God knows where Deirdre and Dan went. Let's ask Him to direct us to someone who can lead us in the right direction."

Rachel nodded.

Liam took her hands in his. "Father, God, we need Your help. Wherever Deirdre and Dan are, please lead us to them. Tell them people are searching for them. I ask that You'll keep them both safe. Bring peace to Rachel and her family. They need Your comfort, Father. In Jesus' name we pray, Amen."

Rachel squeezed his hand and peered up, her eyes watery. "Thank you, Liam."

He leaned over the truck's console and kissed her gently on the lips. "I'll save the rest for after we find these wayward kids."

Kids. Yes. Dee and Dan certainly had acted like children when they didn't tell anyone where they were going. She half-hoped her father would lower the boom on her sister when they found them. She was not being her twenty-two-year-old adult self at all. Rachel's lungs expanded with a deep breath, which she let out slowly. At least her anxiety had dissipated some compared to when they'd set out on this mission.

Liam sprinted to the passenger side of the truck and opened her door. He lifted her down to the ice-packed pavement. "Let's go in and find out what we can. You okay?"

She nodded. He was so caring. Who else would spend his first day off a five-day shift out in the cold with a dogsled in search of someone else's sister?

He wrapped his arm around her shoulders and steered her toward the building. "We'll have to be buzzed in at this hour."

Once inside, Liam kept a firm grip on her hand as he found two rangers still in the building. One of them was a local who knew Dan but couldn't think of anywhere they might have gone. "I seriously doubt he would have taken his team into the park this soon since he's just getting used to the dogs."

Time grew late, and they still had no idea where to hunt for Deirdre and Dan.

Right before midnight, Rachel phoned her parents. "Mom, all but a couple of the rangers had left. But one of them said he couldn't remember Dan ever being on a dogsled, nor could he imagine him running the dogs in Denali. So that could be positive news."

Rachel's foreboding worsened. Her head ached. "We can't do any more here. Liam found the law enforcement ranger. There's nowhere they haven't checked outside of the national park grounds itself. Liam will bring me back to your house. He plans to join the search and rescue team when they go out to locate Dee and Dan." Tears prevented her from saying anything further.

Liam took the cell from her hand and added a few details to the information Rachel had given them. He disconnected the call and took her into his arms. "Let's get you home. You don't want to, but you need some rest. You've had an active day."

She swiped her hands over both sides of her face to brush away the tears. "What about you? You've been on the go for five days straight."

"But I'm used to it. I'll be fine. I don't want you to get sick."

She rubbed her forehead. She'd be uneasy the entire time he was out there.

As if he'd read her mind, he said, "And I don't want you to worry about me. I've volunteered with this team before. We know what we're doing. We'll find Deirdre and Dan."

Chapter Twenty-One

By the time Liam got Rachel back to her parents' cabin, the clock on the dashboard showed just after midnight. The O'Rourkes still kept their vigil in the living room with Kalen, exactly as they'd left them. "I've spoken to the National Park Service Search and Rescue Team, who will make passes over the area to locate Deirdre and Dan. I'm convinced Denali is the only place they could have gone since we haven't found them. But don't fret. He probably wanted to get a feel of how to run the dog team. No doubt got disoriented and lost. We'll find them."

Liam's words downplayed his anxiety. *Heaven help someone find them soon... and unharmed.* The expressions on all the O'Rourkes told him they were grateful. "I'm going with SAR. I'd better hurry so they can take off." He embraced Rachel, smiled at her mother, and shook Kalen's and Mr. O'Rourke's hands. "I'll call as soon as I have a chance."

Rachel squeezed him. "Please be careful." Her eyes brimmed with tears.

"I will. Get some rest. I know it'll be hard, but at least try. Prayer helps."

Her father patted his back. "Prayer will be ongoing, son."

Liam left the cabin and hurried to meet the search and rescue team, who were preparing to leave as he pulled up. *Lord, thanks for getting me here in time. Please lead us to them.*

More than twelve hours later, Rachel paced a circle in the living room, then through the dining room, around the kitchen table, past the doorway into the foyer, and circled the coffee table again as she waited for a call from Liam. She'd honestly tried to rest on the couch, but horrible images and scenarios crept into her mind every time she laid her head back.

Dad, in a constant state of prayer, kept his head bowed at his corner desk in the living room. Kalen had gone to his bedroom to do classwork online. *Something for him to focus on.* Mom was in her domain in the kitchen, cleaning out the cabinets and drawers, her escape whenever something bothered her.

Rachel peeked at the clock. *Almost three p.m., Lord. I'm trying to put all my trust in You. I am, but they've been missing for almost twenty-four hours now.* What if something terrible had happened to Deirdre? And Dan? *Allow Liam and the SAR team to find them. And let them be safe.* They'd been searching for so long. *Keep everyone safe.*

She had to start spending more time with the Lord. Her spiritual life had been sorely neglected... up until now. So, why would God listen to her?

As she paced over and over, her prayers kept time with her steps. She had so much to make up for—with Dee and with God.

After hours with only a few breaks and calls from Liam, Rachel's legs ached, but she couldn't stop. She rounded the kitchen table for the umpteenth time and heard her cell ring. She sprinted through the foyer and lunged for the phone lying on the coffee table. *"Liam!"*

"You sound out of breath. Let me guess. You've been pacing the house again until I called."

"Did you find them?"

"Not yet. We had to take a break. We're refueling now, and then we'll go out again to another section of the park. I'm sure they'll be located soon. Please rest, Rachel. Don't make me worry about you too."

Chapter Twenty-Two

When Rachel's eyes opened a crack, the first glow of dawn on Sunday created a shining frame around the closed drapes on the picture window. A glance at the digital clock on her father's desk told her she'd slept until almost seven. She recalled having dropped onto the couch and stretched out sometime after Liam's last phone call to tell them the SAR team was leaving to make another search. She'd leaned back without realizing it and wound up on her side. Mom, fast asleep in the recliner, had obviously covered her with an afghan. Rachel smiled. How she'd missed her mother since moving away.

Rachel's father was back in the corner by his desk, but now on his knees. He must have been up all night praying. Today was Sunday. How could he possibly preach? Dad had been like this through the terrible moments when Kalen had his accident until they knew he'd be okay. Her father's faith had grown so strong afterward.

Romans eight, twenty-eight popped into her mind. *And we know that all things work together for good to them that love God, to them who are the called according to his purpose.*

Father, how can this work together for good? But if you say it can, I have to believe. Give me strength.

Her cell rang. Everyone rushed to her as she reached for the device. "It's Liam." Her voice quavered. She dreaded the thought of being told they hadn't located Deirdre yet.

"Tell me you found them."

"I'm sorry, honey, but I can't. I don't understand it. I was sure they were somewhere in the park. But we won't give up. Another team is going out. The Army National Guard, which has helped in the past, was called in. A Black Hawk helicopter will be here shortly. It offers their guys training experience in search and rescue. They'll give it their all. I'll go out with SAR as soon as I catch a few winks. Are you okay?"

Am I okay? "No, I'm not okay." Her answer came back harsher than intended. Of course, he'd ask her that. He was worried about her. "I apologize. I didn't have to bite your head off."

"Not a problem. You're under stress because of your sister. It's understandable." He was silent.

Had the connection dropped? "Liam?"

"Rachel, I don't know what else to say, except I will do everything I can to find Deirdre after I've slept."

The sobs burst through the dam she had maintained until now. "I know you will. I didn't mean..."

"Sweetheart, would you like me to come there and stay with you? I could stretch out on the couch for a little while."

Pull yourself together, Rachel. She wiped her eyes with a tissue snagged from a box her mother had on the end table and took a deep breath. "No. I appreciate it. As much as I'd like you to be with me right now, you need to get a decent rest in your own bed."

"Are you sure?"

"Yes." Then she rattled off, "Dad has been in nonstop prayer. He contacted a deacon who started the prayer chain. Several men went out looking for Deirdre and Dan with no success. I'm okay. I want *you* to rest."

"You need to rest too." He was quiet again, as if he wanted to say more, but didn't.

She finally broke the silence. "Will you call when you awake?"

"Of course I will. Did you get any sleep last night?"

"Uh-huh. Some, and I promise to try again."

Liam trudged to his truck, jumped into the driver's seat, and headed for his cabin. He let out an exhausted breath. *Where are they?* Maybe the next team or the Army's would discover them while he slept. He could only hope.

As he pulled into his yard, the thought hit him between the eyes. *We didn't tell Anik.* Had Rachel filled him in on what happened?

Liam hopped out of the truck and ran into the house. "Anik! Are you here?"

A thump came from upstairs. "Yeah. I'm up here. You scared the life out of me, pal. Made me bump into the door. Where have you been?" The man lumbered down the stairs, holding his forehead. "That'll leave a whopper of a bruise. What's all the yelling about?" He plopped onto the couch.

"You didn't hear?"

"Hear what?"

"Deirdre went out to help Dan with the team yesterday and never returned. We've been searching for them all night."

"What?"

"Deirdre never got home. Mr. O'Rourke called the state troopers, and they're out looking. The church has a prayer chain going. I went out with SAR, and we checked areas of the park. Just finished. A different team has gone out now to check another section. I'll eat and get some sleep. Dan's parents have contacted everyone they know."

"Why didn't you call me? I would've joined the search." He slid his hands through the hair on both sides of his head and rested his elbows on his thighs. He jerked his head up. "Where haven't you gone?"

"I can't think of anywhere right now. With so many out there looking, the bases are pretty much covered. I assumed the O'Rourkes might have phoned you, but they're beside themselves with worry. Sorry, I didn't." Liam stifled a yawn. "I suppose we'll search farther out now. SAR requested a team from the Army. They're sending their guys in the Blackhawk, and they can go to higher reaches of the mountain. We didn't think Dan would try that, but..." Liam shrugged.

Anik's brows lowered. "How's Rachel?"

Liam grimaced. "How do you think she is? She made up with Deirdre, but even so, this is her sister. She's racked with anxiety. The entire family is." He dropped into a chair and yawned again.

"You'd better get to sleep, pal. You won't do anyone any good if you collapse. I'll go to church and find out who's doing what. Then I'll run back here after the service and see if you're awake."

Sunday. "I need to clean up and go."

"Oh, no! I don't think so. You can barely stand, and you'd nod off during the sermon. You *need* to rest."

Anik was right. "Okay. Tell Rachel I wanted to be there if they go. And if I'm not up by the time you return, wake me. I promised her I'd find Deirdre."

"Will do, but after a five-day shift and volunteering on SAR, you should lie down and close your eyes. You could use ten hours of sleep, but I know you better than that. Still, if you pass out, who will you help?"

"I'll be all right if I can snatch a few. Remember, I've done this before."

"Right. Maybe we can brainstorm afterward and come up with somewhere no one's checked. Or we can come up with another plan. But you need to sleep... *now.*"

"Yes, you're right. Thanks." Liam rose and headed for the stairs. "Again, sorry we didn't think to call you, buddy."

"Don't worry about it. I can imagine the stress everyone is under."

As Liam pulled himself up the staircase to the bedroom, he shook his head. "Lord, please help us."

Rachel took a hot shower and dressed for the morning service. She gazed into the mirror at her red-rimmed eyes. *Not even a ton of makeup could help.* People would understand.

"Breakfast is ready." Her mother's voice sounded so tired.

As she headed downstairs, the joy she'd felt earlier in the week came to mind. She and Liam had a relationship. Plus, she'd finished the article for the newspaper, thanks to Anik. She gasped. *Oh, no. Anik!* Had Liam called him? She glanced at the clock. Anik was probably on his way to the church now. *I hope Liam is resting.*

Before she sat at the kitchen table, she recalled her boss's words about returning to work by Monday. Already Sunday, and she couldn't leave. There was no way she'd go back to Fairbanks while Deirdre was missing. Tears assaulted her already stinging eyes once more at the thought of what might have happened to her sister. "Excuse me. I should phone Mr. Gibson and tell him I'm staying."

"Take your time, sweetheart," her father answered, his voice as tired as her mother's.

She hurried to the living room, picked up her cell from the coffee table, and selected her boss's number.

"Hello, Rachel. Calling to let me know you're on your way?"

"No. To tell you I won't be back today or tomorrow." She explained the circumstances, fighting for all she was worth to keep the gathered tears from falling. "I'll notify you when we find them, and I can leave."

Mr. Gibson hadn't interrupted as she told him what was being done to locate the pair. When she paused, he said, "I'm so sorry. I understand. I'll drive down there and join the search. Another set of eyes."

Her anxiety reached a new high. "No! Don't. Everyone in the area is looking. Even the Denali Search and Rescue teams are out, and they've called in the Army helicopter. Thank you for your concern. I have to go now. Mom has breakfast ready." She hung up before he said another word.

Chapter Twenty-Three

Rachel sighed. Had she ever sat through a longer Sunday school lesson in her life? The duration seemed unbearable with the soft-spoken deacon, who had filled in for her dad, and her sleep-deprived eyes, which struggled to stay open. *This too shall pass.* She finally understood that old saying. Not in the Bible, but Second Corinthians, four, seventeen was. *For our light affliction, which is but for a moment, worketh for us a far more exceeding and eternal weight of glory.* She bit her lip. *Light affliction. Right.*

There she went, doubting again. She tried to concentrate on the deacon's words.

When her father said he'd made a call to the assistant pastor that morning and requested he preach the sermon, she'd been relieved. Dad was so tired, he wouldn't have been able to stand behind the pulpit even for the shorter sermons he sometimes gave.

The lesson topic had been interesting, but her mind refused to stay focused. She yawned.

The class finally dismissed. Her feet moved like anvils down the hall to the main auditorium. She had to keep moving.

The opening hymn, *All Hail the Power of Jesus' Name*, kept Rachel awake with its powerful message and beat. After the song ended, she gazed around the church, but couldn't find Liam. Anik slipped into the pew next to her. "Is Liam at home sleeping?" she whispered.

Anik nodded, leaned in, and whispered in return, "He was so wiped out. I told him it'd be best for him to snooze instead of trying to stay alert here. He agreed with reluctance. I promised to wake him when I get back so he can go out again with the search and rescue team."

"Again?" The word came out a little louder than she'd meant to. She covered her mouth with her hand. Her former elderly junior church teacher, sitting in front of them, turned to face Rachel and shook her head.

Rachel lowered her voice. "He needs to sleep. He can't push himself like that." Her eyes misted.

Anik's hand rested on her forearm. "No cause for worry. I don't plan to rush to the cabin right after the service. Liam is used to working long hours at the park, but I won't wake him. I only *said* I'd get him up when I got home to convince him to go to bed. He's never slept late since I've been living with him. Don't you add him to your worry list." Anik's brows pulled together. "That's an order from *big brother*." He quietly chuckled. "Where's your dad?"

The junior church teacher half-turned her head.

"We'd better go to the lobby and talk so we don't disturb anyone." Anik rose from the pew.

The deacon finished giving the announcements for the week and reminded everyone to pray for Deirdre, Dan, and their families. He then requested the congregation turn to *Great is Thy Faithfulness* in the hymnal.

Rachel followed Anik out the sanctuary door to the lobby, where they sat on a bench.

"Dad and a few men and women from his Sunday school class, along with the other two deacons, went to the prayer room during the service. Oh, Anik. I—" The tears she'd held burst forth.

He eased her to his shoulder. "Go ahead. Have a good cry. You'll feel better. Don't give up hope, girl. They're out there somewhere, and if I know Liam, he'll find them."

After the message, Anik walked Rachel to her car. The prayers offered for her sister and Dan had drained Rachel. She was helpless. What could she do?

Anik opened the driver's side door for her. "I'll head to the cabin now and see if Liam is awake. If not, I'll have to get him up. I was thinking about this during the rest of the service. I promised him." Anik shrugged.

"But after he leaves to join SAR, I'll take my team out and search for Deirdre and Dan. Would you like to go, or do you think it'd add more strain on your parents?"

She considered it for a second. Her insides sprang to life. "I'll go. I think my being with you will keep them from worrying. Kalen will keep reminding them. Having two more sets of eyes searching should also comfort them."

"Then it's a plan. I'll tell Liam. Can you meet me at the cabin?"

"Yes. I'll run to Mom and Dad's, change, grab a thermos of coffee, and head over."

Anik jogged to his Jeep, got in, gave her a quick wave, and took off out of the church parking lot. Rachel started the engine, released the emergency brake, and left for her parents' house.

Liam may not have taken off to rejoin the search and rescue team yet. She'd fallen head over heels for him. How could she even think of returning to Fairbanks once she knew her sister was okay? *Lord, is there any way I can stay here in Healy and find a job to support myself?* She didn't want to leave but still hadn't heard from any magazines she'd written to. *I promise to get back to my quiet times with You, Lord. I promise.*

Half an hour later, Rachel was on her way to meet Anik. When she pulled up, Liam rushed out the front door. Her heart flipped at the sight of him.

As he reached her, she slipped out of the vehicle. He scooped her up in his arms and swung her around. "I'm so glad I had a chance to gaze on this beautiful face before I head to Denali." He smiled.

He planted his lips on hers in the most wonderful lip-lock she'd ever imagined. Her hands flew to his neck, and she held on as if for dear life.

He embraced her. "You make it hard to leave, but we both know what's at stake." The seriousness of the situation was written on his face. "Anik told me what he planned. Be safe. Don't take any chances. Two people are enough to rescue right now." He kissed her again, ran for his truck, and called over his shoulder, "Pray for us while you're out there. I'll be praying too."

Rachel sighed. "Lord, please help us. I don't care who finds Dee and Dan, as long as they're found." She waved as Liam drove out of the yard.

After she locked the car, Rachel located Anik in the backyard with his team. The dogs were all set and appeared raring to go. They greeted her with a round of yips and barks. "Don't have to ask them if they're ready. It's as if they're saying, 'Give me the trail. I was born for this.' "

Anik stood from a squat. "You've got that right." He placed a .30-06 Springfield in the sled's basket where she was to sit.

She'd grown up with firearms and recognized the rifle. Her father carried the same gun if he was going out in the wild. Cans of pepper spray were also tucked into an unzipped soft thermal bag. "Not taking any chances, are you?"

"Nope. The Springfield's for you. Figured you've been gone from here for so long, you wouldn't think to bring one of your dad's. And I can do with this." He opened his parka and revealed a Ruger Blackhawk revolver with a six-inch barrel strapped to his side. "Ready to go?"

She sat in the basket and zipped shut the insulated container. "Glad you included food for the journey. I didn't." Rachel swung the backpack of other items she thought they might need into the sled and secured it. "Let's go."

Anik released the brake. "Hike!"

The dogs took off with a flurry of excited barks as a mist of loose snow lightly sprayed Rachel.

Again, Father, please allow us to find my sister and Dan. It's so cold. Let them be okay.

Anik had driven the team a couple of miles from the entrance to the national park when Rachel's cellphone rang. *What? There's no cell service here. Must be one of those infrequent spots where a signal gets through.* Perhaps someone found Deirdre. She gestured for Anik to stop.

As she pulled her cell from the zipper pocket of her parka, her ski goggles blurred from the snow spray. She answered without checking the screen. "Hold on for a minute," she shouted to the caller.

The sled came to a halt. "Hello?"

The caller's voice was faint with intermittent static. "Rachel! I'm here at your parents' house. They said you've gone off with Anik on the dogsled to find your sister. I'd hoped to go with you."

"*Mr. Gibson.* What are you doing in Healy? I told you it wasn't necessary for you to come."

"Well, I wanted to be here for you and to help. Are you nearby?"

"No, we've already entered Denali. I can't talk right now. We need to keep moving. There's nothing you can do."

The dogs voiced their irritation at being stopped in their run.

"I have to go." She hung up and tucked the phone back in the small pocket. *Honestly!* What was that man thinking?

She glanced at Anik, whose brows were raised. "I thought there was no service when you got inside the park."

"Apparently, we didn't hit the dead zone yet. Lucky for your boss. Too bad." Anik chuckled.

She huffed, turned forward, and waved her hand.

Anik called out, "Hike!"

The dogs jumped into motion and were off.

Mr. Gibson had become nothing but an irritation. *I intend to have a serious talk with him. Boss or no boss.*

Chapter Twenty-Four

Time crawled as the search and rescue helicopter crossed, recrossed, and doubled back over the frozen land of Denali National Park. Liam shook his head. Where were they? Deirdre and Dan had to be out here. They hadn't been seen anywhere from Healy to the park and now beyond. How could they have disappeared.

"What's that!" Liam shouted as the SAR aircraft flew over a remote expanse near the historic gold-mining community of Kantishna. An object on the ground reflected the bright midday sun and shone like a beacon through the trees. "Circle the area. I think I saw something." Most visitors to Denali rarely ventured this far into the park.

As the craft made another pass over the densely wooded section, two figures came out into the clearing and waved frantically at them.

One hopped, using a branch as a crutch, and held onto the other person.

"That has to be them." *Lord, let it be them.* Boy, were they in for a lecture from more than one front. Still, if it were Deirdre and Dan, everyone would be elated to know they were alive. How *did* they survive for two nights in the frigid temperature? A story worth hearing. *Rachel may have another article to write.* He smiled as the pilot found a suitable place to put the helicopter down.

Before the craft touched down, sonic cracks and thunks blasted through the air. The copter pitched sharply to the right. *Who was shooting?*

Liam held on for dear life as the craft turned again. The pilot managed to bring the chopper down to a flat area behind a ridge farther from the tree line.

A member of the team said, "I believe the shots came from the other side of the hill."

Another crack sounded as Liam jumped out and scurried up the rise. The individuals who had flagged them down rose from the snow and scurried into the timber. In their haste, one of their hats blew off, and a shock of long, bright red hair wafted in the wind. *It's Deirdre.*

Another ranger from the SAR team crawled up beside Liam. The ranger aimed his .30-06 Springfield and fired in the direction of the next crest from where the noise came.

Liam sprang from his position and sprinted toward the woods where Deirdre and the other figure, who had to be Dan, had gone. Right before he reached the trees, another report rang out. Liam fell.

Anik brought the sled to a standstill. "Did you hear that?"

Rachel ripped off her goggles. "Was it gunfire?"

"Yep. I think from over there." He stretched his arm to point. "Have the rifle ready. It may be an indication that someone needs help. Or it might mean trouble."

He replaced his snow goggles and gave the dogs the signal to go. The canines leaped back into action.

Several minutes later, more shots fired as Anik brought the team to a halt at the foot of a small hill. "You stay here with the dogs. I'll check things out before we go any farther."

He scrambled up the slope, lay prostrate on the snow-packed ground, and peered over the edge of the incline. About seventy-five yards away, two people reclined in a similar position, facing away from Anik, their weapons aimed over a ridge. Behind them, a felled moose.

Rotten poachers. Anik unholstered his revolver. He wasn't sure what the thieves were firing at, but the noise of a helicopter's rotors had filled the air moments before. Could be SAR. *These scumbags will wish they'd never entered this park, let alone killed that magnificent animal.*

A return crack from somewhere split the stillness. The poachers ducked. When the miscreants peeked over the rim again, they raised their rifles. Anik aimed at their feet and took the shot. The bullet hit right between them.

The poachers spun onto their backs and dropped their firearms. Anik stood and kept his gun pointed in their direction.

Rachel appeared at his side with the Springfield.

He huffed at her. "I told you to stay with the dogs."

"When you fired, I figured you might need some help, so I secured the team." She eyed the two lying in the snow, their weapons not too far from them, and the dead moose. "No! What a waste of a majestic animal." Then she called out, "*Jerks.*"

One of the poachers slid his hand across the snow.

Anik yelled, "Don't even think of reaching for those. We're both expert shots." Those guys weren't any the wiser. "Get up and step closer to the top of the ridge with your hands held high, then stop."

The degenerates did as directed.

Anik and Rachel cleared the rim and started down the other side toward them.

The same man who reached for the gun crouched as though he'd make a run for it. Anik fired another round near his feet. "Stop right there." The poachers stood like statues. *They're shaking in their boots now. Excellent.*

Rachel picked up the discarded weapons, handed her rifle to Anik, and continued up the incline.

When she reached the top, she said, "A chopper is starting up. It's rising over the next hill. Now it's moving to the clearing between the edge of the woods and this crest."

She shielded her eyes from the afternoon sun. "Anik, there's a body on the ground in front of the forest. The rangers are running to it."

"It's probably someone shot by these two idiots. Go on down, and tell them I have a couple of poachers in hand. Take their rifles with you."

"Liam planned to go with the SAR team. You don't suppose—"

Rachel tore down the slope toward the helicopter.

"*Liam!*" Rachel shouted as she neared the chopper. The pilot pointed to the tree line. She dropped the two guns on the ground, surged past the aircraft, and raced to the rangers hunched over a body. "*No! Liam.*"

Two more people joined the rangers.

Rachel slid to her knees beside Liam. "*No.*" Her eyes flooded.

"What are you doing here, Rachel?" asked a familiar female voice.

One ranger said, "He's breathing, miss. We need to get him to the ER."

Rachel nodded, then glanced up at a face with red hair blowing in all directions. "*Deirdre.* Where have you been?"

The rangers lifted Liam onto a stretcher and headed for the helicopter. Rachel turned to her sister. "Never mind. I'll talk to you later." She ran to catch up with the crew. "Can I go with you? Liam is my... boyfriend."

They nodded and helped her into the chopper. The aircraft began to move. "What about my sister and the musher she's with? And poachers are held at gunpoint over there." She pointed toward Anik, standing behind the men with hands in the air.

"Don't worry, miss. The pilot has already called it in. An Army Blackhawk will be here in less than five minutes. Right now, our priority is Ranger Liam."

She reached out her hand and took his. Tears clouded her vision and rolled down her face. She kissed his cold hand, allowing her lips to linger on his skin. *Please, Lord, keep him alive. He has to be okay.*

Chapter Twenty-Five

As the SAR helicopter flew to Fairbanks Memorial Hospital, Liam's complexion grew paler. Rachel's heart tightened. He had to make it. *Please, Lord.* He had to live. She needed him.

"Rachel?" Liam whispered.

"I'm here."

No more response came from him.

As the aircraft touched down on the helipad, ER staff members rushed forward and transferred Liam to a gurney. Rachel followed the emergency room team like a zombie, everything surreal.

The entrance doors swished open. People yelled orders. She continued to follow, though she didn't understand a word anyone said. Someone stopped her outside two swinging doors. A nurse approached. "We're taking him to surgery."

Tears gushed over Rachel's cheeks as the woman helped her to the waiting room.

The rangers' faces were etched with concern. "Don't worry. Liam's in great hands here. He's a strong man, and he's pulled through injuries before. We have to return to base."

She stared at them as they left. Despite others all around her, anticipating news about whomever they had in the ER, Rachel felt all alone.

After she'd sat frozen in place for an unrealized amount of time, her parents came to mind. She yanked her cell out of the parka and selected their cellphone number. Mom and Dad had no idea where she was or what had occurred. "Mom—" Rachel couldn't force the words out. Another flood of tears ensued instead.

"It's all right, hon. Anik phoned and told us what happened. The rangers filled him in on everything, so he called us. We're leaving for Fairbanks and will be with you soon. Stay calm. We're all praying. Anik should be there about the time we arrive. Dad and I will be praying all the way there."

"I'm so scared he won't make it." Rachel's sobs made it impossible for her to say more.

"Just keep praying for him, honey. We're heading out the door now." The call ended.

Rachel stumbled to the information desk. She took a handful of tissues from the box and trudged to her seat. She wiped her eyes and blew her nose, then focused on her cell.

The same nurse who directed her to the waiting area asked, "Can I get you a cup of coffee? I noticed your hands were half frozen."

Rachel gazed up. The young woman had kind brown eyes. "What did you say?"

The scrubs-clad woman repeated her question.

Rachel nodded. Was this real? Or a nightmare? Where were Deirdre and Dan? Surely they were brought to the hospital too.

Anik stood by while the Alaska State Troopers showed up right after the search and rescue team took off with Liam. As the troopers arrested the poachers, one trooper uttered, "You'll wish you'd never even *seen* a moose before this is all over."

Anik, along with the ranger who had stayed with him, surveyed the process. Anxiety ran high to find out if Liam was going to make it. "Lord, please help my pal."

The ranger voiced a solemn, "Amen."

A second helicopter arrived.

After the troopers left with their prisoners, Deirdre, Dan, and the ranger entered the waiting Blackhawk helicopter. Anik rushed to the aircraft. "Do you have any word on Ranger Liam Chadwick, the one those reprobates shot?"

"Not so far. All we've been told is he's at the ER." The Army sergeant pointed his thumb back at Deirdre and Dan. "We have to fly them to Fairbanks Memorial and contact their folks."

Before the copter's door closed, Anik shouted to Deirdre, "Tell Rachel I'm on my way. I'll leave as soon as I take my dogs home."

"I'll tell her. You be careful, Anik."

He raced to his dogs, who greeted him with eagerness to resume their run. He took Boss and Tracker's heads in his gloved hands one at a time and told each of them what a fantastic job they had done. When he gazed up at the full team, twenty-eight eyes concentrated on him, waiting for his signal to mush again. *Nothing like peering down the barrel of a fully loaded dog team, itching to be off.* He stood in position and called out the word they craved. "Hike!"

The dogs outdid themselves with their speed getting Anik home. He grinned. They had sensed his urgency. If ever he'd doubted his furry brothers had a genuine connection to him, this disproved it.

Anik settled his dogs in, jumped into his Jeep, and took off for Fairbanks. He'd have to call the neighbor to care for them while he was gone. He wished he could have gone with the helicopter, but he couldn't leave his team out there.

What seemed like hours later, he pulled into the hospital parking lot. As he exited the vehicle, a red Chevy Tahoe parked in the slot across from him. "What's *he* doing here?" Anik waited.

Gibson slipped out of the driver's seat. Mr. O'Rourke got out of the passenger side and opened the rear door for his wife.

Anik clamped his mouth shut. *Rachel will not be happy about this situation.* He waved, then rushed to the hospital entrance.

When Anik stepped off the elevator, Rachel ran to him. "*Anik—*" She buried her face in his parka.

He hugged her. "Did they say anything about Liam's condition?"

She shook her head. Uncontrollable weeping followed, and words failed her. Her eyes stung as if on fire.

"I'm sorry, sunshine." Anik held her and rubbed her neck. "He'll pull through this. Liam's as tough as they come. Let's sit."

After her tears were dried, Rachel said, "You haven't called me sunshine since I was a kid. I've missed it."

He motioned toward a chair. "I'll do it more often. You were such a ray of sunshine to me when I suffered from gloom and doom. Always treated me as though I was part of the family... like a *real* big brother. I guess it's why I've been so protective of you."

"You *are* a big brother. Kalen thinks of you that way too."

"Yeah, and he treats me like I'm an annoying one." Anik laughed. "By the way, now that Deirdre has been found, Kalen called and said he had to go back to school. I promised I'd keep him informed of Liam's condition. If you need him, he'll come home."

He was the best little brother a girl ever had. Rachel pressed her lips together and caught a stray tear with a tissue.

"Speaking of siblings, are Deirdre and Dan here? SAR said they were bringing them to Fairbanks."

"I haven't seen them come in. They appeared to be remarkably well at the park in the brief moment I saw them, considering. Praise God. He watched over them." The waterworks restarted, but she mopped her face with tissues.

"The ranger who stayed to help me with the poachers said Dan took outstanding care of them out there." Anik smiled. "Despite the fact he got them lost."

The O'Rourkes stepped off the elevator, followed by Jess Gibson. Rachel sucked in a sharp intake of air. "What's he doing here?"

"My exact thought when I saw him in the parking lot." Anik squeezed her shoulders. "Don't let him rattle you. I hurried ahead of everyone and meant to tell you he was on his way with your mom and dad before they came up. When you were so distressed, I forgot."

She smiled at Anik in return. "It's all right. I needed your strength and support more than a warning about Mr. Gibson." Upon their approach, Rachel stood and hugged her mother. Her dad was next. She nodded toward her employer. Why did he have to show up? This was hard enough without him here.

With a sympathetic expression, her boss remained quiet.

Rachel retook her seat while Anik moved over to allow her mother and father to sit on either side of her. Mr. Gibson lowered himself to a spot next to Rachel's father.

Her mother enclosed Rachel's hands in her own. "Have they told you anything yet?"

"No." Again, her eyes brimmed with moisture. She sniffed.

"Where are Deirdre and Dan?" her father asked. "All we were told was that they were en route to Fairbanks."

Chapter Twenty-Six

Rachel's eyes had closed as she leaned her head on her father's shoulder. When she awoke, she found everyone slumped in the same position as before. How long had she slept? The double two-way doors swung outward, and a man in peacock blue scrubs and a light blue surgical cap covering most of his silver hair stepped out. He headed their way, his expression sober. Rachel jumped out of the chair and rushed to him. "Is Liam okay?"

The rest of the group joined her. The doctor stopped in front of them as his eyes roamed from one person to the next.

Rachel repeated more urgently, "Is Liam all right?"

The surgeon's lips rose in a smile. "Are you Rachel O'Rourke?"

"Yes, I am. How's Liam?"

"I'm Dr. Fenelli. Ranger Chadwick will be as good as new in no time. That's one tough young man. He woke up for a moment and begged me to let you know what happened. He'd heard your voice, though he was unconscious during the flight."

"Is he awake? Can I see him?"

"No, he's in recovery. His condition is still serious. The bullet nicked his liver, and we had a time controlling the bleeding. The flight paramedic onboard with the SAR team did an outstanding job with the wound, but the bleeding started again when we brought him into the OR. He's all patched up now, but you won't be able to see him until he's conscious and stable. Then he'll be in ICU. You should go home and rest. We'll call you when he can have a visitor.

The doctor focused on Rachel's father. "Have any of you been in touch with Ranger Chadwick's family? We haven't been able to get through. One of the staff said Hurricane Idalia had caused significant high winds and power outages in Florida's coastal Big Bend region. The storm may have triggered localized service disruptions."

Her dad nodded. "That's probably what happened. We haven't been able to contact them either. But we'll keep trying."

Rachel felt a hand on her shoulder and spun to see who it was. "*Deirdre.*" Rachel hugged her sister tightly. "I'm so glad to see you. Is Dan here too? Where have you been?"

"No, to 'is Dan here.' His mom and dad came and drove him back to Healy. We're both fine, just tired. They had us in the ER for the longest time."

Her father placed his arm around Rachel and Deirdre, then addressed the surgeon. "We're all from Healy, so we'll be here at least until Liam's out of danger. We'll find a room nearby."

Rachel folded herself into her father's embrace as her tears turned into another waterfall.

Her employer broke through the uncomfortable silence. "Since Rachel's apartment is on the other side of town, and I live down the street from here, you're all welcome to come to my place and get some sleep while you wait."

No. She found her voice. "I'm not leaving." She headed for the chair against the wall and sat.

Her mother shrugged. "It's very kind of you to offer, Mr. Gibson, but I need to stay with Rachel."

He nodded. "Anyone else?"

"I'm super tired, Mom," Deirdre said after a huge yawn. "Maybe I should have let Dan's parents drop me off at home, but I wanted to be here with my sister." Deirdre lowered herself next to Rachel and took her hand. "But I'd still like to stretch out somewhere warm."

"Dee, you should rest, but you can't stay at Mr. Gibson's house alone." Rachel lifted her eyes and took in the group. "Why don't you all join Mr. Gibson? I'll be fine."

"I'm not leaving you, hon. You've had a traumatic day." Her mother turned to her father and hugged him. "Since you've been up for so long, you and Deirdre go."

"Thanks, but there's no way I'm leaving you and Rachel here by yourselves." He tried to stifle a yawn, but it won the battle.

"I had a snooze while Rachel napped." Anik placed his hand on the older man's shoulder. "I'm set for another few hours. You and Deirdre can leave." Anik faced Rachel and her mother. "I'll take care of them."

"If you're sure. I guess I could use some shuteye." Rachel's dad hugged and kissed his wife. "Call me when Liam's awake."

She returned his embrace. "I will, dear."

Rachel's boss moved in front of her and squatted. "I hope Liam recovers soon. Don't worry about your job. Consider these sick days." He covered the clenched hands in her lap with one of his. "I can see how much he means to you." He stood, faced her father, and said, "Don't rush. I'll meet you at my car."

Rachel watched as Mr. Gibson strode to the elevators. He meant that.

Anik held up his index finger. "Be right back."

As the elevator arrived, Anik caught up with Jess Gibson. "Mind if I ride down with you? Thought I'd get a cup of coffee at the cafeteria to keep from dozing while I wait with Rachel and Mrs. O'Rourke."

They stepped into the car, and Gibson pressed the number one button. Silence filled the space.

Anik eyed the man. "You really care about her, don't you?"

"Of course I do. She's my employee." The elevator opened on the ground floor, and Gibson got out.

Anik followed him toward the entrance. When they came to the doors, Anik grabbed the man's arm. "That's not what I meant. You wanted more of a relationship with Rachel than just being her boss. You *wanted* a romantic one. Do you love her?"

Gibson turned and pinned Anik with a stare. "I wouldn't know. Infatuation, or caring deeply for her. I never had a chance to see what could develop." With a hard look, he started for the exit again.

"I believe it's safe to say you were at the care-deeply stage."

The newsman halted, then whirled. "What difference does it make now? She's obviously in love with the ranger."

Anik grinned. "Yes, she is. But your concern for her means a lot. I feel that way about her too. Always have, but not the way Liam does. My desire is for her to be happy. I'm guessing that's where you are. Right?"

A flicker of a smile appeared on Rachel's boss. "You're right. I want her to be happy too. She's a special lady."

Anik held out his hand to Mr. Gibson. "Take care of Deirdre and Mr. O'Rourke. They're pretty special too."

"I will. Tell Rachel I'll bring them back when we receive the call that Liam's awake. Thanks, Anik."

"Thank you, Mr. Gibson."

As Anik saluted him, Rachel's boss chuckled. "Drop the Mister. It's Jess."

The man left the building and walked into the parking lot.

Hopefully, this would make the atmosphere better for Rachel at her job. Anik grimaced. If only she didn't have to work here in Fairbanks.

How long of a recovery would Liam have ahead of him? Her being over a hundred miles away would be hard on him when he returned to Healy. On both of them.

After her sister and father left the floor to meet Mr. Gibson in his car, Rachel and her mother settled in on the waiting room chairs.

Anik strode up with a huge grin. One side of Rachel's lips lifted. "You look like you scored big at a race. What gives?"

"I had a quick talk with your boss. I think conditions will be a lot easier for you at your job from here on."

"Anik! What did you do?" Her insides bristled.

"Nothing." His face lit up. "I asked him if he was in love with you." He showed his pearly whites.

Her mother snickered.

Rachel's jaw lowered. "You didn't." She clamped her mouth shut for a second. "You may have made things worse for me... if I *have* a job anymore."

His head shook. "Don't panic. Gibson knows you love Liam. Your boss wants you to be happy. I *made* him admit he cared deeply for you. He'll not be harassing you."

She sighed. "I hope you're right. I always liked Mr. Gibson before he started hounding me for dates."

Her mother stretched her arm across Rachel's back. "We all owe Anik a thick, juicy steak for all he's done for us today." She patted his cheek. "And I plan on making you one as soon as we're home again. Plus, some of your favorite chocolate chip cookies. How does that sound?"

"Fantastic to me. Thanks." He eased down next to Rachel. "Guess we'd better make ourselves comfortable."

Her brows knit.

She wouldn't be comfortable until Liam awakened, and she could talk to him. *Lord, let him recover quickly.* The dread that had overcome her when Liam was so still in the snow gripped her heart once more.

Chapter Twenty-Seven

It felt as if someone had poured glue into his eyes as Liam pried them open. Noises buzzed in his head, and he forced his eyes to focus. Darkness met him, except for a glow from what he guessed was a nurses' station across a distance from his feet. He strained to sit up but immediately regretted the effort. "O-o-o-oh."

A nurse flew into his cubicle. "Where does it hurt?"

"Everywhere. I tried... to sit up."

"You shouldn't move much. You've been badly wounded. Lie still." She offered him some water from a tumbler with a plastic straw sticking out of the top. Had H^2O ever tasted so refreshing?

"Is Rachel here? I thought... the doctor said... she was in... the waiting room. Can I... see her?"

"It's one in the morning. She's no doubt gone home."

No, she wouldn't. "You don't know... Rachel... like I do." He hadn't known her *long*, but he did know her *well*. "Please check. If she's here... can she come in? She must... be worried."

The nurse peeked in both directions out the doorway, then ground her teeth. "I shouldn't do this, but I'll ask if she's still here. If I let her in, it'll only be for a brief visit." She gave him a sympathetic expression. Then she left the room and spoke to another nurse at the desk across the hall from his bed.

Minutes later, Rachel entered Liam's cubicle. The glow on her face was more welcome than a rainbow after a storm.

"Remember, only a short while." The nurse stepped out.

Rachel was at Liam's side in a flash and held the hand he offered. "I've been so worried about you."

"I can imagine how... I would have been... if you were shot. But God... took care of me. I heard you... talking to me... in the helicopter. The doctor said... I had a close call." He drew in a deeper breath. "But I'll be normal... in no time. Only... I need... to get... rest..."

"I'd better go. You're drifting off. But I won't be far." She smiled at him and gently brushed her fingers over the stubble on his chin. Rachel released his hand and leaned in without bumping him. She softly kissed his lips. "Sleep. I'll see you later this morning." She lifted a lock of hair off his forehead and turned to leave.

"Rachel?"

She swiveled. "Yes?"

"I love... you." His eyes drifted shut.

Rachel's heart pinched. She rushed to his side and touched his chest, but he didn't move. "Liam?" She ran out of the cubicle to the nurse's station. "*Nurse.* Can you check on Liam?" Her pulse raced with fear he'd passed out—or worse.

The nurse checked the monitor. “Everything is stable.” She glanced up at Rachel.

“I’m sorry. He said… something to me, and then his eyes closed. I spoke his name, but he didn’t respond. It scared me.”

Concern spread across the nurse’s face. “I suppose it did after what he’s been through. Judging from the monitors, he’s asleep. Go on home and rest. We’ll take care of him.”

“So he’s out of danger completely?”

The nurse hesitated. “Dr. Fenelli said the bleeding is under control, and all his vitals are stable. The best thing you can do for him is to relax. Then, be here for him after he wakes again. I promise we’ll contact you if there are any problems.”

Anik popped up when Rachel came out of the ICU. He hurried toward her. “How’s Liam?”

Tears flooded her eyes, and Anik’s stomach lurched. He grabbed her shoulders. “What happened?”

“Nothing. I’m sorry. He got tired and fell asleep. But it scared me. Then the nurse said everything was fine.” She swiped the moisture from her eyes with her hands.

“Whew! That’s a relief.”

Rachel eyed the chairs where they had sat with her mother. “Where’s Mom?”

“She woke up and went in search of a cup of cocoa. She’ll be right back.”

Anik led Rachel to the seats. “So… shall we join everyone at Jess’s place? I have a hunch Liam will be out for a while, and you need to sleep.”

“That’s what the nurse suggested. I guess we can. We can tell them where we’ll be. Oh, do you *know* where Mr. Gibson lives? I’ve never been there.”

Anik pulled a business card from his pocket. "He gave me this before we parted downstairs." Anik flipped the card over. Jess had written his address and cell number. "He said to come no matter the hour, so I'll call him. You sit here and wait for your mom. I'll see if the nurses have all our numbers."

A terrified mien came across Rachel's face.

"Don't worry. God's brought Liam through this far. He will not abandon him."

After she sat, Anik strode to the ICU. At the glass entry, he waved to the nurse. When she came to the door, he told her where they'd be until morning. "Take care of my pal. He means a lot to us."

She assured him they would.

By the time Anik returned to Rachel, her mother had arrived with two cups of hot chocolate from a vending machine near the cafeteria. "Be careful, hon. It's steamy. I thought you'd be with Liam longer. This was for Anik, but I'm sure he'll want you to have it." Her brows raised.

He nodded. "Go ahead. I'll grab a cup before we leave."

"Where are we going?" Mrs. O'Rourke's forehead rumpled. "Is Liam all right?"

"He's fine, Mom. He fell asleep. The nurse suggested we leave." Rachel grimaced. "They'll call if anything changes."

Her mother let out a long breath. "I'm so glad. So now what?"

"We go to Mr. Gibson's." Anik helped her sit with the hot liquid in her hand. "I have his address and number. We could all use sleep. Then we'll come to the hospital in the morning. He's in excellent care, and the worst is over."

Chapter Twenty-Eight

As she pried her eyes open, Rachel squinted at the sunlight trying to sneak around the window curtains. Voices came from outside the door. She vaguely remembered her mother having directed her to Mr. Gibson's guest room in the wee hours of the morning, where Deirdre sprawled out on one side of the king-size bed. Her sister hadn't stirred when Rachel joined her, but now, nobody but herself occupied the space.

She threw her legs over the edge and found her boots. Huh! She was still fully clothed. Her stomach let out an unearthly sound and gnawed at her insides. Although she'd had a bite to eat here and there like the rest of the family, she hadn't really thought about food since before Deirdre had gone missing.

Rachel caught a glimpse of her image in the mirror behind the masculine, dark-oak dresser and attempted to tame the unruly mess on top of her head. She straightened her clothes and sped out of the room.

The first face she encountered was her father's. "Good morning, sweetheart. I hope you got enough rest." Her father pulled out a chair next to him in the dining area.

"Yes, thank you, Dad." As she sat, she gazed around the condo, which had an open floor plan with no walls separating the kitchen from the living and dining rooms. Tall French doors, leading to a balcony from the large room, provided a spectacular view of the woodlands that surrounded the complex.

Her mother strolled into the kitchen, and then brought Rachel a cup of coffee. "Did you sleep well? I slept like a rock once my head hit the pillow."

"Where did you sleep, Mom?"

Rachel's boss strode through the front door, arms loaded with a box and three white bags.

"Mr. Gibson was kind enough to give up his bed for your father when they arrived last night. I joined him."

"Not a problem at all, Mrs. O'Rourke. I'm used to falling asleep in my comfortable recliner." Mr. Gibson placed the bakery box on the dining table. He opened it to display an array of pastries and then dumped a pile of biscuits onto an empty platter beside the sweets.

Rachel spotted four kinds of cereal, milk, sugar, orange juice, and chocolate syrup on a credenza next to the wall. She turned to Anik. "Where did you sleep last night? You had to be as tired as the rest of us."

"You'd better believe it. I stretched out on the futon in the living room. It's memory foam."

As Mr. Gibson opened the oven's warming drawer and returned with a huge pan full of scrambled eggs, he said, "Hope everyone is hungry."

"This is wonderful." Her mother smiled at Mr. Gibson. "You are quite the host."

"I've had a lot of experience schmoozing some of our clients." He grinned. "Plus, I eat a substantial breakfast. Don't be shy. I have plenty of eggs to scramble if we run out of this batch."

Deirdre giggled, and Mr. Gibson winked at her.

"Has the hospital called?" Rachel asked.

"Not yet." Her father scooped up a healthy helping of eggs and plopped them onto his plate.

Mr. Gibson brought in a platter of crispy fried bacon and added it to the food on the table. "They probably won't call until Liam is awake and has been checked over. If we don't hear from the hospital by the time we finish eating, I'll call them and find out what I can. I'm friends with quite a few of the staff."

Was this the same man she'd worked with for the past months? She couldn't believe the change in his attitude. "Thank you, Mr. Gibson."

He raised a finger as if to say something, but then dropped his hand and sat down.

Rachel's cell rang.

Rachel walked into the ICU and approached Liam's cubicle. Her heart almost stopped at the sight of an empty bed. *No!* She rushed to the nurse's station. "Where's Liam Chadwick? They said I could visit now. But he's not there. He didn't—"

"It's okay, miss. Mr. Chadwick was transferred to a regular hospital room." The nurse wrote the number on a sticky note and gave Rachel directions.

As her hand covered her heart, Rachel let go of the breath she'd held. She hurried into the waiting area and told everyone the good news. "That means he's finally out of danger, Mom. I'm so relieved." Rachel's chin quivered as tears gathered. She fought to keep them under control.

"I know you are, hon. He'll be up and back to his normal self in no time."

The group found their way to the third floor and located Liam's room. Dr. Fenelli stepped out, allowing the door to close behind him. "Looks like you all got some rest, while my patient did the same. Take turns with your visits. Mr. Chadwick is still pretty weak. Only two of you at a time and for no more than five or ten minutes, with a break in between."

Butterflies took flight in Rachel's stomach. *Thank You, Lord, for taking care of Liam and answering my prayers.*

"Go ahead, sis." Deirdre squeezed Rachel's shoulder. "Liam's no doubt just as anxious to see you. Anik wants to check up on him too. The rest of us can wait." She caught her mother's eye, and both parents nodded.

Rachel hugged Deirdre. Her sister had grown up fast over the last few days.

With Anik right behind her, Rachel entered the room.

A grin stretched across Liam's face. "I was afraid you'd all driven back to Healy after you left early this morning." He held out his hand to her.

She slipped her fingers into his not-too-strong grip, leaned over, and kissed his cheek. "There was no way I was leaving here until I had assurance from the doctor that you were out of danger."

"Yeah. You had us worried for a while, pal. What were you trying to do with those two-legged weasels over the rise behind you?" He reached across the bed and clasped his friend's hand. "Glad you'll be okay. I'd hate to break in a new landlord." He chuckled.

Liam shook his head. "Stupid mistake. I was afraid Deirdre would get shot. Didn't think it through very well, did I?" A weak laugh followed, and he winced. "Remind me not to laugh again for a few days."

As she stroked his arm, Rachel's heart broke at the pain he had to be in. "Mom, Dad, Deirdre, and Mr. Gibson are all eager to visit. We went to my boss's condo while you were sleeping."

Liam gave her a puzzled expression.

"It's all right. Mr. Gibson seems to have had a personality transplant since you were shot. He was a perfect gentleman and quite the host." With the waiting room only a few steps away, she moved close and lowered her voice so only Liam and Anik could hear. "He's changed his attitude."

Liam's head tilted to one side, and he smiled. "I have a lot to talk to you about."

Anik's eyes opened like saucers, and he pressed his lips together for a moment. "Guess that's my cue to leave you two lovebirds alone for a few minutes. Take your time, Rachel." He turned to Liam. "Call when they say you'll be released. I'll come and pick you up."

"Thanks, buddy... for what you did out there and for taking care of Rachel. One of the rangers called and filled me in on everything."

After Anik saluted Liam, left the room, and joined the others in the waiting area, she faced Liam. "While I was still here in the early hours of this morning, you said something to me before you fell asleep."

"I was hoping you heard me. Wasn't sure I said it out loud, I was so woozy."

"Oh, I heard it, but did you mean to say it?"

"If what you heard was 'I love you,' I promise I meant every word."

She sat in the chair next to his bed. "How is that possible? We haven't known each other for more than two weeks."

"Some things are not measured in time, Rachel, but by the heart. I'd do anything for you. I'd go anywhere for you. I love you. It's as simple as that."

If she were any happier, she'd burst. How could this have happened? A tear spilled over onto her cheek. "I have a confession. I love you too, Liam. This is all a little confusing. But there's one thing I'm positive about. I can't imagine life without you." She stood and lowered her lips to his.

He held her head in place with his free hand. When they both came up for air, Liam said, "Sweetheart, those are the sweetest words anyone has ever said to me."

She blushed. "I guess I'd better let Mom and Dad in to see you. They've been concerned. But can we keep our love for each other a secret until you're out of the hospital? Dad will have lots to say, and I don't want him to give you a third degree... yet." She giggled.

"Mum's the word. For now."

Rachel's mom and dad came into Liam's room. Mrs. O'Rourke smiled. "We finally got in touch with your parents and told them you're already on the mend. Needless to say, they were relieved. Your mother wanted to fly out to be with you right away, but your father convinced her we'd let them know if there was any setback. Apparently, they're dealing with some serious storm damage, but are both well." She handed Liam her cell. "Give your mom a call."

He tapped the number she had pulled up for him. "Hi, Mom."

After assuring her he'd call again as soon as he had his own phone, they hung up. "Thank you, Mrs. O'Rourke. It's a comfort to my mom that you're all with me." He gave the cell back to Rachel's mother.

Mr. O'Rourke took his wife's arm. "We should let others visit. Judging by how you look now, I'm sure you'll have a speedy recovery."

Next, Deirdre and Jess Gibson entered. Liam struggled to keep his surprise at bay when he noticed Rachel's boss leading Deirdre into the room with his hand at her back. *Best not make a comment.* "Deirdre, I'm glad you came out of this so well. How's Dan?"

"Dan's fine now except for a broken ankle. We were both worried that no one would find us. When he lost control of the dogsled, and it ran over a cracked, hidden tree trunk, I heard the bone snap. His expression made me hurt all the way to my toes. Somehow, he managed to turn over the basket and get the dogs under control. We were right next to the edge of the wooded area where you found us.

It took forever for me to drag the sled into the trees while Dan scooted himself along." She took a deep breath.

"The two of you might have frozen out there."

"I know. But fortunately, Dan had packed a couple of space blankets. We huddled with the dog team surrounding us, and that kept us all warm. We searched everywhere for our phones, but they must have flew out into the snow when we overturned. I couldn't find either of them."

"You wouldn't have gotten through anyway. You were in a dead zone. What about the poachers? Did you see them before search and rescue showed up?"

"Yes, but we kept a low profile. How did you find us?"

Liam grinned. "The Mylar sheets were a perfect beacon. The sun reflected on them."

"Thanks for searching for us. And I'm so sorry you were injured in the process. Rachel was beside herself with worry. She really cares about you."

His grin grew. "I feel the same about her."

"Duh. I'd never have guessed." She pressed her lips together, but the giggle came through anyway.

Gibson inspected the floor.

Deirdre moved closer to the bed. "Well, I'll leave and let you rest. I'm sure Rachel wants to come in one more time. Can I hug you first?"

"Of course, as long as it's not a tight one." He grit his teeth.

She gave him a gentle squeeze.

Gibson stepped forward. "Liam. I apologize for how I acted when I came to Healy. I have no excuse except for green-eyed envy." The man held out his hand.

Liam eyed the man's hand and then grabbed it. "Are you in love with Rachel?"

Jess shook his head. "After a talk with Anik last night, I realize my feelings were not as deep as love, though I do care for her, both as my employee and because she's such a remarkable person. Competition is what I had a problem with. I resented that you showed up and hit it off with her right away when I'd been trying to get her to go out with me for months. All my life, I've always managed to get whatever I wanted, and I'm competitive by nature. It's how I've gotten where I am. Guess I scared Rachel off with it. But I saw how much she cares for you. Hope we can all be friends."

"Thanks." *I believe he means it.*

"As Deirdre said, Rachel will want to come back in for a while. This morning, I convinced everyone to stay in Fairbanks for another night so they would be fully rested before driving back to Healy. Anik, along with Mr. and Mrs. O'Rourke are welcome to remain at my place. Deirdre wants to stay at Rachel's apartment.

"If it's okay with you, I'll stop in tomorrow. Call if you need anything. Here's my card." He put it on the table next to the bed. "Hope you make a quick recovery. She needs you."

He followed Deirdre out.

Hmm. Not such a bad guy after all.

Chapter Twenty-Nine

While Liam recovered in the hospital the following week, Rachel stayed in her Fairbanks apartment and visited him every day. Her father and Anik had returned her car to Fairbanks, then went back to Healy. Mr. Gibson made sure her assignments at the paper were super light.

Liam took a deep breath and blew it out slowly. What would life be like when he went home to Healy, and she remained in Fairbanks? No telling how long they'd be apart. Not sure he'd handle that well.

The day before he was to be released, Rachel and her boss arrived in Liam's room at the same time.

After a few pleasantries, Mr. Gibson stood from the chair in the corner. "Liam, I've suggested to Rachel that I drive the two of you to Healy. This way, while she helps you settle in, I'll stop over at the Denali kennels. We need more pictures, and I was a cameraman at the beginning of my career. The photos will add more interest when

I run Rachel's article in the paper. Then she and I can drive back home on Sunday."

Rachel's jaw dropped open.

Something didn't sit right with Liam about the arrangement. For one, her *real* home was in Healy, and two, Rachel obviously wasn't in agreement. *Am I the one who's jealous now?* "I hoped Rachel would have more days off to stay in Healy. There won't be much for me to do while I wait to be released for work."

She smiled at him. "I planned to ask for the rest of my vacation." She turned to her boss. "I realize it's short notice, but I don't have an assignment yet. All I've written lately are those small items to fill spaces in the columns—fun facts, inspiring quotes, etcetera. That job could be done by anyone on the staff. I'd appreciate it, Mr. Gibson."

"*Tsk tsk.* You will *never* call me Jess, will you?"

She gave him a half-grin. "Not while you're my employer. Regarding the trip to Healy, Anik offered to drive up until I called and told him I'd bring Liam home myself. I'll need my car in Healy. Mom will have me running all over creation in preparation for Thanksgiving dinner in a week."

Mr. Gibson narrowed his eyes.

Liam took Rachel's hand in his and waited for the man's reaction and answer to her petition for more time off. *This should tell us where Rachel's boss stands since it goes against his plans.*

Her boss pressed his lips into a straight line. "If you were any other reporter for the *Star,* I'd say no. But... because you've proved yourself valuable to our publication—and under the circumstances—yes, you may take your vacation. Put in your request. You're fortunate my sister is part of our team and in charge of scheduling. She won't say anything to anyone about the break in protocol once I talk with her." He picked up his parka and stepped to the door. "I'll see you both in Healy."

"Thanks for stopping by, Mr. Gibson." Liam tilted his head.

With a chuckle, Rachel's boss halted. "Please drop the mister. You're not my employee, so you can call me Jess." He strode out. His footfalls clicked down the quiet hall to the elevator.

Rachel hadn't left Liam's side. He peered up at her. "What do you make of that?"

"What? The part where he wanted to drive us to Healy, or that he wanted to drive me back to Fairbanks, or when he let me have a vacation to stay in Healy with you, or—"

Liam laughed, though it pulled on the tender areas of his wound. He winced. "All of it."

"I'm not sure. Perhaps he's trying to make up for how he acted before you got shot. But he also acts like the old Mr. Gibson, as he did when I first started working at the paper. He was polite and kind then. I doubt he has any ulterior motive if that's what you're worried about. At least I don't think so."

As she sat in the chair next to Liam, he kissed her hand. "My only concern is that he'll hit on you again the way he did before once, once I'm back at work in Healy and you're here. You're probably right, though. He's being considerate."

The nurse poked her head in the door. "Ready for your exercise?"

Liam grimaced. "Definitely. Even if it's only to get from one end of this unit to the other and back." He raised the head of the bed higher and swung his legs over the edge.

She retrieved a second hospital gown from the cabinet and helped Liam put it on backward to fully cover him, though he could have managed on his own.

The nurse reached out into the hall and slid a walker into the room. His grimace deepened. "I keep telling you I'm not ancient yet." But he supposed they couldn't take the chance of his getting a dizzy spell.

With a titter she said, "Now you know this is hospital policy—to ensure you don't have an accident. I suggest you use a cane or two at home for the first couple of days."

He huffed. "Okay, nurse." He glanced at Rachel and shrugged. "Time to do my laps."

She pressed her lips together in an obvious attempt to keep her mirth under control.

When Liam returned from his exercise around the hospital floor, his facial features were as relaxed as when he left the room. Joy at how he'd come through his injury flooded Rachel. "You bounced back fast." Eleven days ago, her heart had almost broken in two as she watched Liam lie unconscious in the helicopter as they rushed to the hospital. *I'll never stop saying thank You for this gift, Lord.*

"I've always been a fast healer." The nurse took the walker, and Liam sat in the armchair in the corner. "The few times my folks had to rush me to the ER with a gash or deep cut, my skin was closing up when we got there." He shrugged. "By the way, did your parents tell you they invited my family to Thanksgiving dinner?"

Rachel nodded. She grabbed one of the blankets from his bed and tucked it over his bare legs. "It's cold in this room. Yes, Mom told me this morning when I called with an update on your release tomorrow. They can't wait for you to be up and around."

"Neither can I. Any news on Dan's ankle? I hope he won't have trouble with it once it heals."

She shook her head. "Deirdre says his doctor expects a full recovery with no problems, but she'll never go in his sled again." Rachel chortled.

"Well, accidents happen to mushers, hikers, and climbers. It's one of the reasons we rangers are out on patrol. Still, when I see Dan on Sunday, I'll talk with him. He needs to gain more experience before he tries mushing in such an isolated area again, especially if he plans to participate in the Iditarod. Maybe Anik should chat with him too."

"He's already beaten you to it. Anik says he'll spend some time with Dan."

"Anik's guidance is exactly what Dan needs."

Liam's dinner arrived, and Rachel rolled the bedside table in front of him. "I think I'll run down to the cafeteria and grab a bite."

He lifted the dish cover and took a whiff. "Mmmm. Smells great. They do have tasty food here at the hospital. I'll give them that."

When her stomach voiced its complaint, she hurried to the door. "I'm going to find the cafeteria. Be back in a little while."

Rachel hadn't eaten since five a.m., when she gave up trying to sleep. The anticipation of Liam going home tomorrow had made her toss and turn all night. And up until she got her own whiff of Liam's dinner, she'd been too excited to eat. After she woke up, she'd had only a piece of toast with a cup of coffee for breakfast before leaving for the hospital.

She stepped into the elevator, and her stomach let out a loud, angry growl. "All right, I'll feed you."

When she entered the cafeteria, she spotted Mr. Gibson sitting at a table not far from the entrance. He seemed perplexed.

Rachel chose a hamburger, chips, and a fresh pear for dinner. Mr. Gibson would probably be gone by the time she got through this long procession of hungry hospital staff members and guests of patients.

It took almost twenty minutes before she stood before the register and paid for her food.

When she entered the seating section, Mr. Gibson still sat in the same place. She approached him. "Thought you went home."

He held a startled expression, as if he'd been caught with his hand in the cookie jar. "Ah, yeah. I had planned to do that, but caught the aroma of food as I neared the door to the parking lot. Hard to resist. Grabbed a quick bowl of soup and was letting it settle while I did some people watching." He grinned in a sheepish manner.

Uh-huh. Could it be possible he'd fallen for her? Maybe that would account for the perplexed expression. Had he been hurt because she chose Liam over him? She hadn't considered it and never meant to hurt him.

"Look, Mr. Gibson. If I hurt you in any way—"

"Hurt me? Why would you say that? Oh, Liam must have told you about my apology to him. No, I wasn't hurt. Let's just say I competed with him to get a date with you and lost. That's all. Don't worry about it." He jumped up from the chair as if it had been loaded with a spring. "I'd better go before the mice at the paper become too playful without the cat around." He snickered.

The attempted jovial sound struck her as a little too nervous. Was she thinking too highly of herself to believe he had actually been interested in her romantically? The stories circulated at work portrayed Mr. Gibson as some kind of playboy.

She kept her eye on him as he rushed out of the hospital and into the parking lot. He turned his head left, then right, and left again, as if he'd forgotten where he parked. *So odd.*

Had her imagination gotten the best of her where Mr. Gibson was concerned?

Chapter Thirty

Liam sat on the edge of the bed, fully clothed in the fresh outfit Anik had run over earlier in the week. He glanced at the clock on the wall. When would the doctor come in, give him his final checkup, and release him? Everyone had been super here at the hospital, but he was ready to leave.

He gazed at Rachel in the armchair, reading an outdated magazine from the waiting room. She seemed relaxed... and so confoundedly patient. He laughed to himself. "Come on, doctor. Sometime early this afternoon would be nice."

She peered up at him with a radiant smile. "Patience, handsome. We'll be heading to Healy before long. Mom said she's making a special dinner to celebrate your release. Anik informed her—after a call to your mother—that your favorite dinner is shepherd's pie." Rachel bit her bottom lip. "Your impatience makes you appear as though you've been imprisoned."

He chuckled. "Well, in a way, I have. Can't make a move without permission around here. But the staff has been wonderful."

Dr. Fenelli waltzed into the room, followed by a nurse. "Always glad to know our staff is doing their jobs well, Ranger Chadwick."

"Doc, I'm thrilled to see you." Liam grinned wide enough that his cheeks almost hurt.

The doctor went through his routine of final checks, then shook his head.

Liam's nerves tightened. "What's wrong?"

"Oh, nothing. I'm only sorry a compliant patient will leave us. There are a couple of patients on this floor I'd rather send home."

Rachel's brows rose.

Dr. Fenelli smiled at her. "Kidding." He focused back on Liam. "You're good to go. Heed all the instructions the nurse has gone over with you in the discharge packet."

The nurse handed the folder to Liam. "Take care of yourself, Ranger."

Liam clutched Dr. Fenelli's offered hand. "I will. Thanks for everything."

After the doctor left, the nurse brought in a wheelchair.

"What's that for?" Liam scrunched his eyebrows together. "You're joking, right?"

"Again, hospital policy." She snickered.

"Come on, big guy." Rachel laid the magazine on the chair and stepped to the bed. She picked up a bag of items Liam would take with him. "The sooner you get into the chair, the faster we can vacate the premises." She gave him a light tap on the top of his head.

"Okay, okay." He maneuvered into the wheelchair with the nurse's assistance. "But I feel foolish."

As the nurse wheeled him down the hallway, Liam thought about the ride to Healy. He and Rachel. Alone. They could have a serious discussion with no interruptions from anyone.

The nurse pressed the elevator's Down button. A couple of minutes later, the doors opened, and Mr. Gibson stepped out. Rachel narrowed her eyes at him. What was he doing back here? He said he'd drive to Healy this morning. "I thought you'd left. Do you have another acquaintance here?"

He grinned at her and then at Liam. "I slept late. Then I ran over here to find out if you'd already gone. Found out Liam hadn't been discharged yet, so I came up. It occurred to me that the sensible thing would be to follow you to Healy, in case you had to make a stop somewhere... to stretch... or something."

"Why do we need you to be with us?" Rachel led the way into the elevator car.

"Because last night I came up with a new idea for an article. A series on the problems with poachers. I'd like Liam's take on it."

"You couldn't wait until we reached Healy?"

Mr. Gibson shrugged. "Spur-of-the-moment."

"The article sounds interesting." Liam leaned back in the wheelchair as they entered the elevator, and the nurse pressed the main floor button. He glanced up at Rachel and raised his brows.

"Hey, if you two don't want me to follow you, no problem. Say the word, and I'll leave now. I didn't mean to intrude." He stood straight and rigid as a stick as the elevator descended.

When the elevator doors opened, her boss slipped by the nurse and hurried out the doors.

"Mr. Gibson." Rachel shadowed the nurse and Liam, then stopped next to her boss. "I'm sorry if I offended you. Your reasoning sounded odd to me, but that's fine... if you want, we'll drive there together."

He turned and faced her. "That's me. Mr. Odd-fellow. It was only a suggestion."

They stopped at the hospital entrance while Rachel retrieved her key fob from her purse. "I'll pull up the car."

"I parked next to you." Mr. Gibson swung his arm for her to precede him out the door. Together they strode to the vehicles in silence.

After she got in her blue Subaru, buckled her seatbelt, and drove out of the parking space, she entered the queue at the entrance of the hospital and picked up Liam.

When she glanced out the rear window, Mr. Gibson had driven his red Tahoe to a spot where he could fall in line to follow them.

The first few miles of the trip passed quietly as Rachel drove to Lathrop Street and then on to AK-3 S. Mr. Gibson stayed right behind her. As she set the cruise control, she wondered why her boss was so insistent on taking photos of the kennels at Denali himself, or why he wanted to write an article on poachers when he could've assigned the task to another reporter. Baffling.

"Rachel." Liam stared at her. "What's wrong?"

"I'm curious about Mr. Gibson's actions. They're strange."

"I thought we decided he was trying to make up for the way he treated us before. And he did say he needed more pictures in the article."

"Yeah. I guess so." Something still nagged at her.

"Could we talk for a while? Without our conversation cluttered with your boss. I might get jealous." He smiled.

She quirked her lips. "No need to be. What do you want to discuss?"

He sighed. "I hate the idea of your returning to Fairbanks after Thanksgiving. We've spent so much time together, it'll be hard not to be with you when I'm not working. We promised to keep in touch, and we'll see each other on Zoom or FaceTime, but—"

"I've been thinking about it too. What else can we do? I have to work, and my job is in Fairbanks. Yours is in Denali." She gave an over-exaggerated shrug.

"I guess you're right." He sighed. "I wish you could find another position closer to home."

They fell into a comfortable silence for the next half-hour. Liam finally dozed off. Rachel hummed a few hymns as she followed a dump truck in front of her, Mr. Gibson's Tahoe still behind her.

After another quarter of an hour, the taillights on the vehicle before her lit up. She pressed on her brake pedal. It went to the floor. *"Oh, no!"* The brake function light on the dashboard flashed on and off.

Liam bolted straight up from his napping position. "What?"

She pumped the pedal to no avail. Rachel pulled to the left to go around the truck. A line of traffic coming at her made her swing back into the correct lane. She inched farther onto the shoulder and tried to slow down by running the tires along the edge of the rocky wall without flipping the car over. Screeching made her skin crawl. The tires were ruined, but better that than—"This is insane."

"Stay calm, honey. Try to use the emergency brake."

"Stay calm? There's a bridge coming up fast. We have to stop."

Rachel yanked up on the parking brake lever in the center console. Dinging from the brake warning began.

The dump truck picked up speed. As soon as the line of cars coming in the other direction whizzed past, Mr. Gibson's Tahoe zoomed ahead and got in front of her. His taillights lit up as he gradually slowed the vehicle until her Outback tapped his bumper. His Chevy slowed down, and they came to a stop on a flat surface next to the rock face to their right—the bridge dead ahead.

Her boss hopped out of the vehicle and ran to her window. "Are you okay? When you swerved and the brake lights didn't come on, I figured your brakes had failed."

Liam twined his arm around her and kissed her forehead. "She used the emergency brake to slow the car, but I'm glad you pulled in front of us and helped to stop the vehicle."

"This happened to my sister once while I followed her to visit our parents in Canada. Déjà vu set in. The flashback unnerved me." He took a deep breath. "I'm glad I followed you."

"What'll we do now?" Rachel peered into Liam's eyes.

"We'll have to leave the car here and continue to Healy in Jess's truck unless you want to call your dad or Anik to drive out here and get us."

"Seems a little silly when my boss is here." Though she'd rather go with anyone else. Had paranoia set in?

Liam looked past Rachel at her boss. "I'm glad you followed us too. Healy's still a bit too far of a walk for me." He gave Jess a weak grin.

Chapter Thirty-One

Of all the ways to finish the trip, riding with Mr. Gibson was not what Rachel had imagined... nor wanted.

After she secured her car, she joined Liam and her boss in the Tahoe.

Twenty minutes past the town of Nenana, her boss pulled into the parking lot of a roadhouse off AK-3.

She frowned. "Why are we stopping?"

Liam's brows knit. "We're only about an hour from Healy, Jess. Why not continue?"

"Because the tension in this truck is about as thick as lava. I need a break. We can drink a cup of coffee and relax before we continue on to the O'Rourkes' cabin." He glanced from Liam to Rachel. "Besides, I have to relieve myself."

They got out of the Tahoe and headed for the restaurant. When they entered, Mr. Gibson took off for the restrooms.

"Liam, this trip has turned into a nightmare. What do you think went wrong with my brakes?"

"Any number of things." He put his arm around her, and they waited to be seated. "Brake line damaged by road salt or debris? You probably don't find a lot of debris on the streets in Fairbanks, but you drove home for your assignment. The car made another run back to the city when Anik and your dad brought it to you. Now this trek. We'll see what the mechanic says."

She sighed. "I guess I've watched too many crime movies. I thought Mr. Gibson had done something—"

"Shhh. He's coming." Liam squeezed her shoulders. "We'll talk later."

Her boss grinned. "Talk about what later?"

Rachel peeked at Liam. "Oh... nothing important." She bit her lip. Only a small fib.

The hostess returned. "Three?"

Mr. Gibson nodded.

"Right this way." They followed her to an empty table.

"Your waitress will be with you in a moment." She laid their menus in front of them as they sat.

Rachel placed her hand on the folder. "I'm not eating here. Mom has dinner waiting for us in Healy."

"I'll wait too." Liam pushed the menu away.

"Well, I need food." Her boss picked up his menu and perused it. "The motel where I'll stay doesn't have an eatery on-site."

"Mr. Gibson, of course you're invited to dinner at my parents' cabin. Please, can we order coffee and finish the trip?"

He peered up with raised brows. "Well, sure. If you don't think I'll be intruding."

"No intrusion at all."

Liam's knee bumped into hers.

He must've known how difficult it was to tell her employer he was invited. She smiled at him.

The server came to their table and took orders for two black coffees and a caramel cappuccino to go, plus one chocolate chip cookie.

After Mr. Gibson paid for their drinks and the cookie, they followed him back to the truck. He took a bite of the cookie, then pulled onto the highway—now dark and empty.

A chill coursed up Rachel's spine. She'd be glad to get to Healy.

Between the vibes emanating from Rachel and Jess's constant meaningless chatter, Liam was anxious to reach the O'Rourkes' cabin. The man obviously had consumed way too much caffeine today. He'd turned into a motormouth.

"I meant to ask you." Jess glanced at Rachel in the rearview mirror. "When did you last have your brakes checked?"

"When I had my oil changed a few months ago. They were fine."

After a breath, Jess moved on to another senseless topic. Liam let his head fall back and rolled his eyes. Would this trip never end?

When they finally arrived in Healy, Jess turned onto the side street that led to the O'Rourkes' cabin. He pulled into the front yard. "We're here." He hopped out of the driver's seat and hurried to the porch.

"Whew!" Liam eyed Rachel and chuckled. "I've never heard a man talk as much as he did." Liam exited the Tahoe and opened the rear door for her.

"It's not his talking that bothers me."

"What then?" Liam intertwined his fingers with hers as they walked.

"I don't trust him anymore."

"Why?"

"Something's off. Mr. Gibson is hiding something. He could've messed with my brakes when parked next to my car before we left

Fairbanks." She huffed. "Maybe all that's happened lately has made my imagination run wild. My nerves are on edge."

"We'll figure things out when you come over tomorrow. I can't see him wanting to harm us."

"Why does my boss insist on more pictures of the kennels? We have plenty. And why write the article on poachers himself when he has an entire staff of reporters, any one of whom would do a terrific job? It makes little sense."

"Let's go in. I haven't had shepherd's pie since Mom last visited me." Liam grinned at her. "We'll hash this out in the morning."

"You're right, honey." She giggled. "Do you mind if I call you that?"

"I called *you* that, too, but I like it. Then again, I'd treasure any endearment you'd choose."

"Maybe I'll find something better." She slipped her arm around his elbow and hugged it to her side. "Did Mr. Gibson say where he has a reservation? I hope it's not close."

Liam agreed. "I don't recall him mentioning a place."

Anik showed up at the O'Rourkes' in time for dinner. "Mmmm, I know that aroma—shepherd's pie." Perfect.

Rachel welcomed him into the cabin. "I figured you'd waltz in any moment." She laughed. "You must have radar that detects Mom's cooking."

He ignored her tease. "Where is he?"

"Who?"

Anik peeked into the living room. "Hey, pal." He entered the room and sat down next to Liam. "I expected a call hours ago. What took you guys so long?" Anik gave Liam a gentle shoulder hug. "You look more recovered than when I saw you last."

"Yeah. I feel healthier too."

"Welcome back, Kalen." Anik shook his hand. "Nice that you were able to come home again for Thanksgiving week."

"Always great to be home."

Anik's jaw clenched when Gibson waltzed into the room. What? Why was he back? He'd better not cause trouble for Rachel and Liam. "Jess. I'm surprised to see you here. What brings you to Healy?"

The man pumped Anik's hand with vigor. "I decided to get additional pictures of the kennels to go with the fantastic article Rachel wrote." He explained how his career in the news business began as a photographer. "I'm also looking for information about poachers for another article to run. I'd like your slant on the crime, along with Liam's."

Gibson parked himself in an armchair. "I've been bored at the paper. Not enough to do. And now with my star reporter unavailable, I'll step up and do my part."

Hmm. Sounded reasonable. "I'd be happy to expound on my *vast* experience." He chuckled. "The rangers and state troopers are the ones you should interview though."

"He's right," Liam added. "You'll get more perspectives."

Jess nodded. "I planned to contact them, but I want to start with you two first, then fill in the gaps."

"Where are you staying?" Anik's brows rose. It had better not be here with the O'Rourkes.

"I reserved a room at a local lodge. How about meeting for lunch tomorrow so I can ask you a few questions? I'll let Liam get settled in before I pull info from his experiences."

"Won't work. Tied up. I promised Dan Harris—the young man Deirdre was with when they got lost at Denali—to review some information about mushing. Why don't we meet for dinner at The Brown Bear Restaurant in Ferry at six? Does that suit you?"

"Yes. Great!"

When everyone finished eating, they retired to the living room to enjoy dessert. Deirdre and Rachel brought in the plates and utensils, and their mother delivered a Black Forest cake.

Kalen wheeled his chair in with a tray of vanilla ice cream and a scoop. Rachel took the items from his lap. "Mom, you created a masterpiece."

Half an hour later, Anik finished his cake, licked residue cherry glaze off his bottom lip, downed his cup of coffee, and rose. "Time to return to the cabin, pal. You're still recovering, remember?"

Liam opened his mouth, but Anik spoke first to Mrs. O'Rourke. "Thank you for the wonderful dinner and dessert. We need to go. I promised the doctor… and Rachel… I'd make sure this guy gets enough rest this week. Just call me the *interim nurse* until Rachel arrives at our place in the morning." He shook Mr. O'Rourke's hand, then held out his arm for Liam to grab onto. "Come on, patient." Anik chuckled.

Liam grimaced. "May I finish my dessert, *Mo-o-om*?" He swallowed the last forkful, drank his coffee, and glared at his friend. "Now I'm finished." He stood and shrugged at Rachel.

She wrinkled her nose. "He's right. You really need to rest as much as possible if you want to be released for duty. I'll be at your place first thing tomorrow and make breakfast for you two."

At the door, she helped Liam with his parka and boots.

Anik donned his coat, hat, and gloves. "I'll wait in the Jeep." He spun and headed for the vehicle.

So, Rachel's boss would be here for a while. Anik cranked the engine and pulled up to the cabin's porch. What was that guy's angle? He sounded sincere, but something was off.

As Anik was about to exit the SUV, the front door of the cabin opened. Rachel had slipped into her coat and walked Liam to the Jeep. The couple took a few moments for their goodnight kiss.

Anik smiled. Made for each other. And no one was going to mess things up for these two, especially not her employer. *Not if I can do anything about it.*

Rachel returned to the living room and helped her mother gather the dirty dessert dishes. She was eager to make breakfast for Liam and Anik. Never thought anticipation of a domestic chore would bring such joy?

Jess entered the kitchen with the remaining cake plates. "I'll make my way to the lodge now. Thank you, Mrs. O'Rourke. Wonderful dinner."

"You're welcome, Mr. Gibson."

"Please. If your daughter won't call me Jess because of her high ethics, can I at least get the rest of you to?" He grinned.

Rachel's eyes narrowed. The suspicion that her boss had tampered with her brakes still nagged at her.

Mom tittered. "Okay, Jess. Since I'm not your employee."

He nodded. "Rachel, the mechanic should put your car back in running order pronto. And I'm glad I was with you to give a hand. I'll say good night."

"Good night, Mr. Gibson. Thank you for bringing us to Healy... and for the assist on the road."

"It was the least I could do. Good night." He left the kitchen.

"Aren't you going to escort him to the door, hon?"

"He knows the way. He's been here before."

Her mother looked at Rachel as if she'd grown another head. "What? Something's wrong. Do you want to tell me about it?" Mom shut off the faucet, her eyes still on Rachel.

Rachel rubbed her neck. "It's probably nothing. I need to think about it."

"Well, when you're ready to explain, I'm here." Mom twisted the water knob on again.

A few minutes later, Deirdre stepped into the kitchen and picked up a dishtowel. Her cheeks glowed as if she'd been outside. She dried a couple of plates before saying, "My, it's quiet in here. What's up? Missing Liam so soon?"

Rachel stuck out her tongue at her sister, but the smile that would have accompanied the action—their way of teasing each other—didn't form. Her mother wiped her hands and left the room.

"Hey, sis." Deirdre stopped drying the dishes. "What's wrong? Liam's okay, isn't he?"

"Yes, he's fine. Or at least he will be once he finishes his recovery at home."

"Then what has you all tied up in knots? You've always made a funny face after you stuck out your tongue in the past."

"Dee... I have this horrible suspicion that Mr. Gibson tampered with my brakes in Fairbanks. It won't leave me. And I don't understand why, except he'd been trying to get a date with me, even here in Healy when he first came. And the way he treated Liam and Anik while he was here the last time—"

"Hey, wait a minute. You're talking like a speeding freight train. Rachel, you've nothing to worry about."

"Why? He was so strange at the hospital. Then, all of a sudden, he acted normal."

"Well, there you go. He was a perfect gentleman this evening. And he helped save you from a crash. If he'd wanted to harm you, he wouldn't have helped stop the car. He drove you and Liam safely here. Doesn't it tell you he didn't do anything to your Subaru?"

"I guess... but why is he still here? Writing his own article? It doesn't make sense."

Deirdre wrapped her arms around Rachel and hugged her. "I heard him say he was bored at the paper. Sis, you're overtired." She let Rachel go. "You need a good night's sleep as much as the rest of us. I'll bet you haven't slept much at all since Liam was shot. First you worried about me, then Liam. I've caused so much trouble for everyone."

"You could be right about fatigue, but it's not your fault. Now, I'm riddled with guilt for thinking my boss had committed a crime."

"Rachel Amber O'Rourke! Don't you start. I mean it. If anyone has anything to be guilty about, it's me. If I hadn't been so angry about you leaving for college without saying goodbye to me, and just talked to you instead, none of this would've happened. We'd have gone on as we always had, without my assuming I'd been neglected. I wouldn't have felt the need to go off with Dan either... maybe. Hope I've grown up since then." She gave her sister another hug. "Please forgive me."

A few seconds passed as they embraced each other. Rachel stepped away and shook her head. "Sis, I've already told you at the hospital I forgave you. All of this could have come about even if you hadn't been mad at me. There has to be a reason God allowed it."

"I guess so."

"Maybe you should pray about it." Rachel crumpled her brows. "I should take *my own* advice." She smiled at her sister. "I'm going to turn in. It's been a day."

On the way up to her room, Rachel pressed her lips together. *Lord, please help me understand what's going on.* It was a terrible thing to accuse her employer of doing. *And, Lord, let the mechanic prove my fears wrong.*

Chapter Thirty-Two

The next morning, Jess waited in the dining room at the lodge, nursing his third cup of coffee. Would she come? She might have had second thoughts about this.

He ran fingers through the clean, tousled hair on his head, now free of the gel he'd used for years to achieve the spiky style as his trademark. He did it for her. She had asked what his hair was like without spikes.

Why was he so nervous? He'd never been like this over a woman before. Not that he'd seen so many. The rumors that floated around water coolers at the paper, saying he was a lady's man, weren't true.

The dining area faded from view as the most beautiful woman Jess had ever met entered. He grinned. She'd come. It hadn't taken this city boy long to realize she was something special.

With graceful steps, her gorgeous, fiery red hair loose around her shoulders, Deirdre sashayed to his table. "Good morning, Jess."

He rose to his feet. "Give me a minute to compose myself. At the sight of you, my pulse sped to the finish line."

She giggled. "You're cute. I like your hair without all the points."

He took a deep breath and pulled out her chair. "Thank you. Have a seat. Did you come hungry? I'm starved."

"Yes, I did. Mom entered the kitchen as I was leaving the house. She was surprised I was up so early. I said I had a meeting and rushed out the door."

Jess shook his head. "At least you didn't tell her a lie. I'm not sure how your family will accept your being involved with me. After all, I am ten years—minus a couple of months—your senior." One side of his mouth hitched upward.

She laughed. "Is that all that's bothering you? I figured your nervousness was over Rachel."

"Why would I be nervous about Rachel?" He frowned.

With the menu in hand, Deirdre leaned forward. "I thought maybe you still wanted her, even though she's head over heels for Liam." Deirdre's eyes locked onto his. "I don't want to play second fiddle to my sister."

"Their ardent attachment is no secret. Plus, Anik made it doubly clear to me. I'm well aware of how she and Liam feel about each other."

He recalled the day the native Alaskan coerced a confession of his true feelings for Rachel out of him. "Your sister's cleverness and character attracted me, but I was never in love with her, though I hated getting beat out by Liam." He grimaced, then chuckled. "You are the *only* fiddle in my orchestra."

She'd told him she never blushed and yet... she blushed. The color made her even more beautiful.

Conversation halted as the waitress, a young teen with a pixie haircut, stopped at the table, order pad in hand. Deirdre placed her index finger on a breakfast offering. "I'll have Eggs Benedict with Greek yogurt and fresh fruit, a cup of coffee with cream, and a glass of orange juice."

"And for you, sir?"

Sir? He pursed his lips. Little Miss Pixie just made him feel older than he already was. *Humph.* "I'll have the short stack pancakes, two eggs over hard, bacon, a bowl of oatmeal with fried apples, espresso, and a glass of chocolate milk." He handed her the menus.

The girl took them and left.

Deirdre stared at him. "Do you always eat so much for breakfast?"

"Yes, I guess I do." He laughed. "I've a high metabolism."

"Chocolate milk too?"

"My mother used to make chocolate milk for breakfast as a treat on holidays." He leaned in. "As an adult on my own, I can drink it whenever I want." He leaned back again. "What did you mean by 'is that what's bothering you'?"

"Huh?"

"When I mentioned our age difference."

"Oh, yeah. Don't worry about my parents' concern about our ages. When Mom and Dad were married, she was eighteen, and he was twenty-seven."

Warmth filled Jess's chest. Then they wouldn't have a problem with his dating Deirdre. He'd been apprehensive ever since the night Deirdre and her father had stayed overnight at his condo. It was a night to remember.

Jess had awakened in the middle of the night to find Deirdre seated at the kitchen table, wiping tears from her eyes. She said she couldn't sleep for fear Rachel's heart would break if Liam died. Jess stayed with her for the rest of the night while he assured the dazzling redhead everything would be okay.

Tears flowed while she told him how she had treated Rachel. He scooted closer and hugged her. Something had happened to him in that moment. It was obvious she felt it too when she gazed up at him.

He had backed away and enclosed her hands in his, though he wanted to hold on to her in the worst way.

Hard to believe how the affection he had for Deirdre came on so fast—so strong. As the old adage said, it had hit him like a ton of bricks.

As he pondered, she chatted, then stopped. She was waiting for a reply. He'd missed whatever she'd said. "I'm sorry, Deirdre. I was lost in the memory of when we stayed up talking all night at my condo. What did you say?"

She started to answer, but the server slid their breakfast plates in front of them. Deirdre closed and puckered her mouth. When the waitress left she said, "It wasn't anything important. I was just rambling on about Mom and Dad."

He smiled. "Let's eat and then we'll take a ride to Denali. We can talk more as I drive."

"Okay. We actually need to discuss a problem concerning Rachel. It's important."

Rachel woke abruptly. She'd slept later than planned. She jumped out of bed and ran to the bathroom. Rushing around to get to Liam's brought back her days at college, when she had overslept. Then she'd have to race to class.

She hadn't reminisced about those days in a long time. Her life had become nothing but rush here, rush there, articles to write, deadlines, and stress, stress, stress. Especially with the way Mr. Gibson had hounded her to go out. Hopefully, his mild harassment had ended.

As she pulled on her jeans, she shot a peek at the clock on her nightstand. *"Hurry, hurry, hurry."*

She ran down the stairs and grabbed her parka.

Her father sat in his recliner in the front room with the paper spread across his lap. "Where are you going in such a five-alarm rush, sweetheart?"

"I promised Liam I'd be over this morning to make breakfast for him and Anik, remember?" She slipped on her boots. "I'm late."

She opened the door and ran out before her dad could say another word.

A quick ride later, she pulled into Liam's drive, exited the loaner car, and hurried to the front door. When she knocked, Liam called out, "Come on in. It's not locked."

He reclined on the couch, propped against a collection of bed pillows, covered in a Sherpa blanket, with two wooden canes stationed next to him. Classical music played on the stereo.

"Don't you look comfy."

He laughed, then winced. "Still hurts if I laugh too hard, so don't make me do that." He grinned.

"What are you listening to? I don't recognize it."

"*The Lark Ascending* by Ralph Vaughan Williams. One of my favorites."

"Nice." With gloves in hand, she pointed at him. "I'm glad you've taken the doctor's orders seriously." She listened but heard no other noise in the house. "Where's Anik? I didn't notice the Jeep where he usually parks."

"He had to meet with Dan a little earlier than planned. He figured you'd be here any minute."

She nodded. "I'll bet Anik set you up like that on the sofa as soon as you woke up this morning." She removed her coat and entered the living room.

"You'd win the wager. He's worse than a mother hen."

"Relax, and I'll get busy in the kitchen. I'll have to apologize to Anik for my being late and his missing breakfast."

Liam took her arm and pulled her down to sit next to him. "Rachel, can we talk first?"

"You sound solemn. Should I worry?"

He traced the side of her face with the side of his index finger, from her high cheekbone to her chin. "Nothing to be uneasy about."

She released the breath she'd held. "What is it?

"We've already talked about how we haven't known each other for long… and you know I love you. I've never felt this way for anyone until now. It's not only a physical thing—although you are the most desirable woman I've ever met." He winked at her. "Like I said, it's something in here." He placed his hand over his heart. "I'm empty when you're not with me, like a part of me is missing."

Tears formed in her eyes. She pressed her lips together. Empty was the same impression she'd gotten when Liam wasn't around... even before he was shot. She assumed she had imagined it. But if it happened to Liam too, it had to be real.

"Liam, I—"

He raised a finger and placed it over her lips. "Let me finish, and then you can tell me to go fly a kite if you don't agree. I'll probably botch this up royally, but I have to say it. I don't want you to go back to Fairbanks. If you do, think I'll shrivel up or go crazy."

Tears spilled over and trickled down her face. She leaned in and gave him a feather-light kiss. As she swiped her wet cheeks, Liam reached out and brushed away the remaining drop with his thumb. "Is this you saying goodbye to me?"

"How could I say goodbye to the only man for whom I've ever felt such love? Those same emotions run through me. The nightmare of your almost dying has nothing to do with—you scared me half to death. Do you know that?" She cupped the sides of his face.

Careful not to lean against him, she wrapped her arms around his neck and kissed him again with more passion.

When they came up for air, she shook her head. "But not going back to Fairbanks is a problem. I have a job... and an apartment. Where would I work here in Healy? And, as much as I love them, I don't want to live with my parents. That was the reason I didn't return after I graduated in the first place."

He took her face in both his hands, cocked his head, and smiled. "I do have some ideas, but I need research. Do you trust me?"

She mimicked his action with her head and ran her fingers over his chin. He hadn't shaved when he got up. The stubble tickled her skin. She giggled. "I trust you with my life, Mr. Chadwick."

Jess escorted Deirdre to his four-wheel-drive Tahoe and helped her climb in. "Shall we find Mount Denali? We'll stop and view it, and you can explain what troubles you."

He hopped in on the driver's side and started the engine.

Once inside the wilderness area, they drove for a while on Park Road before he spotted a beautiful outlook of the mountain and pulled in. "Here's the perfect spot." He turned off the motor. "Tell me if you get cold."

Deirdre clasped her hands and kept her focus on her lap.

"Hey, what's got you so tied up? You said you needed to talk. I'm a great listener... remember?" He tilted his head and searched her face. Her eyes were flooded with tears.

Jess took off a glove and pulled her chin his way with the index finger. "Talk to me."

"Rachel feels super guilty about... well, let's say she... dissed someone... suspected—it's terrible. She's having a rough time—"

"Huh?" He threw his hands up like a traffic cop. "Hold on for a minute. Your sister feels guilty, right?"

Deirdre nodded, and the tears fell.

"About what she suspects someone has done, right?" He opened the storage compartment in front of her, pulled out a few napkins, and handed them to Deirdre.

"Yes." She wiped her face. "She confided in me last night. As she was telling me how guilty she felt, it reminded me of how wrong I was for how I treated her after she went to college."

Jess lifted her left hand to his lips and kissed her palm. "Sweet, adorable Deirdre. Didn't you tell me you already apologized to your sister about your anger... and she forgave you?"

More nodding came with the tears that slid down her cheeks. "I can't get over how unfair I was." She blew her nose. "I put her through so much unneeded pain when she'd done nothing to deserve it. I did. I'm the one who should've called *her*."

Hmm. Rachel was torn up because she suspected someone of—*probably me she has negative ideas about.* He couldn't blame her after the way he treated her friends and hounded her to go out with him. "Deirdre, your sister has adverse thoughts about me, doesn't she?"

Her eyes widened. "I shouldn't have said anything to you about this. Rachel's going to kill me."

He slipped his arm around her shoulders and hugged her. "It's okay. She has license to think of me as she does. I made a fool of myself when I first arrived in Healy, not to mention how I annoyed her with constant invitations to go out to eat, both in Fairbanks and here. And now, with her not aware of my real reason for returning to Healy—to be with you—Rachel came to the wrong conclusion. Then there was the accident. And I'll bet she blames me for that in some way. What a disaster!"

Deirdre leaned her head against Jess's shoulder. "We've both created a mess of things."

"Sweet thing, it's time to tell her how you still feel. Also about us. I'd like to set her mind at rest about me."

Deirdre's eyes flicked to him. "I can't tell her I told you."

He chuckled. "Don't. Tell her I had some negative vibes from her—which is definitely true—and guessed. Perhaps talking to your parents about us should be our next step."

Hopefully, Deirdre's right that they won't mind a ten-year difference between us.

Chapter Thirty-Three

The following morning, a knock at the front door had Rachel scurrying from the kitchen to answer. She pulled the door open to find her boss on the front porch with a long, flat box in his hands. Now what? "Uh... Mr. Gibson?" He sure looked different. Nice.

"Good morning. I brought a dozen cinnamon rolls to add to your day." He grinned.

"Come in." She stepped back and allowed him to enter. What had brought him here now?

Deirdre descended the stairs with a glow on her face, a smile, and a sparkle in her eyes. *Hmm*. What was going on here?

After Rachel took the box from him and placed it on the entry table, she hung up her boss's parka and directed him to the living room. Deirdre followed them and sat in an armchair facing the couch where he'd planted himself.

The expressions he and her sister were giving each other spoke volumes. But Rachel wasn't sure what language they were speaking, nor how she felt about it.

"Morning, Jess." Her father came down the hallway and took the matching seat to Deirdre's. "You're sporting a new style today. And you're in time for breakfast."

"Thank you, sir. It was time for a change. Um, there's something I'd like to ask you. In private."

"Can it wait until after we eat? My wife said she's ready to put everything on the table." He glanced at Rachel and pointed to the box on the table. "What's that, sweetheart?"

"Mr. Gibson brought cinnamon rolls."

Her father's face lit up. "Good timing, indeed. Your mother said she got up too late to make anything sweet today, and we'd have to settle for toast." He laughed as he stood. "Let's go into the kitchen." He turned to Mr. Gibson. "We'll have our discussion in my study after we've eaten."

Deirdre followed the men until Rachel grabbed her arm and pulled her back. "Sis, the way you and Mr. Gibson looked at each other—please tell me you're not involved with my boss. I told you my doubts, and... he's a playboy."

With a hand on Rachel's shoulder, her sister said, "Those are your suspicions. Not mine. Anyway, he said you've every reason not to trust him after the way he treated you, Liam, and Anik."

"You *told* him?" Rachel's heart clenched. "This is my employer. What will he think? Everyone around here is determined to get me fired."

"No, I didn't, exactly. I wound up having a blubber-fest yesterday morning when he and I had breakfast together." She ducked her head. "When we went for a ride after eating, He asked me what was wrong. I said I'm the one who's guilty of treating you the way I did. When I mentioned you suspected someone of something, he guessed the rest, and... well, everything came out, and we're all fine, except I'm still guilt-ridden for what I did." She frowned. "And he's not a playboy. He's wonderful. He admitted the rumors at work but said they're not true."

Rachel's brows rumpled. "Sis, stop with the guilt trip. I should have made an effort to spend time with you before I left for college, and also to keep in touch while I was gone. I don't blame you for anything. Please, Dee. No more guilt, all right?"

"Okay." Deirdre gave Rachel a side hug, and they ventured down the hall.

"But you and Mr. Gibson?" Rachel squinted at her sister, then sucked in a long breath. *He said the rumors weren't true? Really?*

After breakfast, Jess followed Mr. O'Rourke into his study. Jess tightened his jaw as he walked behind Deirdre's father. Was she right about her parents not having a problem with his dating her? Maybe this wasn't such a good idea after all. He should've let them become more accustomed to him.

His and Deirdre's emotions had spiked so fast. Everyone would assume he was only coming on to her. No doubt, the rumors at work about him had reached Rachel's ears. He'd never denied them. How would he convince Deirdre's family he was just a regular guy who cared for her... a lot?

Mr. O'Rourke sat and motioned for Jess to sit. He took a chair across the desk from the clergyman.

"Now, son... what did you want to ask me?"

Here goes nothing. Jess leaned forward with his elbows on his knees and clasped his hands. "Sir, ah... you see... Deirdre and I have decided we enjoy each other's company."

Her father raised his brows.

Jess waited for a response that didn't come. *What are you, fifteen years old, asking her father if you can ask her for a first date?* "It happened the night when everyone stayed at my condo. She couldn't sleep. Me neither. We spent the night talking in the kitchen. You have a very sweet daughter."

"*That* I am aware of. I've *two* very sweet daughters."

"Yes." Jess produced an awkward grin. He recognized the quality in Rachel as well. "But Deirdre is sensitive. She needed someone to talk to that night. And I enjoyed listening to her. I thought about how much I wanted to protect her, though all we talked about was how she'd mistreated Rachel."

"So, what you're trying to tell me, in a roundabout way, is that you and Deirdre want to be a couple. Is that it?"

Heat rose in Jess's neck. How did he—? "I'm making a mess of this, aren't I?"

Mr. O'Rourke chuckled. "Let me go out on a limb here and say you haven't had many conversations like this with fathers in your lifetime."

"No, sir. Actually, I haven't dated much. The rumors of my exploits are greatly exaggerated. And I confess, encouraged by me. I put on a bad-boy persona to make people believe I was somewhat of a playboy. But the truth is, I've only taken women out a handful of times. Tried to get Rachel to go out with me because I realized she was different from all the other women I've ever met. But she wasn't interested. It became a challenge to me after a few turn-downs." He grimaced.

"When I met Deirdre, and we spent the evening talking, we clicked."

The man stared at him. Heat intensified in Jess's neck under Mr. O'Rourke's scrutiny. "I'm asking if it's okay with you that I date Deirdre. When we can, that is."

Her father still didn't say anything. He didn't move. Only blinked.

Rachel opened the door to the study. "Dad... Mom says we should hustle if we don't want to be late for services."

While Rachel accompanied her parents to church, neither of whom said much, Deirdre opted to ride in Mr. Gibson's truck. It gave Rachel time to think. Her boss and her baby sister? Why? Of all the guys Dee had chasing her, why had her sister chosen him? A guy at least ten years older than her. Rachel shook her head.

Even if he had cleaned up the bad-boy look—Rachel bit her bottom lip—she had no reason not to trust the rumors at work about him. *He'd better not hurt Deirdre.*

They pulled into the parking lot at the same time Anik's Jeep did. Her heart filled with warmth as Liam smiled from the passenger seat.

She slid out from the rear seat of her father's sedan and met him as he carefully got out of the Jeep. "Hi, handsome. How are you feeling today?"

"More restored each day that passes, when I see your sweet face." He leaned closer and whispered, "I've been lonely ever since you left my place."

Her face heated. Last night, her dreams had been about Liam, surely prompted by yesterday. Such a beautiful day together. They'd talked, watched a DVD, and played a board game. When Anik came home that afternoon, he and Liam had peeled potatoes at the kitchen table, while she made the rest of dinner. Then Anik had left to meet Mr. Gibson that night at The Brown Bear to discuss poachers, but their friend wasn't gone long. It had felt natural to be at the cabin with Liam as though she belonged.

They entered the church and found their way to the auditorium for Sunday school. Dad would be giving the sermon for the morning worship service today. She loved her father's strong messages.

Deirdre glided into the pew where they sat every Sunday. Mr. Gibson shadowed her. Anik took the seat next to him, and Rachel followed with Liam. Gradually, the sanctuary filled, and the adult Sunday school lesson began. One of the deacons taught from Luke 15:1-7, after which they took a ten-minute break.

Rachel remained seated.

Her boss turned to Deirdre and said, "I've never heard the story about the lost sheep. I haven't been in a church at all since my parents died. My sister keeps after me to join her church, but I keep putting her off. I'm glad I came with you today."

Organ music signaled the morning worship service was about to begin. Another deacon led in an opening hymn, gave announcements, and led the congregation in a couple more hymns.

Then Pastor O'Rourke rose to give the message. "The bulletin says I'm to preach a message titled 'Go into All the World,' but early this morning, I had a long talk with a gentleman regarding his dating a younger girl. That discussion prompted me to change my topic."

As the auditorium grew silent, Deirdre's and Mr. Gibson's faces morphed into a progression of varying shades of pink. Rachel's sister looked at her father with wide eyes and gritted teeth. Her stage whisper came out loud and clear as she leaned toward Mr. Gibson. "I should've warned you about Dad's strange sense of humor."

He whispered back at the same volume, "I like a preacher with an odd and good sense of humor." Mr. Gibson grinned.

Her father directed his gaze at Deirdre. "Daughter, pay attention to the sermon." Her dad chuckled when she saluted him.

With her hand pressed to her mouth, Rachel barely held in her laugh. Her poor boss. *If he sticks around after this, we'll have proof that he really cares for Dee.*

Her father continued. "The gentleman had been keeping company with the younger girl... on the sly." Rachel's father lowered his head and peered over his glasses toward her boss. "Then he told said younger girl he needed to tell her father and mother they were seeing each other, and ask for their blessing... which the parents appreciated. But the admission didn't come until the said younger girl mentioned the parents wouldn't have a problem with an age difference... which was true."

It seemed everyone in the sanctuary wore a puzzled look.

"After the gentleman had dug a hole for himself, he asked permission to date said young lady. Of course, it was given. He said he was grateful to get everything out in the open. That's when I decided to preach on A Time for Everything.

"In the case of these two young people, the *right time* would have been before they decided to keep their relationship secret from her parents." Mr. Gibson gave a thumbs-up, signaling he was in agreement.

Her father chuckled again. "Please turn to Ecclesiastes three, one. 'To every thing there is a season, and a time to every purpose under the heaven:' "

The sermon ended with an invitation for all who needed to pray to come forward to the altar and talk with the Lord. A twinge pierced Rachel's heart. She and Liam were as guilty about not being honest and forthcoming as Deirdre and Mr. Gibson. She rose when they did.

Liam stood also and took her hand. As he led her out of the pew, his cane clicking on the tiles as he walked, he whispered, "*Time* to come clean with your parents after church." He smiled.

"You're right."

They went to the altar and kneeled. How would her parents handle both their daughters in sudden relationships? All they needed now was for Kalen to announce he had a fiancée. And what of 'Big Bro' Anik?

Chapter Thirty-Four

After the unusual sermon, Rachel and Liam rode to her parents' home in Anik's Jeep. She hoped Liam was prepared for the onslaught of questions her father would no doubt have for him when she and Liam admitted their attachment.

With a puzzled expression, Anik scratched his head as he drove, then chuckled. "That was quite the lineup at the altar." He peeked at Liam, who peered back at Rachel in the rear seat.

Heat traveled up her neck. She feigned a smug countenance with raised brows. "I'm surprised you didn't join us, Anik. After all, we all have things we probably need to confess every day."

He laughed. "Nothing I do is in secret."

"How would *we* know? A *secret* is a secret from everyone else." She smirked. "We have no idea what you do each day, or where you go, or who you're with."

"You've got me there." He pulled off the road into the O'Rourke front yard.

Once they were in the house, she sought out her sister, who had gone to her bedroom to change. Rachel knocked on the door. "Dee, can I come in?"

"Sure."

Rachel sat on the bed. "What did Mr. Gibson want to see Dad about?"

"We decided it would be better if Jess asked permission to date me and form a relationship with their blessing. He was nervous about it and afraid Mom and Dad would assume the worst because of the difference in our ages until I told him nine years separated them. Dad wasn't exactly his *subtle self.*"

She giggled. "Jess found what our father said from the pulpit amusing. He likes Dad's sense of humor. We're both glad it's out in the open."

Deirdre gazed at Rachel from under her long, dark lashes. "You're okay with this, aren't you? Please say you are."

Rachel moved her head from side to side. Was she okay with it? This was her baby sister... with her boss. How bizarre was that? "I'm not sure. Are you positive about this, sis?"

"I am. Something clicked between us in Fairbanks. I can't explain it. Probably the same thing that happened with you and Liam."

Oh, no! She'd left Liam out there all alone with her father. Liam wanted them to explain their affection for each other together. Rachel jumped up and ran out the bedroom door.

Liam used his cane to follow the pastor into his study. "I guess Rachel's with Deirdre and forgot we had planned to talk to you."

"And what would that be about, son? Perhaps the fact you and my older daughter are definitely now a couple, judging by the hand-holding at the altar?" Mr. O'Rourke had a gleam in his eye.

"Obvious, huh?" Liam chuckled.

"Only to about... the *entire congregation*, from the comments I received as people left the sanctuary. People have been asking when the wedding will take place."

Uh-oh. They should've approached her father before this. "Sir, I'm sorry we didn't say anything to you earlier."

"Liam, why don't you sit down?"

Rachel burst into the study. As she slipped into the chair next to Liam and faced him, she panted. "Sorry. I got sidetracked with Deirdre."

Her father leaned on the elbow he'd propped on his desk and covered his mouth, but his eyes crinkled.

He must find humor in the events of this day. Liam twisted his lips.

"Sweetheart, Liam here tells me you two are an item, and I've had several people ask if you've set a wedding date. When were you going to let your mother and me in on your plans?"

Liam didn't think it possible, but Rachel's eyes spread wider. Her jaw dropped. "I... ah... we—"

"I believe what she's trying to say is... we haven't gotten that far yet in our discussions." Liam's heart was so full of joy, he barely held in his own mirth. "However, if you've no objection, sir, it's the direction I'd like to take." He peered at Rachel. "If you're agreeable."

Her face blossomed from a delicate pink to rose red in a flash. She smiled and nodded.

"Hmm... seems my daughter, the reporter, can't find any words to express herself. How unique." Mr. O'Rourke glanced at Liam. "Son, from what I've learned about you, I can't imagine anyone better in a relationship with my Rachel. Slow the progress down a notch, which shouldn't be difficult since she lives and works in Fairbanks."

Liam reached for her hand and grinned. If he had his way, she wouldn't be so far away for long, but that would be another discussion with her father they'd have later.

In the evening, everyone retired to the living room. Anik surveyed the couples. Loneliness almost overwhelmed him, though these were the people who had all but adopted him into their family.

Mr. O'Rourke and his wife, deep in conversation, occupied matching easy chairs with a small round table between. Liam and Rachel sat together at one end of the couch, while Jess and Deirdre were perusing a picture album on the other. Why did Kalen have to go out to dinner with a friend this evening? If he hadn't, there'd be another unattached buddy to talk to.

Anik slouched in the third chair by the fireplace. Alone.

He recalled the comments Liam had made a month earlier about dating. One corner of Anik's mouth pulled up. He'd lied when he said he'd seen several ladies during his travels. His mind had been too focused on racing and his dogsled team. Then he'd concentrated on his friend and Rachel.

His grandmother was right. He'd better get busy and find someone if he was ever to start a family of his own. He certainly couldn't live in the cabin with Liam and Rachel when they took the plunge. They'd need extra room when the inevitable happened.

Anik's parents and *Aanaa* were always on his back about settling down. She would pinch him and say, *"Grandson, I won't live forever, and I want great-grandbabies."* He laughed to himself. Then sighed.

"Oh." Jess held up a hand. "Almost forgot. Rachel, I heard from the mechanic who retrieved your car from Nenana. Things were so tense on Saturday evening, I completely dismissed the message from my mind. This morning... well, anyway, he said your Subaru is ready to be picked up."

Rachel's eyes narrowed. "Why did he call you and not me?"

Jess showed a Cheshire Cat grin. "I told him to charge all repairs to the newspaper and not bother you. I left *my* phone number." His brows rose. "You were so focused on Liam, I took care of it."

She tilted her head as her expression relaxed. "Thank you, Mr. Gibson. That was kind of you."

"I've got some good points. Anyway, the guy said road debris did your brake line in. He also changed the fuel line, which showed wear. She's ready to go, and you can return his old rattletrap of a loaner."

Rachel's lips wrinkled.

Anik's did the same. *Bet she carries a load of guilt now.* She suspected Jess of having tampered with the brakes. *I would have wondered the same thing under the circumstances.* But he was relieved that Jess was guilty of nothing more than secrets.

Rachel rose from the couch. "Mom, you sit and relax. Deirdre and I will get dessert for everyone."

"Thank you, dear. I hope you both are blessed with daughters someday as helpful as mine."

Anik kept his eyes on Rachel as she left the room with a smile a mile wide. Liam winked at her.

Hmm. Anik's eyes narrowed. Something was on that boy's mind, and it wasn't dating. Why had they gone down to the altar? He'd vouch for Rachel and Liam's character any day. They wouldn't have—but there was definitely a plan in the works, a major change in both of them. Was he about to lose his current home sooner rather than later?

"Liam, would you come outside and look at what I saw?" Anik hopped up from the chair and headed for the front door. "I'm not quite sure what to make of it."

"What is it? Where are we going? Can I view it from the window?"

"No, this is important." He flipped on his parka and waited for Liam on the front porch.

Liam stood, grabbed his cane, and followed. "Okay, buddy. What's this urgent thing you want me to look at? All I see out here are cars and the same scenery we've seen before when we've visited."

Anik turned and pinned Liam with a stare. "Time for you to confess, pal. What's going on between you and Rachel?"

"What do you mean? You're aware we've been dating."

"Your trip to the altar had more than dating in the message." Anik lowered his brows and pointed at Liam. "What've you done?"

With his hands held up in front of him like a barrier, Liam backed away from his friend. "Whoa! I haven't done anything to earn the kind of glare you're giving me. What's all this about?"

Anik's expression softened, and his shoulders relaxed. "I'm worried about Rachel. You two act mighty suspicious."

A laugh burst out of his friend. "I guess our secret is safe with you."

Again, all the muscles in Anik's face drew tight. *"What secret?"*

Chapter Thirty-Five

With his hand on Anik's shoulder, Liam said, "Calm down before you blow a gasket, buddy. The only secret we have, although it's not one to Mr. and Mrs. O'Rourke anymore, is that Rachel and I confessed our love for each other. It happened in the hospital. We planned to keep it quiet while I was still an infirmary captive."

Liam lowered his arm to his side. "The reason for the secrecy was because she didn't want her dad to bombard me with questions until I felt up to it. Also because of our short acquaintance. We both wondered if people would assume it was just a physical thing. It's the way some people are. Pastor's sermon caused us to wind up at the altar and pray. As with Deirdre and Jess, we were remiss. Pastor O'Rourke counseled with us after church. As our best friend, we should've told you too. Satisfied?"

Anik dragged his pal into a bear hug.

"Yeouch!" Liam pushed away and rubbed the area of his wound. "Easy on the merchandise. I'm not ready for roughhousing yet."

"Sorry. I was so happy the situation wasn't... well, you know. I forgot about your injury. I didn't want to believe the thought that crossed my mind." He patted Liam on the back. "Hope I didn't cause you any serious pain."

"Nah." Liam laughed. "Only a twinge. More of a fear that you were going to crush my ribs." He grimaced. "But seriously. I love Rachel so much, I could never hurt her like that."

"I figured as much, but the evil demon works hard on Christians to make them fall. And some couples listen to him." A sheepish appearance came over Anik. "Then there are friends who think the worst... like me, who allowed him to get into their mind." Anik sported his infamous Cheshire grin. "So, did you set a date for the wedding?"

"Not you too. Slow down, guy. We're not even engaged... yet."

"Well, what are you waiting for? I was positive you two belonged together the first time I saw you with her. Outside of when Kalen was in the hospital, of course. And I suspect you did too."

Liam chuckled. "All I can say right now is... I'm glad you talked me into going to dinner with you when Rachel came home. Let it go at that." He reached his arm around Anik's broad shoulders and pulled him toward the door. "We should go in before someone wonders what we're up to."

A thumbs-up was Anik's response.

Liam quirked his lips. *I doubt this Inuk considers the wedding discussion over.*

After evening service, Liam said good night to Rachel and left with Anik for the cabin. He'd better work on a fix for the long-distance problem that loomed on the horizon. This was Thanksgiving week, so he needed to touch base with people before they left for the holiday. If she had to go back to Fairbanks next Sunday, he'd go nuts without her until Christmas... at the earliest.

Anik walked into the dining room. "What's this? Your wedding list already?" He bent over Liam's shoulder and scanned the names of contacts for magazines, newspapers, journals, and the National Park Service.

Liam didn't bother to glance up at his smart-aleck friend. "Very funny. I'm making a list of places to call on Monday. I'll find out if they accept articles from freelance writers." *One of the best uses of the internet so far.*

"What a super idea. If Rachel were employed here—wait. Have you told her what you're doing? Does she want to stay in Healy?"

Liam stopped the pen and gazed at Anik. "Yes, she knows. We talked about it after church. You really are a pesky big brother type, aren't you?" Liam snatched his ballpoint and resumed jotting down names of contacts.

Anik left the room for a few minutes and returned with his laptop. "Let me help. I might come up with some places you didn't. Move your notepad close enough so I can see it."

As Liam leaned into his chair, he smiled. "Thanks, buddy." He tapped his finger on the wooden table as he stared at his friend.

"What?" Anik peered up at him.

"Just thinking. When are you going to find your own girl to give all this attention to? Time's a-wasting."

"Get back to the list, and leave my love life alone. When we have you and Rachel hitched, then you can play cupid for me."

Liam laughed and continued his task, but noted the forlorn expression on Anik. "So, you admit you aren't dating anyone right now."

Anik's cellphone rang, and he picked it up. "Hello. Yeah, speaking." His face went sour. He rose from the table and walked away.

Hope it wasn't bad news about his friend. The one who was supposed to visit and help him prepare for the Iditarod.

Anik disconnected the call. Liam had gone into the living room and clicked the TV remote. Anik took a seat on the couch. "Hey, pal. I hate to tell you this, but those poachers I helped catch escaped. It was during a transfer from one correctional facility to another late this afternoon. They notified me because one of the guards overheard the men vow vengeance on me."

"Are you kidding?" Liam's brows almost met.

"Nope. Not kidding. Don't worry about me. I can take care of myself. And the state troopers have set up extra patrols around here to watch for the lowlifes. Those losers probably have no idea where to find me."

Liam rose and hurried to the front door. "All the same, we need to secure the cabin… and keep our guns handy. If they shot me once, they'd do it a second time in a heartbeat."

Anik went to the back door and double-locked it. Liam drew the shades on the windows.

As Anik picked up his cell from the table, he retook his seat in the living room. "I'm nervous about Rachel. She was with me."

Liam's eyes rounded. "You didn't let her know?"

"Only found out and told you. I'll call now." Anik pressed the button for the O'Rourkes.

He waited and fidgeted while the phone rang in his ear. Where could they be at this hour? Had they gone out somewhere? Was he overreacting? Rachel would be with her family. Her father was no one to tangle with, and these poachers would have to go through him to get to his daughter. Anik frowned. He didn't want that to happen either.

Liam's face grew pale. "They're not answering?"

"Hello. O'Rourke residence." Anik breathed again. "Mrs. O'Rourke, is the pastor in?"

"Yes, Anik. He's in the kitchen having a late-night snack with the girls. Hold on."

The sound of her hurried footsteps helped Anik ease his grip on the cell.

A few moments later, Mr. O'Rourke's voice said. "Anik. What makes you call this late? Is Liam okay?"

"He's fine, but we received unwelcome news. The poachers escaped, and one of the guards at the correctional facility had overheard them vow vengeance on me. I'm concerned about Rachel since she was with me when we caught the poachers. The state troopers are patrolling the area. Still, your family should be on alert."

"Thank you for warning us, Anik. We'll take extra precautions. Let us know if you hear—"

The sound of glass breaking resounded through the phone. The line went dead.

Chapter Thirty-Six

Liam grabbed Anik's shoulder. "What's wrong? What did Mr. O'Rourke say?"

Anik's eyes widened. "I heard glass break, and the line went dead."

Liam sprinted for the front door and snatched his parka off the hook, ignoring the twinge of pain in his lower back. "Come on. We have to get over there."

"Right behind ya, pal."

They rushed to Anik's Jeep, hopped in, and raced to the O'Rourke residence.

When they pulled into the yard and slid to a stop, Liam spotted a hefty birch branch broken off the tree and leaning against the side of the cabin. No doubt from the high winds. It may have accounted for the crash Anik said he heard, but why had the line gone dead?

After his haste to leave the cabin, Liam gingerly stepped out of the Jeep's passenger seat and speed-walked to the front porch, followed by his friend.

It only took a couple of knocks before Mr. O'Rourke answered. "Anik! Liam! Come in out of the cold and wind."

They entered the foyer and wiped their wet feet on the entrance rug. Liam blurted out, "We got worried when the phone went dead after the sound of broken glass."

"I tried to call Anik back after we found out what caused the crash." Mr. O'Rourke turned to Anik. "But you didn't answer. The old birch tree next to the house has been dying for some time. It dropped one of its larger branches, which toppled over and hit the kitchen window. With the harsh, icy wind blowing into the house, I had to cover it immediately. Must have touched the End Call button in my excitement and disconnected."

Anik patted his pockets and parka. "Guess I forgot my cell on the dining table."

"I tried Liam's phone as well, but also no answer."

Liam checked for his phone and chuckled. "I left mine at the house too. We were in such a rush. That's a first... but we're relieved to find everyone's okay."

Rachel strolled into the living room from the hall. "Everything's cleaned up, Dad. You should have that dead tree removed."

Her face lit up with a smile when she saw Liam. "Hi. When did you arrive?"

Liam returned her smile. "Just now."

Her father took her arm and led her to the couch. "Sit down. I need to tell you something."

As she lowered herself onto the sofa, she lost her joyful expression and looked at her father. "What?"

Liam took the seat beside her and held her hand.

Anik explained what the authorities had told him earlier, that he called to warn her father, and then they heard the crash and hurried over.

The color in her cheeks paled. The grip on Liam's hand intensified. "Do they know where any of us live? Is my family in danger too?"

Liam's heart ached at the fear in her voice. First, it was the trauma of his getting shot, then the suspicions that Gibson had messed with her brakes, and now this happens. "Honey, the state troopers are patrolling the area for these guys. I'd appreciate it if you didn't go anywhere until they're caught. They might exact revenge on you because you were with Anik when they were detained. They weren't the most intelligent beings, from what my buddy here told me."

"That's for sure." Anik arched an eyebrow. "While I held them for the authorities, I had to fire at their feet again and threaten to end their argument when they started to shove and blame one another for their predicament."

Kalen rolled into the room. "I heard what you said about the poachers escaping. Why don't we *all* stay together?"

Mr. O'Rourke sat on the other side of Rachel. "That's a good idea. Boys, I'd be more comfortable if both of you would remain here for the time being. I believe having you sharpshooters around will reassure my girls and wife while the criminals are loose. It would also add to Rachel's peace of mind with you still on the mend, Liam." Her father squeezed her shoulders. "Anik can sleep in Kalen's room upstairs. He has twin beds."

"Yeah. There's plenty of space in my bedroom, Anik."

Mr. O'Rourke pointed down the hallway. "And we've a guest room down here you can use, Liam. No stairs to climb. How about it?"

Liam couldn't have devised a more satisfactory plan if he'd tried. "Sounds fine to me. Anik and I can run to my place and grab some clothes."

"Under the circumstances, an ideal strategy." Anik headed for his coat. "It doesn't hurt to have reinforcements." He displayed his infectious grin. "We'll be right back."

As Anik drove onto the road from the O'Rourke property, two dark shadows ducked into a copse of trees.

Liam slapped the dashboard. "Did you see them? It could be the poachers."

Without a word, Anik spun the Jeep around and drove back to the O'Rourkes'. "Stay here with them. I'll go home and pack for both of us. You can call the state troopers and tell them what we think we saw. I'll be back ASAP."

Liam jumped out of the vehicle, wincing, and raced for the front door.

All this running around is not helping my pal. All this activity had to be painful for Liam. Anik's lips tightened.

As he drove away again, he watched his friend enter the house. Sure would be glad when those rotten miscreants were behind bars permanently. Someone must've let their guard down. These guys weren't bright… but they were sneaky.

He arrived at Liam's cabin and whipped into the drive. He had to remember to pick up both cell phones, guns, and ammo. Trouble could show up before the troopers reached the O'Rourkes'. He'd better hurry.

In no time, Anik had flown through the house and gathered the clothes they'd need for at least four days—for good measure.

He took out two rifles and two handguns, laying them across the couch in the living room, and secured the rest in the gun safe.

After a security check of the windows and doors, Anik loaded the Jeep and took off.

When he approached the O'Rourkes' home, a state cruiser was in the yard. The hair stood on the nape of Anik's neck. He parked close to the trooper's car and ran into the house. "What's happened now?"

"A couple of potshots." Liam turned to face his friend. "When I peeked out, I didn't see anyone. The trooper got here a minute after the last shot. The idiots are long gone by now."

Anik strode outside. Sure enough. Twin bullet holes in the wood stared at him from the entrance, the lead lodged in the solid wooden door. One aperture at the top and one midway down and to the right. Not very accurate shots. How did these clowns ever take down a bull moose? Unless… someone else made the kill.

He stuck his head into the house. "Liam. How many shots did you hear?"

"Three. Two at first, and then a couple of minutes later, a third."

Another spot caught Anik's attention between the door frame and the picture window to the left. Good thing they didn't shoot out the window.

Either one of those nut-jobs had shot twice, or there was a third shooter. He opened the front door again. "Trooper! Check this out."

The trooper stepped onto the porch and examined the newly found depression. "I called in the report, and our detachment will have contacted Alaska's state forensic services. Don't touch anything. The crime lab with the Alaska Department of Public Safety will be out to go over the scene as soon as they're available. In the meantime, I've been assigned to patrol—guard, so to speak. I doubt the shooters'll be back again tonight. The first two shots may have been to get someone to open the door. The last one, just for effect."

Anik followed the trooper into the house. *Or there's a third culprit.*

"Mr. O'Rourke told me you and Ranger Liam plan to stay with them until we catch the escapees. I'm sure your presence will comfort them in this situation."

Anik nodded and stared at Liam. "There could be three poachers. One who might have left the scene before we spotted the downed moose that day. Might be only the two of them, but my hunch says otherwise."

Liam's brows raised.

Prickles ran up Rachel's neck. Why had all this come about? Couldn't the authorities keep a grip on two irresponsible, thoughtless men? Remorse settled in her consciousness. That wasn't kind. *Mistakes happen, even to the most competent people. Still... why this, Lord? Now, with Liam recovering. He has to be in pain.* Some Thanksgiving week.

All she'd wanted last month—and she *hadn't* wanted the assignment in the *first* place—was to come home, get the article on the Canine Rangers done, and return to Fairbanks to her peaceful life...without complications. Well, except for the thing with her boss always asking her out. *And now look.*

Her eyes moistened. Here she'd fallen in love with this extraordinary, handsome man, who'd been shot by those creeps. Oh, great! Now she blamed Liam for her dismay. She lowered her head into her hands, elbows braced on her knees.

As if he sensed her frustration, Liam eased in next to her and circled her shoulders with his arm. "Are you okay?"

A tear seeped out and landed on her pant leg. "No." She rested her head against his chest.

He pulled her into his embrace and hugged her. "It'll be all right. Anik and I will be here with all of you. Plus, I heard your dad and Kalen are both good shots with a rifle. We'll keep you, Deirdre, and your mom safe. Not to mention the state trooper will police the area until they have the criminals behind bars."

"I know we're safe with all of you. Plus, the Lord's watching over us, but the stress has caused adrenaline to hit the top of my cup, and it has overflowed."

He kissed her hair and traced his fingers down her cheek. "Go ahead. Cry if you need to. It's okay. Remember, we all have phones to call the troopers."

Anik came into the room. "I've taken Liam's things to the guestroom and dropped mine off upstairs."

"We should keep the cells on the coffee table." Liam held out his hand.

Anik slapped his forehead. "I didn't bring them."

"What?" Rachel was stunned.

"You're kidding." Liam shook his head.

Anik flipped on his parka. "Back in a few." He was out the door in a flash.

If it weren't such a serious situation, she could've laughed her head off. This was so unlike Anik. *He must be feeling the stress too.*

"I can't believe he forgot the phones." Liam shook his head again. "For someone so OCD about everything else in his life—"

She let a snicker slip out. She was grateful that he and Liam would stay with them. Having both of them here with her family was a comfort, especially with Liam hurting as he was.

Someday, she and Liam would make life together permanent. All they had to do was survive this crisis... this *trial. Lord willing.*

Chapter Thirty-Seven

Sunday night came and went without another sighting of the poachers on the loose. It had been eerily quiet. Too quiet for Liam's liking.

On Monday morning, after a check-in with the state troopers, he made a call to the national park magazine.

After being transferred to an extention, elevator music played in his ear while he waited in the queue and let his mind wander to Rachel. He could picture her helping to clean up in the kitchen after the morning meal they'd all eaten. And what a meal it had been! Pancakes, sausage, blueberry compote—like Mom's when they lived in Minnesota, from freshly picked blueberries on the farm—coffee and cream.

Someday, he'd have breakfast like that every day, when the gorgeous correspondent would become his wife. They'd—

"Editor's office. May I help you?" The woman came across the line with a professional tone to her voice.

"Yes, thank you. I'm Liam Chadwick, a Denali Park ranger. I have a question. I don't write myself, but I know an excellent reporter who would love to write for your publication. She's already written a fantastic piece about the Canine Rangers, which will appear in *The Fairbanks Star* soon. How does one send in articles to your magazine? Do you have that information, or do I speak to someone else?"

"I'll be happy to direct you to what you need." She gave him a link where he could download instructions to submit stories and explained what he'd find in the downloaded document, including how the stories had to have an original slant.

"Since Rachel is a reporter with the newspaper, I doubt she'll have trouble with the requirement in the least."

"I'm sure she won't. She'll send a query via email with each submission, attaching two or three samples of her work." The woman included several other requirements to take note of. "Each article must be unpublished elsewhere."

What? Oh, well. Guess that excludes the one she did on the pups. Too bad. The story was a winner, in his opinion. But she could use a different angle of some kind on the dogs to submit.

The young woman spelled the link to their website. "At that site, she can peruse what others have already written."

"This is exactly what she needs. Thank you."

"Our printed edition has a circulation of around three hundred and twenty-five thousand."

"Wow. Terrific. Thanks for all your help."

"You're very welcome. I look forward to reading some of your friend's stories in our park magazine soon."

They disconnected the call, and Liam made a few more calls on Rachel's behalf. This was going to be a perfect plan for her. With her skills, she could submit pieces with no trouble. Then she wouldn't have to live in Fairbanks.

A knock came at the guestroom door. "Come on in." He laid his cellphone on the nightstand.

The woman who had stolen his heart stepped into the room, happiness written on her face. "And what've you been up to secluded in this lonely room?" She giggled. All her stress and fears from last night seemed to have dissolved with the morning's sunshine.

He rose from the overstuffed chair and wrapped his arms around her. He could get used to this every morning. "I've been making inquiries for you about writing articles for various magazines."

Her eyes opened wide. "What? What magazines?"

"Remember, we discussed this as being one way for you to remain in Healy and write?" He held her at arm's length. "You don't recall that conversation?" His heart dropped to his stomach with a thud. *Didn't she want to stay here with him?*

"Yes, we had a conversation about it, but I said I'd still like to be a reporter. My job thrills me, as I search for information and see my byline in the paper." Her brows rumpled. "I don't know. Maybe you're right." She sighed. "I guess I'd have a byline."

He cupped her face in his hands and kissed the tip of her nose. "Rachel. I'm not trying to pressure you into doing something you're not ready to do. If working for *The Fairbanks Star* is that important to you, we'll work things out. I was only trying to help."

She slipped her arms around his waist and gently squeezed. "I realize that. Let me think about it. Perhaps the best thing to do would be to come home. At any rate, I'll be here until the Monday after Thanksgiving, and back again for Christmas. By then, I'm sure I'll be able to make up my mind what to do."

Oh, Lord. I sure hope she doesn't want to leave. He held her close. He couldn't stand the thought of her so far away, but he couldn't *make* her stay. *Father, help us.*

Stay in Healy and write? Wasn't it what she really wanted to do? Or continue to travel on assignment for the newspaper? She loved Liam, but would she be satisfied with a life that kept her in one place? Her parents wanted her to come home to the family cabin. If she were honest with herself, she'd rather live with Liam in his. Her lips curled at the corners. She'd have to marry him first. She bit her bottom lip. And he hadn't asked—not yet anyway. Then there was her father's request. *"Slow the progress down a notch..."*

She stared at the two park magazine links on the paper Liam had handed her with samples of what she'd find at those sites, along with a list of other publications that accepted submissions from freelance writers. She'd at least check them out and gather more information to help her make a decision.

Tomorrow. She'd start tomorrow. Today, she had promised Mr. Gibson she'd finish a piece about the lives of transplants from other parts of the United States to Alaska. It appeared she was to become the resident authority on all aspects of Alaska living... and jobs. She laughed to herself.

But first... lunch.

As she hit the last step and pounced onto the wooden floor of the foyer, she heard banter coming from the dining room. When she'd told them she'd go upstairs to concentrate on the piece she was to email to the paper by the end of the week, Liam, Anik, Mom, Kalen, and Deirdre had been playing a lively game of Monopoly. The game hadn't ended. This was what she loved. They were like a big family.

Anik told them he'd postponed his training for the Iditarod for the time being, and Liam was still on medical leave. She'd enjoy the togetherness regardless of the situation. Mom was happy they were with them too.

Deirdre—already missing Mr. Gibson, or *"her Jess,"* as she called him—would no doubt be distracted by the guys.

Lord willing, there'd be no need for the guns Anik had brought.

Kalen! Part of her wished he'd stayed in school until Thursday. Rachel's heart raced. She couldn't bear the thought of him being hurt again. After all, he wasn't involved in this mess.

When would they find and jail those criminals? How nerve-wracking. None of them could go out without fear of being shot.

Anik and Mrs. O'Rourke spun and stared at Rachel after a loud rumble came from her stomach. She blushed, grabbed an apple from the bowl on the kitchen counter, and left the room.

He snickered to himself as he hovered and sampled a piece of fruit from the tray Mrs. O'Rourke set out for a late lunch. "I have to admit, I'm glad your daughter's tummy voiced its opinion about not having eaten for so long." He snickered.

"You're always hungry, aren't you, Anik?" The lady laughed. "Well, lunch won't be long now."

"After we eat, please write down whatever you might need from the grocery store. I'll go out for supplies. After all, Liam and I added two more extra mouths to be fed. And I'd rather go than have you or one of the girls run around with the possibility of those escapees out there. Pastor should stay home with all of you."

She turned, the wooden spoon she'd used to mix potato salad in her hand. "That's kind of you, Anik. You've always been such a help... *when* you were here instead of gallivanting to the far reaches of the world." She winked and resumed her chore. "I'm pretty well set. We always prepare to be socked in during winter at some point—in case of a blizzard. But I suppose we could use some fresh items. Okay, I'll make a list for you."

"Good. I'll check if anyone else needs anything. Where's Pastor?"

"He had to run over to a church member's house after breakfast. His family has a complicated situation to handle and needs counseling. He should be home anytime now, but we won't delay lunch for him. He can eat later."

Anik frowned. None of them ought to be out there with those criminals loose. Then again, Mr. O'Rourke had nothing to do with the capture of the poachers. The man was capable of his *own* defense with a Marine training background. Though middle-aged, he was still formidable.

Chuckling to himself, Anik recalled a time before he left for the Air Force when he'd wrestled with the pastor at the church gym. The older man had pinned him down in two seconds flat with one of his martial arts moves.

Anik paused the memory. That wouldn't help if someone took a shot at the pastor. Anik's neck hairs lifted. *Lord, please protect Mr. O'Rourke while he's out doing work for You.*

Chapter Thirty-Eight

Almost a week had passed with no word about the poachers. Liam's fingers combed through his hair as he relaxed on the couch in the O'Rourkes' living room after breakfast. He and Anik had kept watch, but it seemed the criminals must have fled the area.

"Smells like a feast in the making back there." Liam tilted his head toward the sounds that came from the kitchen, while Anik prepared to leave and join his family for their holiday celebration.

"Sure does. I'm getting hungry again." Anik laughed. "My *aanaa's* house will have the same aromas."

"So what are you going to do about your practice schedule for Iditarod?" Liam leaned forward, elbows on his knees.

"Since we've heard nothing about those poachers, who've probably left the state, I guess it's time to continue my training, but

I'll do that on my own now. Rachel will leave for Fairbanks on Monday, and I don't want to take her away from you or her family."

Liam smiled. "Thanks. I appreciate that. I'll head back to work next week as well... on light duty." His joy faded. Not a word had come from the magazines Rachel had contacted, though she'd sent several samples of her writing to each. She'd followed all their guidelines for submissions. *It might take a while before they contact her.* She'd have to be patient. Him too.

The reality of Rachel's departure and the distance that would exist between them descended on him like a wet blanket. After the holiday weekend, she'd be so far away.

Mr. O'Rourke slipped into his parka. "Time to pick up my son and your family at the Healy River Airport, Liam."

"Is it that late?" Liam jumped up from the couch with barely a stitch of pain, flipped on his jacket, then turned to Anik. "Drive safe, and say hello to your family for me. I'll see you here later for your second dessert."

Anik lightly punched Liam's arm. "You betcha, pal. Don't eat too much turkey."

While Mr. O'Rourke and Liam got in the church van, Anik drove away.

Liam was anxious to reunite with his family. After more than twenty hours of traveling, they'd be worn out. What would they have to say about his relationship with Rachel when they got here? Liam laughed to himself. They'd been pretty flabbergasted when he'd talked to them on the phone.

Everything was coming together. His family would get to meet his beautiful lady and her family. *Hopefully, this long holiday weekend will be a quiet one, so they could relax and enjoy themselves.*

In the living room, Rachel took a breather from helping her mother and sister with dinner preparations. Tires crunched on the snow-covered gravel driveway. As she flew to the window, laughter filled the outside air. Her heart burst with excitement.

"Did I hear car doors slamming, hon?" Her mother stepped into the room. "Are they here?"

Rachel spun to her. "Looks like everyone is present and accounted for out there."

Snatching her parka from the hook over the bench in the hall, Rachel rushed out the front door. Liam exited the van. She ran to him and wrapped her arms around his waist. He kissed the top of her head.

Their guests had all moved to the rear of the vehicle to unload luggage. Liam took Rachel's hand. "Come and meet my family. They'll love you."

With her stomach full of butterflies, she followed Liam to the group behind the van. Kalen had retrieved his wheels from the lift on the passenger side and rolled up to her. "Hey, sis. Load me up with some of those bags."

She grabbed a small lock of his hair and pulled.

"Ouch!"

"Okay, you pest." She kissed his cheek. "You're always ready to do your part, aren't you? So glad you're back."

He whacked her on the bottom with a duffel bag. "Oops." Then quickly rolled away.

Liam chuckled, then turned to a tall blond lady, whom Rachel assumed was his mother. "Mom, I'd like to introduce you to Rachel O'Rourke."

The glow of a brilliant smile spread over the face of the woman with a lot of white streaks in her dark blonde hair. Her crystal blue eyes sparkled. "I'm so happy to meet you, dear. When Liam called to tell us about you, he couldn't stop singing your praises." Mrs. Chadwick reached out and wrapped her arms around Rachel as she whispered. "I was beginning to wonder if he'd ever discover a special someone up here."

Heat flooded Rachel's chest and settled in her face.

Mrs. Chadwick drew her to a handsome man with salt-and-pepper hair and dove-gray eyes like his son. He wore a wide grin as he lowered the suitcase he was hauling. "Bruce, this is Rachel, the girl who captured our Liam's heart."

Rachel swallowed hard. Her face had to be bright red. She glanced at Liam, and he shrugged, then laughed.

"No need to be embarrassed." Mr. Chadwick embraced her. "You'll get used to my Emma. She calls 'em as she sees 'em." He gave her a kiss on the forehead and winked at his wife.

Liam placed his hands on Rachel's shoulders. "Excuse us, Mom, Dad."

Mrs. Chadwick patted her son on the cheek, then she and her husband joined Mr. O'Rourke.

Rachel followed Liam to a young woman who had the same color hair, eyes, and smile as his. "This is my kid sister, Ainsley. Although at twenty-two, I guess you're not much of a kid anymore."

A mischievous expression overcame the younger girl. "Did our mother embarrass you enough? She does that to me all the time." Ainsley giggled and gave Rachel a hug. "I'm anxious to hear all about your experiences as a reporter for a big newspaper."

"You may be disappointed." Rachel took one of Ainsley's two pieces of luggage. "*The Fairbanks Star* is not a big publication, although its readership is growing all the time."

"I want to know all about it. It sounds exciting." Her gray eyes glistened.

Rachel's heart swelled. What a beautiful family. *I already love them.*

Liam took his sister's suitcase from Rachel. He stretched his arm over her shoulders and pulled her toward the man rearranging suitcases in the rear of the van. A petite lady and two small children waited at his side.

The mouths of Liam's niece and nephew hung open as they stared at the snow-covered range, draped in clouds, more than eighty miles away. Rachel knew how they felt. The little ones would undoubtedly never forget their first sight of Mount Denali from her parents' property—one of the rare places around town that offered a glimpse of the peak.

"Meet my older brother Lucas and his family." Liam slapped his sibling on the back.

The man resembled his father, except for chestnut-colored hair.

After more hugs from Lucas, his wife Tammy, and the children's shy peeks, Rachel and her father led everyone into the cabin.

When she spotted Liam in the living room a few minutes later, he stood in front of the picture window. What was he searching for?

As they sat down to dinner, Liam gazed at Rachel, whose brows wrinkled. Something had her uptight. "What's on your mind?"

"I saw you staring out the window before Mom called me to help her. What were you watching? You didn't see someone in the woods, did you?"

"Watching but not seeing. It's all quiet. Nothing to worry about."

After dessert, everyone got ready to depart. Rachel sidled up to him. "I thought Anik was stopping by tonight. He must be having a wonderful reunion to make him forget Mom's carrot cake. It was always a favorite of his."

"He may have been too stuffed to make it here for more food. Besides, he knows your mom will save a piece for him."

"Ha! For sure."

Rachel rested her head on his shoulder. "I hate that you're not staying here tonight. It was such a comfort and fun to have you and Anik with us, but I understand. You want to spend some time with your brother. And the threat *has* gone away."

"It was a tough decision. I don't want to leave you, but I haven't seen Lucas in so long."

Rachel peered up.

Liam softly kissed her, then deepened the kiss. *Someday we won't have to part.* Soon, he hoped. "But... we'll all return for breakfast tomorrow. Time to get my folks and brother's family to the lodge for the night. Sweet dreams, fair maiden." He grinned at her. "I know what *mine* will be about." She squeezed him extra hard. He was glad that side didn't hurt anymore.

After he helped his family get settled in their lodgings, had a long chat with Lucas, and said good night until morning, Liam drove to his cabin. He entered the yard and parked next to Anik's vehicle.

Huh. Strange. Anik's dog team barked as if they hadn't eaten in a week. Maybe he forgot to feed them earlier and was out there now.

Liam shut the truck door. *What's this?* The snow around the Jeep was trampled, as though a group of people had been there. A knot gripped his gut. He surveyed the area. Lights weren't on in the house. Anik could have gone to bed already, but why were his dogs still barking? He wouldn't ignore them like that.

Liam hurried to the cabin's front entrance, through the arctic entry, rushed inside, and flicked on the light switch in the foyer. He tiptoed upstairs. The tightness in his stomach worsened with each step. He listened at Anik's bedroom door. No sounds of his customary snoring. Liam knocked. No response. He peeked into the dark room, engaged his penlight, and shined it in the direction of Anik's bed. Empty. *Where is he?*

"Something's not right." Liam searched every room.

Anik's team. They're not hungry. They're upset. Liam raced out of the cabin.

As he neared the shed, a trail of blood drops in the snow led to the partially open door. He cautiously crept inside. Anik lay amidst his team, face covered by his cap.

The dogs quieted down a tad but kept as close to their master as possible. "Okay, gang. Let me find out what's wrong with your brother here." The canines parted enough to allow Liam to kneel next to Anik and remove the hat. Their master's face was swollen and bloody. He groaned. Tracker and Boss whined.

One of Anik's eyelids lifted. His eyes shut again.

"I've got you, buddy." Liam reached into his parka pocket, pulled out his phone, and hit 911.

The paramedics arrived in a flash. After they checked Anik's vital signs, an EMT advised him, "Your vitals are good, but we'll take you to the ER."

Anik declined with a slow shake of his head. "I'll be all right. I'd rather stay here, but thanks. Nothing's broken, only bruised and battered... and sore."

When the responders moved him into the cabin, one of the team shook his head. "I advise you to at least see your doctor. Have you called the state troopers to report the crime?"

"We'll be sure to call." Liam shook the EMT's hand. "Thank you for the help."

As the unit went out the door, he thanked them once more.

Liam rejoined Anik in his bedroom. "You should've gone to the hospital like they said. You look terrible."

"I look worse than I am, no doubt. It was those two poachers with another guy, who seemed familiar. Likely the ringleader who downed the moose by the way he talked to the others. I think I've seen him hanging around town before. I'll report it to the state troopers tomorrow. Right now, I need rest. Did you lock the house and shed up tight?"

"All secure."

Thunk...thunk

As the hair rose on his neck, Liam spun away from Anik. "Stay here. I'll check if a shutter is loose." He ran down the stairs, two at a time.

Thunk

Back door. *Man! My cell's upstairs.* He grabbed his handgun from a desk drawer in the hall and sprinted through the house to the garage entry. The sound stopped. *Thank you God for the solid doors on this place, but it could be a window next.*

Seconds later, bangs and scrapes began at the front entrance. Liam rushed down the basement stairs to the exit, hidden from outside view at the rear of the cabin. He emerged and inched past the raised deck off the dining room, quiet as a rabbit. When he peeked around the corner toward the entrance, three men grunted as they pushed and whacked the door with a heavy section of tree.

"Hold it right there." Liam pointed the firearm at them. He closed the distance between himself and the poachers. Recognition hit. The third man had applied to be a ranger months ago, but was turned down. He'd loitered around the station afterward with a scowl.

Liam focused on the other two. "Remember me? The guy one of you shot when I was helping search and rescue?"

The ranger wannabe launched the branch straight at Liam. It landed on top of his gun hand. The pistol fired, the bullet hitting the poacher's foot. He screamed and fell backward into the snow, curling up and holding his foot. The other two men froze.

If only he could charge them like a linebacker and pin them both to the ground, but with his injuries, that wasn't possible. All he could do was keep the gun trained on them and hope Anik called nine-one-one. Now what should he do?

From the corner of his eye, Liam saw Anik lean on the deck rail, his revolver in hand. "Don't either of you two move!"

Wee-oo-wee-oo

The siren got louder as a state trooper patrol vehicle pulled onto Liam's property. Two troopers jumped out. A second car screeched to a stop behind them.

After the two troopers secured the poachers and hauled them away, the remaining trooper followed Liam and Anik into the cabin. Liam brought Anik and the trooper a cup of coffee.

Anik gave his statement about the assault. "I'd fed my team, locked the shed, and turned the corner of the cabin to find the three reprobates standing at the porch. They were arguing, and the leader of the pack had a gasoline can in his hand."

Liam's chest burned with a flood of anger.

Anik continued. "When they saw me, the big guy lowered the gas can, and they rushed to surround me. I was taught self-defense in the Air Force, but there was one too many of them. Just as I thought I'd black out from the beating they were giving me, a siren sounded and two cruisers came barreling through on the road. The three misfits disappeared into the woods, but the troopers must have seen them because they veered off in their direction. Liam came along later and found me with my dogs."

The trooper made a final note and stood. "We received an anonymous call from a female, who said she spotted three hoodlums get out of a beat-up truck pulled off the road and walk down your driveway, carrying a gasoline can."

Anik's jaw dropped. "Had to be Mrs. Kaitaq, the Inuit widow who lives down the road from us and watches *everyone*. Tomorrow, I'll send her a big bouquet of roses, even if she complains that they make her sneeze."

Liam nursed his aching side from laughing and the night's activity.

The trooper drank the final dregs from his cup. "Glad we finally found these characters. They've given us the slip ever since they escaped. One of their family members had to have helped them. You two take care. Make sure you see a doctor about those injuries."

Liam nodded. "He will, if I have to drag him there."

When the trooper had left, Liam dialed the O'Rourkes' residence and updated them on what had happened. "No doubt, the authorities will throw them in the slammer and toss the key to their cells in a drift, after all the grief they've caused. They won't get loose again."

Chapter Thirty-Nine

As Rachel approached Healy to celebrate Christmas Eve with everyone, her thoughts drifted to the Monday after Thanksgiving. It hadn't been the holiday they'd all hoped for. She'd fought tears when Liam showed up on their doorstep that morning, wrapped her in his arms, and said, "I have to be at work soon, but I couldn't let you leave without..." His kiss had been filled with such fierce emotion. She still felt his lips on hers. Oh, how she loved that man. She'd missed him these past weeks beyond measure. Contact over the miles was just not the same.

But now she was on her way home, and she had no intention of departing again after the holidays.

Rachel sighed. Still two long miles to her parents' cabin. Seemed like she'd never arrive. Her mom and dad had given her their full support in her search for other employment. They offered her old room for as long as she wanted or needed. Rachel took a deep breath and exhaled slowly. *As long as I need it. How* long would she and Liam keep dating… and nothing more?

He'd been ecstatic when she told him of her decision to quit her job and come home. He insisted she would hear from one of the magazines soon, *"As sure as shooting, beautiful."* She hoped so.

She glanced at the rearview mirror. Mr. Gibson… guess she really should start calling him Jess, now that he wasn't her boss. After all, he did plan to marry her sister, after a decent interval of dating… or until he could convince her dad to consent. Rachel snickered. Anyway, Jess was still right behind her, his Chevy Tahoe loaded to the max with more of her belongings than her Outback could hold.

After the life-threatening accident the last time they'd traveled this road, she was comforted by his presence. "Boy, how things have changed." She smiled.

As they turned the vehicles into her parents' front yard, her mother ran to her. Mom must have been waiting at the window. Rachel giggled to herself. Deirdre followed in their mother's wake.

"Hi, Mom. We're here." Rachel rolled her eyes. When did she turn into Captain Obvious?

Her mother grabbed and hugged her. "Yes, I see that and couldn't be happier."

Jess got out of his vehicle and swung Deirdre around in his arms when she reached him.

Her father came out and gave Rachel a squeeze. "I'm glad you're home, sweetheart." He strode to Jess's truck and extended his hand to the man who would no doubt become his son-in-law sooner rather than later. "Good to see you, my boy. Any problems on the drive?"

"No, sir. It was smooth all the way." Jess neared Rachel. "I'll bring everything in for you."

After a hug from Deirdre, Rachel dropped her fob into his outstretched hand. "Thank you… Jess."

He arched his brows, his body went stiff as he slapped his fist over his heart. "You called me Jess?" He laughed.

"You've become a real comedian, *Mister* Gibson."

He pouted with one eye squinted, walked away, then laughed again.

She was tired after all her packing and decision-making. If only Liam could have been here to greet her. But he'd be here as soon as he got off his shift, and they'd enjoy Christmas Eve and Day together.

Deirdre had managed to get the two days off from her new position at the park. Liam had taken a week's vacation to spend with his family, who had already arrived yesterday. Kalen came in the week before. What fun this holiday would be.

Anik, whose bruises and wounds had finally healed, had called and told her he was finishing up practice runs and would join them later.

With all the people she cared about present for Christmas and the poachers awaiting trial, things couldn't be better.

Returning from his family's traditional Christmas Eve breakfast in the village of Talkeetna, about two and a half hours south of Healy, Anik neared the Denali National Park. He thought about how fortunate he was to have grown up in this area. He loved his family, the O'Rourkes, his pal Liam, mushing, racing, and his team. "What more could he ask for?" He couldn't think of anything to take the place of his dogs and their loyalty to him. It was his team that had kept him from freezing to death last month when the poachers caught him by surprise and beat him to a pulp, then left him lying in the snow.

The miscreants had been frightened away by approaching sirens, but the authorities didn't stop at the cabin in their pursuit of the criminals.

Nothing but pure determination enabled Anik to crawl toward the shed he used to house his dogs as a kennel. By a miracle, his lead dog, Tracker, had managed to open the latch on the gate, and instead of the team running out to freedom for a while, Boss and Tracker dragged him inside the pen. All fourteen of his furry brothers had lain down next to him and kept him warm until Liam found him. *Thank You, once again, Lord.*

The criminals were fortunate they didn't come back and try to finish him off when the sirens stopped. His team would have torn those misfits to shreds.

Tears filled his eyes. He pulled off to the side of the road and wiped his face. *I love those four-legged hunks of fur—the brothers he'd never had.* Those dogs *were* more like siblings to him than canines. He continued his trek to Healy.

Half an hour later, he parked in the O'Rourkes' yard. The roof was lit with colored lights. A huge decorated tree stood in the middle of the living room's picture window. *I love Christmas.*

He slipped out of the driver's seat and heard music coming from the house. His favorite carol, "Hark the Herald Angels Sing." As he lifted a box of gifts, he hummed. He was counting on this to be a wonderful night, even if he and Kalen—in their mutual state of singleness—were outnumbered by couples.

Out of the corner of his eye, he noted movement along the timberline across the road. The hair on his neck stood on end. His previous month's beating invaded his thoughts. He hurried to the porch, ran up the stairs, and knocked on the door.

Liam pulled the door open. "Hey, buddy. You sounded like you were in a double-quick hurry to get inside." He took the box and placed it on the floor.

Anik shrugged out of his parka. "I thought there was something at the edge of the woods. Guess it spooked me."

"Rachel said she'd seen something out there too, but her mom said it was hunters looking for rabbits. Don't worry. Let's get you warmed up by the fire. Mrs. O'Rourke said dinner is almost ready."

He led Anik to a chair by the fireplace in the living room and left to get him something warm to drink.

Anik couldn't shake the sense that someone was watching the house. He clamped his teeth together. He refused to ruin the festive evening with speculation that those poachers might have escaped again and returned to seek vengeance. He wanted tonight to be a wonderful Christmas Eve.

Liam sat next to Anik. "I see the worry lines, my friend. It's only natural, like post-traumatic stress disorder. With the crisis we all went through, especially you, it's to be expected. PTSD will take time to wear off, but we'll all be fine."

Anik accepted a cup of cocoa from Liam's sister's hands. "Thank you." She smiled and sat across the room from him. *Man, it's warm in here.* He pulled at the collar of his turtleneck sweater. Ainsley sure was pretty… and sweet.

Kalen was telling the Chadwicks the story of how he lost the use of his legs through an accident, and how he came very close to being eaten by a bear. "Of course, I do exaggerate just a tad, but that was the gist of what happened."

"Kalen," Anik interjected, "you forgot about the part with the Ijiraat."

"The what?" Ainsley asked.

"Shape-shifters who change into arctic animals but can't disguise their red eyes." Anik turned to Kalen. "Wasn't that what you originally said was responsible for attacking you that day?" He winked at his younger friend.

"Don't listen to him, Ainsley." With a glare, Rachel pointed at Anik. "You know very well there is no such thing as an Ijiraat… is there, Liam?" She faced him.

"Well, I hate to contradict Anik, but Kalen's dogs were all safe, and they wouldn't have been if there was some fiendish shape-shifter out there who caused his accident." He shrugged at Anik. "But I did find bear tracks when we got to Kalen that day."

Anik bent his head forward and stared at Liam from under his brows. "The Ijiraat could've left and decided he wasn't mad at the dogs."

Kalen raised his hands. "Hold on, guys. Let's not scare poor Ainsley to death with your tall tales. She'll be up all night with nightmares." He burst into guffaws. "But I will say, I will never forget the bear I surprised when I came around that huge bush. It's burned into my memory." Kalen shifted his focus to Anik. "And the grizzly did *not* have red eyes."

Everyone laughed. Mrs. O'Rourke, who sat next to Ainsley, patted her arm. "These boys are always trying to outdo each other with their spooky stories. Ignore them."

Ainsley glanced at Anik, and her smile grew.

"Simply livening up the atmosphere, dear lady. Christmas Eve isn't Christmas Eve without stories to tell." He grinned, then peeked at Ainsley. She still smiled at him. *What a strange sensation.* He'd never felt like this before. *What's with the almost unbearable heat in here?*

Liam leaned over and whispered to Anik, "You're acting peculiar, buddy. I think you just got some color back in your face." He chuckled.

Anik's face heated even more. What would his pal Liam say if he knew his sister was the cause? Couldn't ask for a better friend than Liam, but how would he react if he found out this Inuit was attracted to her?

When her father announced it was time to give out presents, Rachel's body tingled with excitement the same way it did when she was a kid. Would Liam appreciate the gift she chose for him? All indications had led her to believe he would when she'd covertly asked him questions. It was a risk, but she wanted something very special for him.

Her father passed out the packages from under the tree. He handed her the type of box that might contain clothing. Ooo, from Liam. Her heartbeat accelerated. He hadn't asked her for suggestions. What could it be?

"Everyone?" Her father raised his hands. "I thought it would be nice if we opened our gifts one person at a time. That way, we'll all get to see what they are. Is everyone okay with that?"

The question met with approval all around.

"Good. I think the best order should be by age in the individual families represented here. Perhaps the oldest first. I think the Chadwicks should go first—as our new guests—then Jess Gibson, Anik from the Amarok clan, and the O'Rourkes last."

Anik held up his hand. "Ah, that would be band or tribe in my case. Whichever you prefer, sir." He chuckled.

"Thank you for that information." Rachel's father laughed and shook his head. "Now. I will not ask you ladies what your ages are. I know how sensitive you can be. You'll just have to jump in where you think you fit." He winked at his wife. "I suggest the head of each family go first and then pass the baton to the next in line. Now, let's start with the Chadwicks. Bruce?"

"Aw-w-w, no fair." Trace, Lucas's five-year-old son, protested and dropped to the floor, where he sat with his legs crossed at his grandfather's feet, and pouted. His three-year-old sister, Evie, rushed from her mother's side and plopped down in her brother's lap as if to give moral support.

His granddad laid a hand on the boy's head. "Trace, you and Evie can go first when we unwrap our family gifts tomorrow."

The pout changed from a poochy-lip to a happy expression of curiosity as he quickly turned to Mr. Chadwick. "What did you get, Grandpa?"

Mr. Chadwick's brows raised. "Well, let's see. I haven't gone first since I was a little kid. Here goes." He ripped into his first package.

After expressing his thanks to everyone, his wife unwrapped her gifts. Then Lucas, his wife, and at last it was Liam's turn.

Rachel bit her lip as he held the small flat box in his hand and lifted it as if weighing the package. "Hmm." He read the tag. "To Liam, from Rachel." He gave her a smile that made her pulse dance a jig, and then he took off the wrapping paper and opened the lid.

He pulled out a silver heart-shaped charm with a lobster claw clasp and glanced at her. Questions filled his eyes. Then he picked up the note inside and read, "Take this symbol of love to the guest room where it can be attached to the rest of your gift."

Although question marks still resided in his eyes, he rose and followed the instruction. When he returned, he held a wiggly Husky pup in his arms and wore a huge grin. "Thank you. He's perfect."

"He's from the litter sired by Anik's lead dog, Tracker. I thought you'd like him. His name and your number go on the charm. You can drop him off here to stay with me on the days you're on duty."

Liam gave her shoulder a squeeze. "Now he's extra perfect."

Trace and Evie ran to Liam as he lowered himself to the seat he'd left. "What'cha gonna name him, Uncle Liam?"

"I'm not sure." He glanced at everyone around the room. "Any suggestions?"

Rachel sighed in relief.

Liam's nerves could barely stand the pressure. It was finally Rachel's turn. She opened every gift at a painstakingly slow pace and left his for last. His hands grew damp as she brought the Christmassy-wrapped package to her lap and untied the ribbon.

She lifted the lid and gasped at the fluffy white cashmere sweater. "It's beautiful, Liam. Thank you. Exactly what I'd pick for myself."

"Check the sleeve," he told her. He was about to burst with anticipation.

She slid her fingers over the fuzzy material. "There's a lump inside." She narrowed her gaze at Liam as she pulled out a small square velvet box and gasped.

He kneeled in front of her, took the object from her trembling hand, flipped open the lid, and turned it toward her. “Rachel Amber O’Rourke, will you marry me?”

Silence filled the room.

Her jaw drooped. Her eyes blinked rapidly and darted from the sparkling pear-shaped diamond ring to Liam’s face. Her eyes became glassy, then closed. As she fell forward, Liam caught her in his arms.

Chapter Forty

After Rachel fainted on Christmas Eve when he'd proposed marriage, a whirlwind had ensued. Liam shook his head at the memory. Her mother ran and grabbed a cold, wet dish towel from the kitchen and laid it on her forehead. Everyone else hovered. Rachel regained consciousness before anyone could call nine-one-one, but it sure had shaken him.

The next thing he knew, her arms flew around his neck. He folded her into his embrace as she shouted, *"Yes, I'll marry you."*

The family all laughed. Too many events had transpired at once for his sweet Rachel's nerves. But his lovely lady was fine now, and here it was the last Sunday before the New Year. A summer wedding was on the horizon, with the reception to be held at The Brown Bear.

He grinned at his reflection in the mirror and eased into his suit coat for the New Year's Eve breakfast at the O'Rourkes'. "You are one very fortunate man, Ranger Liam."

"You are that indeed." Anik stepped into Liam's bedroom with an equally wide grin. "I hope someday I'll find someone just like Rachel. And you're lucky I only ever saw her as a sister, pal."

They laughed all the way out the door and into Anik's Jeep.

"Mom." Rachel's heart filled with anxiety. Everything had happened so fast. "There's not much time between now and summer to prepare for the wedding. Can we get it all done? There's the wedding dress, a cake to decide on, bridesmaids and their dresses to pick out... oh... and so many more things to think about."

"Hon, calm yourself. You don't want to pass out again, do you? Stop worrying about the details. Now that Dee's your maid of honor, she and I can work on what you need, and then let you and Liam make the final decisions. In the meantime, search for your perfect job. It'll turn out fine."

Thank You, Lord. Mom was so structured. Over the years, she'd organized weddings and all kinds of events for Dad, like tonight's New Year's Eve celebration at church. It came as second nature to her. She'd even arranged the accommodations for the Chadwicks' visit this holiday season, so they could relax and enjoy the trip here.

Rachel shook her head. Would she ever be that efficient? Not like Liam, with all he had to do and think about at work. She was more like Anik, reacting on the spur-of-the-moment, except with her writing. She giggled to herself.

As if they'd heard their names, Liam and Anik walked into the foyer from their patrol around the O'Rourkes' cabin and grounds. They'd continued being diligent even though the poachers were incarcerated. They hung their coats and made their way into the kitchen, where they poured themselves cups of hot coffee from the urn on the counter.

Liam announced in a singsong baritone voice, "All's clear on the O'Rourke grounds fro-ont."

"That's good to hear, dear." Mom patted him on the arm.

After a tight hug and kiss from her betrothed, Rachel rolled a serving cart with place settings and condiments into the dining room and unloaded the items.

Liam had said it helped him and Anik feel better to continue their security strolls whether at home or here, with the PTSD still playing on their nerves. She could understand that. What an exceptional guy she'd marry soon.

She called to her mom, still in the kitchen, "Looks like everyone has gathered for the New Year's Eve breakfast. How's the smoked brisket?"

"Ready." Her mother walked into the room and placed a platter piled high with slices of savory meat in the center of the dining table.

Liam snatched a piece of brisket and popped it into his mouth.

Her mom took the cart from Rachel, pushed it into the kitchen, and returned with serving dishes full of scrambled and poached eggs, English muffins, hollandaise sauce, Canadian bacon, fruit, and yogurt parfaits. "Come and eat, everyone."

After they'd eaten and helped clean up from the meal, Rachel told her father, "We're ready to go to church. Anik is loading Lucas's family in his Jeep."

She turned to Liam. "Since my folks will go with yours in Dad's car, that only leaves Kalen, my sister, and me riding with you in my Outback."

He leaned in. "I figured Jess would want to take Deirdre."

"I'm sure you presumed right. Not thinking." Rachel dangled her key fob in front of him. "I'll drive." She grinned.

"Oh, no. I'm well enough to handle that chore now. Hand 'em over."

He snatched the fob and then held her parka for her while she shrugged into it. "The way to a man's heart is to put him in charge. Remember that, sweetheart."

She turned and smacked his biceps. *Don't think you'll be in control of everything, dear.*

He laughed as if he'd heard her thoughts.

That night, after a brief New Year's Eve service, Rachel and Liam entered the fellowship hall adjacent to the church for a period of fellowship. Aromas mingled in the air as they walked through the large ancillary building's door.

"The food the ladies prepared for tonight smells outstanding," Liam crowed. But then it would be. It was all homemade. Even his mom had made his favorite, shepherd's pie, at the O'Rourkes'.

The crowd moved through the line quickly and settled into chairs placed next to the walls.

Liam smirked to himself. They sure had fantastic cooks in this town, including his soon-to-be wife. He forked a mouthful of barbecue venison Rachel had roasted to his lips.

He was so blessed to have a wonderful girl like her. *Lord, I promise, with Your help, to try my best to make each day of our lives together better than the last.*

"Okay, everyone," Pastor announced, "Time to get our watch night service going so we can pray in the New Year at the stroke of midnight."

Members of the congregation swallowed their final bits of food and disposed their paper plates, napkins, plastic tableware, and cups in the trash. They streamed into the sanctuary.

Hymns were sung, a short message on living for the Lord, and a musical special by one preteen on piano, preceded a time of prayer. At ten minutes before the old year would end, one by one, the people clasped hands in their pews. With heads bowed, Pastor led in prayer with others following.

The sounds of fireworks and occasional gunfire outside infiltrated the auditorium. Liam prayed all the harder. *Hope that noise is only in celebration and not more criminals out there doing their unlawful deeds.*

As the congregation made its peaceful way into the New Year, the loud booms continued. Rachel leaned in close to Liam. "Let's get a head start on everyone so we can pick the jobs we want during cleanup." She winked at him.

Before anyone else rose from their seats, he and Rachel headed to the church kitchen, or so Liam thought. When they stepped into the rear of the building, he spun on his heels. "Shhh." He whispered in her ear. "We're not alone."

Inside the kitchen, Jess held Deirdre in a gentle embrace and lowered his lips to hers. She responded as he'd hoped she would.

She pulled back a few inches. "I thought we were going to make a dent in the cleanup before everyone else got here." Her eyes narrowed. Then she gave him a lopsided grin. "Not that I'm complaining, you understand." She hugged him.

"That was the excuse I used to get you here." A Cheshire Cat smile stretched across his face, and he bounced his brows.

"Ah ha! You lured me by deception. Is this what I should expect from you in the future, Mr. Gibson?"

"Not all the time." He tightened his arms around her. "But it can add a certain element of excitement." He laughed. "The real reason I *lured* you here," Jess reached into his pants pocket and pulled out a ring box, "is this."

Her brows rose.

He took both her hands in one of his and placed the case in them. "Deirdre... sweet, wonderful Deirdre. Please marry me."

As she lifted her gaze to his, tears filled her eyes. "What will my parents say? Have you told them? My father said to slow down."

He tilted his head and spoke in a quiet voice, almost inaudible. "That's not the answer I expected, but yes, your dad and I discussed it. I think he's checked on me ever since the first day I visited his office. We're good." He kissed her forehead. "Now, would you like to see what's inside, and then tell me the words I hope to hear?" He cocked his head.

She nodded and opened the lid. A delightful squeal came from her. "It's gorgeous."

Jess slipped the two-karat marquise diamond onto the third finger of her left hand. "It belonged to my grandmother. Granddad had excellent taste. And the ring fits you perfectly."

Before Deirdre could give him a yes or they could even kiss, the sound of feet running across the kitchen floor interrupted them. Rachel rushed to her sister. *"Dee!"*

Liam joined them with a grin.

Jess held up his hands like a traffic control cop to stop them. "Hold it! She hasn't answered me yet." He turned to the girl he loved. "Now, angel. You were saying?"

She laughed. "You know I'll marry you." She jumped into his arms.

Rachel latched onto her sister's arm, her pulse doing another jig.

Liam sidled up next to them. "Well, this is the last thing I thought we'd find in the kitchen."

"What are you two doing, sis? Didn't Dad tell you both to take your relationship slow? This is *far* from slow."

"You and Liam didn't."

"She's got you there, beautiful," Liam said.

Deirdre exchanged her narrowed eyes for a smile. "Calm down, dear sister. Jess told me he spoke to Dad. Everything is kosher."

With her hand on her forehead, Rachel leaned against a counter. Liam held her shoulders. "Are you okay? You're not going to faint on me, are you?"

"I'm fine, but I wonder what Mom is going to do with *two* weddings to organize. and Deirdre was supposed to help her." Rachel turned to her former boss. "Did Dad tell you how long you'll have to wait?"

A chuckle came out of Jess as he took Dee's left hand in his and kissed it. "I told him I want to get married as soon as he will allow. The idea of Deirdre here in Healy, and me in Fairbanks—except when I can get away—is killing me." He looked pleadingly at Liam. "You know how it is."

Rachel blew out a stream of air. Both she and Liam said in unison, "Yes, I know," then stared at each other.

She addressed her sister again. "But what did Dad say?"

With her free hand, Dee shrugged, then latched onto Rachel's arm. "I don't know whether you'd consider this or not. Please be honest with me. What do you think of a double wedding in the summer?"

"So soon? Our father agreed? You don't want your own special day?"

"I'm sure Dad will agree. What I'd like is to share this important event with my big sister." She turned to Jess. "Maybe these two guys would remember their anniversaries that way." She arched her brows.

The rest of the cleanup committee entered the building. Anik led the pack. *This must be where Liam and Rachel disappeared to. There they*

are. He rushed through the kitchen doorway and grabbed his friend by the shoulder. "I need to talk to you."

Rachel gasped and covered her mouth. "Tell me they didn't escape again."

Liam's face grew pale.

"Don't worry." Anik gave a thumbs-up. "Those reprobates are locked up tight this time."

"Whew!" Liam closed his eyes and shook his head.

"Thanks to Mrs. Kaitaq." Anik beamed. "And she loved her roses, by the way." His smile became a grin.

"Who's Mrs. Kaitaq?" Dee asked.

"She's a Native American widow who lives down the road from us. She watches everyone, and the minute she sees something she doesn't like, the entire town hears about it. 'Anik, your Jeep kicks stones into my yard. Liam, your truck is too loud. Anik, you drive too fast down the driveway.' We hear about it all the time. You name it, she complains about it. But I'll tell you what." Anik smiled. "The day after the poachers were arrested, she received a gigantic bouquet of roses from me. She's changed her tune."

"So, what do you want to talk to me about?" Liam picked up a dish towel while several women entered the room and started washing dishes and sealing up leftovers.

Anik glanced around at all the people watching him. His neck warmed. *No way.* He'd seek Liam's advice later. "Ah... perhaps now isn't the best time. See you later." He hurried from the kitchen.

At five o'clock in the morning on New Year's Day, Rachel and Liam said their goodnights on the O'Rourkes' front porch with an embrace and soft kisses. They'd stayed up the rest of the night in the living room with Deirdre and Jess, talking about the double wedding ceremony. Rachel sighed. Barring all the work to be done, their being joined as one couldn't come fast enough for her.

She leaned on Liam's shoulder. "I hope you don't mind sharing our wedding day with my sister."

"As long as you don't, I'm fine with it." He nuzzled her ear. "The most important things to me are for you to become my wife… and for me to make you happy."

"I'm overjoyed that my relationship with Dee is now as it should be. Sharing one of the most significant events in our lives means a lot. Obviously, to her too."

The soft sound of a snicker slipped past her lips. "I can't believe the stars in Jess's eyes whenever he looks at my sister. Who would've known a few months ago? He always tried to act like such a "bad boy". Now, his hair is perfect, and there's no more black leather clothing. He even smiles all the time. He's actually quite handsome in a suit and dress shirt."

Liam pulled her to his chest. "You're making me jealous."

Rachel's head popped up, and she smiled. "You have nothing to change your handsome gray eyes to green about. He's still not my type, but now I view him as more of another brother. A nice one too, I might add."

"Yes, he's proved himself to be trustworthy and certainly in love with your redheaded firecracker of a sister. I'm happy they found each other. They both needed someone special. The stars have lined up for a beautiful start to this year."

In the predawn hours, on the first day of January, Liam and Rachel shared one more emotion-stirred kiss. As they paused for air, Rachel gazed into the dark expanse above them. "Look!"

In the Healy, Alaskan sky, over the Denali Mountain, the Quadrantid meteor shower soared like fireworks on the 4th of July.

Liam squeezed her tightly. "It's as if all of heaven is here to celebrate our two lives that will soon become one."

Epilogue

The week after New Year's Eve, Rachel couldn't wait to tell Liam the news. He arrived at the O'Rourkes', and she led him into the area of the dining room her parents had designated *her office* space. "I'm so relieved. I finally got word from the national park magazine where I submitted my articles, as well as two other popular publications. They want regular articles from me as a freelance writer, Liam."

With a wink, he smirked and boasted. "Told ya so."

Liam rushed into the living room of his cabin, where Rachel and Anik discussed topics she might write about for more submissions to magazines and newspapers. They glanced up at Liam as he announced, "I received information from the Department of Justice that the court has convicted the three poachers of attempted murder and violation of federal and state wildlife laws for killing the bull moose. Also, first-degree assault and escape from custody after arrest."

"About time," Anik muttered.

After a nod, Liam continued. "The criminals were imprisoned for a minimum of twenty years, with charges of thousands of dollars in fines."

He huffed. "I think it's way too lenient for the atrocities they committed against God's creatures." Still, the stress oozed out of Liam's body, knowing the three men would be under lock and key.

"I've no problem with those who hunt game for food, but not for sport." He ground his teeth. "Certainly not to sell their hides and leave the meat to rot." But the degree of their punishment wasn't his call. "The offenders were each charged with the assault on Anik. Glad they got their due for what they did to you, buddy."

Rachel said, "And you."

"But there's more." Liam sat in a chair and held up a printed page. "The report says, 'After consideration of all the factors in the case, an additional twenty years had been added to the miscreants' sentences for attempted arson.' " He dropped the sheet onto his lap. "Everyone's PTSD should soon fade away with support from our families, the church, the community, and most of all from God." He let out a cleansing breath.

"August fifth, our wedding day, has finally arrived." Rachel hugged her sister for a moment as they stood well back from the chairs lined up and filled with guests. A multitude of friends and family had come to rejoice and give their blessings at their ceremony.

The sun shone on Denali Mountain in the background while, on a grassy knoll of the Healy Bible Church grounds, Mr. O'Rourke prepared to cue the guitarist to play.

Rachel leaned over and whispered to her sister, "It was so nice of you to agree on Ainsley for our maid of honor."

"It was an obvious choice." Deirdre squeezed Rachel's hand. "It was nicer of Lucas to defer his place as Liam's best man to Anik. Jess told me he considers Anik his closest friend now, too, since Liam will be his brother... in-law." Deirdre's joy made her emerald eyes sparkle.

Two bridesmaids, who the O'Rourke girls had grown up with in church, started down the aisle to the music of "Jesu, Joy of Man's Desiring."

Liam's favorite Husky from his Denali team, Flame, headed toward him with head held high as she wore a small poofy veil and toted a basket of rose petals. Evie loosely held a white leash attached to Flame and carried a matching basket. White flower petals littered the aisle when Flame bobbed her head and Evie bounced her basket up and down.

Right behind the flower girls, Trace carried a ring pillow as if it were made of crystal.

Deirdre giggled. "Were there ever more perfect flower girls or a serious ring bearer?"

"They're the best." Rachel grinned as the sisters locked arms. "Here we go, Dee. The first day of our new lives." A warm sensation flowed up and throughout Rachel's body. She was about to become Mrs. Liam Chadwick.

With their father as the minister, Rachel and Deirdre decided to walk each other over the rose petals to meet the grooms.

The vows were spoken by each couple. Rings exchanged. Kisses exchanged. And Mr. O'Rourke announced, "By the power vested in me by the state of Alaska, and having witnessed your promises to each other, I now pronounce both of these couples married." He had the newlyweds turn and face the guests. "It is my honor to present to you, for the first time, Mr. and Mrs. Liam Chadwick and Mr. and Mrs. Jesse Gibson."

Liam pulled Rachel closer. "You won't faint on me, will you?" He smiled.

“Of course not. Why would I? This day is a dream come true, my love.”

At the reception line, Anik’s dogsled team and Liam’s fast-growing Husky pup gave yips and licks, decked out in bow ties and pretty bows for the occasion.

Anik’s *aanaa*—and the rest of his family—supplied many native food dishes for the feast afterward to accompany the catered foods at The Brown Bear.

During a quiet moment in the restaurant’s reception hall, decorated to the hilt in green, white, and purple, Liam leaned toward Rachel. “Now that you work from home, will it be okay with you if we adopt a retired Denali Canine Ranger? From my team? My sweet Flame is up for adoption next year. I don’t have the heart to lose her.”

“Oh, Liam. Did you have to ask? I’d love for her to become part of our household. She’d be a good role model for Sleuth.” Rachel laughed. “That’s such a great name for your puppy. Sleuth.”

He joined her in laughter. “Hey. Tracker... Sleuth. It went with his sire’s moniker, and he resembles Anik’s lead dog too.” He kissed the tip of her nose as he led his wife in the bridal waltz around the floor. “I’ll let the canine crew know Flame is ours when she’s officially retired. We’ll be a happy family. With more members to come, I’m sure. Not only of the four-legged variety.” He showed a Colgate smile. “She and Sleuth might make great babysitters.” He whisked his blushing bride away before she could respond.

Anik was flying high on emotion at the Chadwick-O’Rourke-Gibson wedding. He’d danced most of the night with Liam’s sister Ainsley. The Inuk’s heart had been captured. Liam grinned. From what he and his parents could tell, so had Ainsley’s. There was nothing he could do but give his best friend his blessing after the crazy-in-love man made four trips to Florida *on vacation*.

During a break in the reception music, Anik approached Liam. "Pal, I plan to ask Ainsley to marry me by the end of the year."

"Buddy, why does that come as no shock to me? But you'll have to convince Mom and Dad first."

The two of them glanced at the senior Chadwick couple. Liam leaned in so that only his friend could hear him. "My parents have worn huge smiles and nodded toward you and Ainsley the entire time you danced. I don't think you'll have any opposition from my folks at all."

Liam slapped Anik on the back and returned to his beautiful wife.

The End

Fun Information For My Readers

Musher commands (not all of which have been used in the story):
Hike: A common command to start the team or increase speed.
Gee: A command to turn right.
Haw: A command to turn left.
Easy: A command to slow down.
Straight Ahead: A command to move forward.
Whoa: A command to stop.
On By: A command to pass another team or distraction.
Line Out: A command to the lead dog to tighten the gangline and pull the team out straight from the sled.

Aanaa: Grandmother in Inuit

Inuk: The singular form of Inuit.

Eskimo: Increasingly outdated term, considered offensive by many Inuit, *and only used as a derogatory term in my story.*

Ijiraat: Pronounced "ee-yi-rahk" or "ee-ji-rahk"
A shape-shifting spirit in Inuit mythology, known for transforming into various arctic animals or humans, though its eyes remain red. Some say these shape-shifters are helpful and bring messages to travelers, but others say they are dangerous. The shape-shifters are believed to live between the worlds of the living and of the dead. They stalk lone travelers.

Note: There is no actual town called Ferry, Alaska. Ferry is a point of interest, and you will find it on the Alaska map. It is a census-designated place (CDP) located in Denali Borough, Alaska. I've chosen to make it an actual town for purposes of the story.

Other Works by This Author

Novels
A Very Present Help
Paths of Righteousness
There Abideth Hope
His Perfect Love
Treasure in a Field
Ko'olau's Secret
Tall Pines Sanctuary
Trust Never After
Wyoming Called

Novella
Icicles to Moonbeams

Novelette
Amethyst Lights

Short Story Collection
Sharon's Shorts
~
A Multi-Genre Collection of Short Stories

Short Stories in Anthologies
"Ding-A-Ling Holiday Blues"
In *Tales of Texas, Vol. 2*

"Spirit Lake"
In *Dark Visions*

Cookbook
Simply Cooking

About the Author

Sharon K Connell writes stories about people who discover God will allow things in their lives to bring them to a saving knowledge of Jesus Christ and/or increase their faith. Her genre is Christian romantic suspense, always with a dose of humor and very often with a mystery. She also writes short stories in a variety of genres.

Born in Wisconsin, raised in Illinois (where she attended college in Chicago), Sharon has also lived in Missouri, California, Florida, Ohio, and Texas. Her travels have taken her to all but six states in the United States, and she has visited Canada and Mexico.

Sharon is a graduate of the Pensacola Bible Institute in Florida and holds a certificate in fiction writing from the International Writing Program through the University of Iowa.

Let the words of my mouth, and the meditation of my heart, be acceptable in thy sight, O LORD, my strength, and my redeemer.
Psalm 19:14

Member of:
American Christian Fiction Writers
Houston Writers Guild
Christian Womens Writers Club
CyFair Writers Group

Links:

Amazon Author Page: http://www.amazon.com/author/sharonkconnell
Instagram: https://www.instagram.com/sharonkconnell/?hl=en
Facebook Group Forum:
https://www.facebook.com/groups/ChristianWritersAndReadersGroupForum/
Facebook Author group, The Works of Author Sharon K Connell (for all my books): https://www.facebook.com/groups/516338614013516
Twitter: https://twitter.com/SharonKConnell
Goodreads: https://www.goodreads.com/SharonKConnell
LinkedIn: https://www.linkedin.com/in/sharonkconnell
Pinterest: https://www.pinterest.com/rosecastle1/
BookBub: https://www.bookbub.com/authors/sharon-k-connell
Blogging on WordPress: https://sharonkconnell.wordpress.com/
YouTube:
http://www.youtube.com/@authorsharonkconnellcreates

Thank you for reading

www.ingramcontent.com/pod-product-compliance
Lightning Source LLC
Chambersburg PA
CBHW031157020726
47499CB00002B/404
* 9 7 8 1 9 5 7 2 4 6 0 6 2 *